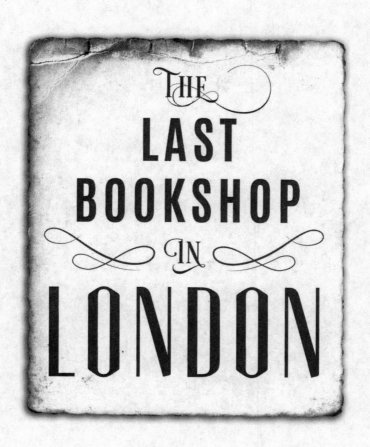

THE
LAST
BOOKSHOP
IN
LONDON

Also by Madeline Martin

Borderland Rebels series

Borderland Ladies series

The London School for Ladies series

Highland Passions series

Wicked Earls' Club series

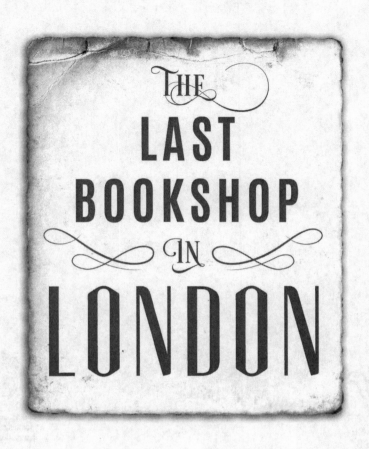

THE LAST BOOKSHOP IN LONDON

A NOVEL OF WORLD WAR II

MADELINE MARTIN

HANOVER
SQUARE
PRESS

HANOVER
SQUARE
PRESS™

ISBN-13: 978-1-335-65304-8
ISBN-13: 978-1-335-63097-1 [Canada Edition]

The Last Bookshop in London

This edition published by arrangement with Harlequin Books S.A.

Hanover Square Press
22 Adelaide St. West, 40th Floor
Toronto, Ontario M5H 4E3, Canada
HanoverSqPress.com
BookClubbish.com

Printed in U.S.A.

To the authors of all the books I've ever read. Thank you for the escape, for the knowledge and for shaping me into who I am.

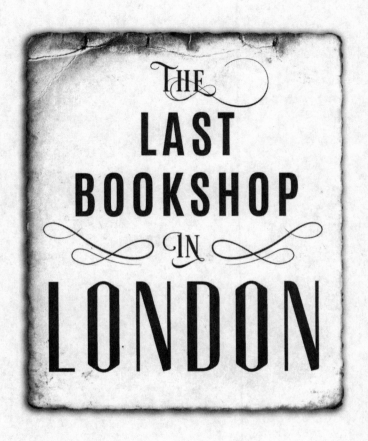

ONE

GRACE BENNETT HAD ALWAYS DREAMED OF SOMEDAY living in London. Never did she imagine it would become her only option, especially not on the eve of war.

The train pulled to a stop within Farringdon Station, its name clearly marked on the wall inside a strip of blue set within a red circle. People hovered on the platform, as eager to get on as those within were to get off. They wore smartly cut clothing in the chic styles of city life. Far more sophisticated than in Drayton, Norfolk.

Equal parts nerves and eagerness vibrated about inside Grace. "We've arrived." She looked at Viv beside her.

Her friend clicked the top on her lipstick tube closed and gave a freshly applied vermillion smile. Viv glanced out the window, her gaze skimming the checkerboard of advertisements lining the curved wall. "After so many years of wishing we could be in London." Her hand caught Grace's in a quick squeeze. "Here we are."

Back when they were mere girls, Viv had first mentioned the notion of moving away from dull Drayton for a far more exciting life in the city. It had been a wild concept then, to leave their slow-moving, familiar existence in the country for the bustling, fast-paced pulse of London. Never had Grace considered it might someday become a necessity.

But then, there was nothing left in Drayton for Grace anymore. At least nothing she cared to return to.

The ladies rose from their plush seats and took hold of their luggage. Each had only one case with them, faded things, beaten down more by age than use. Both were stuffed to the point of near-bursting and were not only impossibly heavy, but awkward to manage around the gas mask boxes slung over their shoulders. The ghastly things had to be brought with them everywhere, per the government, to ensure they'd be protected in the event of a gas attack.

Lucky for them, Britton Street was only a two-minute walk away, or so Mrs. Weatherford had said.

Her mother's childhood friend had a room to let, one she'd offered a year ago when Grace's mother first passed. The terms had been generous—two months for free while Grace acquired a job and even then, the rent would be discounted thereafter. Despite Grace's longing to go to London, and despite Viv's enthusiastic encouragement, Grace had remained in Drayton for nearly a year after in an attempt to pick up the pieces of her broken existence.

That was before she learned the house she'd lived in since her birth truly belonged to her uncle. Before he moved in with his overbearing wife and five children. Before life as she knew it shattered even further apart.

There was no room for Grace in her own home, a point her aunt had been eager to note often. What had once been a place of comfort and love became a place Grace felt unwelcome. When her aunt finally had the temerity to tell Grace to leave, she knew she had no other options.

Writing the letter to Mrs. Weatherford the previous month to see if the opportunity still held was one of the hardest things Grace had ever done. It had been a surrender to the challenges she faced, a terrible, soul-crushing failure. A capitulation that had rendered her the greatest failure.

Grace had never possessed much courage. Even now, she wondered if she would have managed her way to London had Viv not insisted they go together.

Trepidation knotted through her as they waited for the train's gleaming metal doors to part and unveil a whole new world.

"Everything will be brilliant," Viv whispered under her breath. "It will all be so much better, Grace. I promise."

The air-powered doors of the electric train hissed open and they stepped onto the platform amid the push and pull of people coming and going all at once. Then the doors shushed closed behind them, and the gust of the train's departure tugged at their skirts and hair.

An advert for Chesterfields on the far wall displayed a handsome lifeguard smoking a cigarette while another poster beside it called on the men of London to join the service.

It wasn't only a reminder of a war their country might soon face, but how living in the city presented a greater element of danger. If Hitler meant to take Britain, he would likely set his sights on London.

"Oh, Grace, look!" Viv exclaimed.

Grace turned from the poster toward the metal stairs,

which glided upward on an unseen belt, disappearing somewhere above the arched ceiling. Into the city of their dreams.

The advert was quickly forgotten as she and Viv rushed toward the escalator and tried to tamp down their delight as it effortlessly carried them up, up, up.

Viv's shoulders squeezed upward with barely restrained happiness. "Didn't I tell you this would be amazing?"

The enormity of it hit Grace all at once. After years of dreaming and planning, here they were in London.

Away from Grace's bully of an uncle, out from under the thumb of Viv's strict parents.

Despite all of Grace's troubles, she and Viv swept out of the station like caged songbirds ready to finally spread their wings.

Buildings rose into the sky all around, making Grace block the sun with the palm of her hand to see their tops. Several nearby shops greeted them with brightly painted signs touting sandwiches, hairdressers and a chemist. On the streets, lorries rattled by and a double-decker bus rumbled in the opposite direction, its painted side as red and glossy as Viv's nails.

It was all Grace could do to keep from grasping her friend's arm and squealing for her to look. Viv was taking it in too, with wide, sparkling eyes. She appeared as much an awed country girl as Grace, albeit in a fashionable dress with her perfectly styled auburn curls.

Grace was not as chic. Though she'd worn her best dress for the occasion, its hem fell just past her knees, and the waist nipped in with a slim black belt that matched her low heels. While not as stylish as Viv's black-and-white polka-dot dress, the pale blue cotton set off Grace's gray eyes and complemented her fair hair.

Viv had sewn it for her, of course. But then, Viv had always seen to both of them with an eye set toward grander aspirations. Throughout their friendship, they had spent hours sewing dresses and rolling their hair, years of reading *Woman* and *Woman's Life* on fashion and etiquette and then making countless corrections to ensure they "lost the Drayton" from their speech.

Now, Viv looked like she could grace one of those magazine covers with her high cheekbones and long-lashed brown eyes.

They joined the flurry of people rushing to and fro, heaving the bulk of their suitcases from one hand to the other as Grace led the way toward Britton Street. Thankfully, the directions Mrs. Weatherford had sent in their last correspondence had been detailed and easy to follow.

What had been missing from the account, however, were all the signs of war.

More advertisements, some calling for men to do their part, with others prompting people to disregard Hitler and his threats and still book their summer holidays. Just across the street, a wall of sandbags framed a doorway with a black-and-white sign proclaiming it to be a Public Air Raid Shelter.

True to Mrs. Weatherford's directions, they arrived at Britton Street within two short minutes and found themselves in front of a brick townhouse. It had a green door with a polished brass knocker and a flower box filled with purple and white petunias in the window. Based on what Mrs. Weatherford had written, this was unmistakably her house.

And their new home.

Viv charged up the stairs, her curls bouncing with each

step, and rapped on the door. Grace joined her at the top, spurred on by the anticipation jolting through her. After all, this was her mum's dearest friend, the one who visited them in Drayton several times in Grace's youth.

The friendship between Grace's mother and Mrs. Weatherford had begun when Mrs. Weatherford had lived in Drayton. Even after she moved, it had continued on through the Great War that took both their husbands' lives and through the illness that had finally taken Grace's mother.

The door opened and Mrs. Weatherford, looking older than Grace remembered, appeared in the widening doorway. She'd always been pleasantly plump with flushed apple cheeks and sparkling blue eyes. Only now she wore round spectacles and her dark hair was laced through with strands of sparkling silver. Her gaze homed in on Grace first.

She gasped softly and touched her fingers to her mouth. "Grace, you're the spitting image of your mum. Beatrice always was so pretty with those gray eyes of hers." The older woman opened the door wider, revealing her white cotton dress with blue sprigged flowers and matching blue buttons. Behind her, the entryway was small but tidy, filled almost entirely with a set of stairs that went up to another floor. "Please, do come in."

Grace murmured her thanks for the compliment, downplaying exactly how much that praise tugged at the part of her that still mourned her mother.

She heaved her suitcase through the doorway and into the home that held the savory aroma of meat and vegetables in the warm air. Grace's mouth watered.

She hadn't had a proper homemade meal since her mother's death. Not a good one, at least. Her aunt hadn't been much of a cook, and Grace spent too many hours running her uncle's store to prepare anything decent.

A rug underfoot softened Grace's steps, cream colored with pastel flowers. Though clean, it appeared to be somewhat worn in patches.

"Vivienne," Mrs. Weatherford said as Viv joined Grace in the entryway.

"All my friends call me Viv." She offered a smile at Mrs. Weatherford with her one-of-a-kind Viv charm.

"What beauties you both have become. I reckon you'll set my boy blushing." Mrs. Weatherford motioned for them to rest their bags on the floor. "Colin," she called up the polished wood stairs. "See to the ladies' effects while I put the kettle on."

"How is Colin?" Grace asked politely.

Like her, he was an only child, left without a father after the Great War as she had been. Though he was two years Grace's junior, they'd played together as children. She recalled those memories with great fondness. There had always been a gentleness to Colin, a genuine kindness behind the sharp intelligence of his eyes.

Mrs. Weatherford threw her hands up in exasperation. "Trying to save the world one animal at a time and bringing them all home." The good-natured chuckle that followed implied she didn't mind it as much as she claimed.

Grace took a moment to admire the entryway as they waited on Colin. A table sat beside the stairs with a glossy black telephone atop it. The wallpaper was a cheerful blue-and-white brocade, somewhat faded, and matched the white painted doors and doorframes. While simple in design, everything appeared immaculate. In fact, Grace was certain she would be hard-pressed to find a speck of dust on anything her mother's friend owned.

A creak sounded, followed by footsteps coming down the stairs as a tall, slender man appeared. His dark hair was combed neatly, and he wore a collared shirt and brown trousers.

He gave a shy smile, which softened his features and made him appear even more youthful than his twenty-one years. "Hullo, Grace."

"Colin?" she said, incredulous. He was almost a foot taller than her, towering over her as she once had over him.

He blushed.

His reaction was endearing, and it warmed her to know he hadn't lost his sweetness in the years that stretched between them.

Grace gazed up at him. "You've certainly grown since I saw you last."

He shrugged his skinny shoulders, looking perfectly bashful before offering a slight nod to Viv, whom he'd played with as well since the two girls had always been inseparable. "Viv. Welcome to London. Mum and I have been looking forward to your arrival." He slid a grin at Grace, then bent to grasp the two suitcases the ladies had set aside. He hesitated. "May I take these for you?"

"Please," Viv said. "Thank you, Colin."

He nodded and took one suitcase in each of his hands, carrying them easily up the stairs.

"Do you remember visiting with Colin?" Mrs. Weatherford asked.

"We do," Grace said. "He seems as kind as he's always been."

"Only much taller," Viv added.

Mrs. Weatherford looked up the stairs with adoration shining in her eyes, as if she could still see him. "He's a good lad. Come, let's have some tea and I'll show you around."

She motioned for them to follow and pushed open the door that led into a kitchen. Light spilled in from the window above the sink and at the back door, filtering in through parted gauzy white curtains. Everything was as pristine in her narrow kitchen as it had been in the entryway. The sun shone off clean white countertops, and a few dishes had been neatly set in a rack to dry. Towels the color of lemons were draped on a rack, and the scent of whatever she was cooking was even more tantalizing.

She indicated the small table with four white chairs to Grace and Viv and lifted the kettle from the stove. "Your uncle picked a fine time to lay claim to your home with a war soon upon us." She carried it to the sink and turned on the tap. "And so very like Horace," she said with evident distaste over the rush of water. "Beatrice was worried he might attempt such a thing, but her illness was so sudden—"

Mrs. Weatherford flicked a glance from where she'd been watching the water level in the kettle to Grace. "I shouldn't be going on like this, what with you just getting in from traveling. I'm so pleased to see you here. I only wish it was under better circumstances."

Grace bit her lower lip, uncertain what to say.

"You have a lovely home, Mrs. Weatherford," Viv said quickly.

Grace cast her a grateful look, which she answered with a conspiratorial wink.

"Thank you." The older woman cut the tap and scanned her sunny kitchen with a smile. "My Thomas's family owned it for several generations. It's not as fine as it once was, but one makes do."

Grace and Viv each slid into a chair. The lemon-printed cushion was thin enough to feel the hard wooden seat beneath. "We appreciate you allowing us to stay with you. It's very generous."

"Think nothing of it." Mrs. Weatherford set the kettle on the stove and spun the knob to turn the burner on. "There's not a thing I wouldn't do for the daughter of my dearest friend."

"Do you think finding employment will be difficult?" Viv asked. Though she kept her tone light, Grace knew how much her friend longed to be a shop assistant.

In truth, the idea was appealing to Grace as well. It seemed so glamorous to work in a department store, something fine and grand like Woolworths with floors of items that extended the length of an entire block.

Mrs. Weatherford gave a secretive smile. "It just so happens I'm well acquainted with quite a few shop owners in London. I'm sure I can do something to help. And Colin works at Harrods. He can put in a good word as well."

Viv's eyes lit up as she mouthed the store name to Grace with barely restrained excitement.

Mrs. Weatherford took one of the yellow towels and lifted a plate from the rack, rubbing away the few remaining drops. "I must say, the two of you don't sound at all like you're from Drayton."

Viv tilted her chin a notch higher. "Thank you. We've certainly tried. We're hoping it will help with our employment."

"How delightful." Mrs. Weatherford opened a cabinet

and replaced the plate within. "I trust you've procured letters of recommendation already?"

Viv had spent the day before their departure to London with a borrowed typewriter, carefully typing a letter of recommendation for herself. She'd offered to do one for Grace as well, but Grace had refused.

Mrs. Weatherford turned back to the drying dishes once more. Viv lifted her eyebrows at Grace, indicating she ought to have agreed.

"We do have letters of recommendation." Viv spoke confidently for both of them, no doubt already scheming how she might produce a second one for Grace.

"Viv does," Grace amended. "Unfortunately, I do not. My uncle refused to write a letter of recommendation for the time I spent at his shop."

It had been his final offense, a retaliation for her "abandoning the store" where she'd worked for most of her life. He didn't seem to care that his wife had insisted Grace find another place to live, only that Grace would no longer be at his beck and call.

The kettle gave a shrill cry and emitted a cloud of steam from its nozzle. Mrs. Weatherford pulled it from the stove, immediately cutting short its scream, and set it on a trivet.

She tsked as she scooped a spoonful of leaves into the tea ball before adding the boiled water to the teapot. "That's a shame, a terrible shame." She muttered something under her breath about Horace and settled the teapot on a silver tray with three teacups and a sugar and creamer set. She offered Grace a resigned frown. "They won't take you at a department store without one."

Grace's stomach dropped to her toes. Perhaps she ought to have allowed Viv to forge her a letter after all.

"However," Mrs. Weatherford added slowly as she carried the tray to the table and poured them each a steaming cup. "I have a place in mind where you could work for six months to obtain a proper letter of recommendation."

"Grace would be ideal for whatever you're thinking." Viv took a lump of sugar from the bowl and let it plunk into her tea. "She always had the highest marks in school. Especially in maths. She practically ran her uncle's entire shop on her own and improved it greatly while doing so."

"Then I think this will work out wonderfully." Mrs. Weatherford took a sip of her tea.

Something nudged against Grace's shin. She looked down to find a young tabby cat gazing imploringly up at her with large amber eyes.

Grace stroked her hand over the soft fur behind the kitten's ears and a purr vibrated to life. "I see you have a cat."

"Only for a few more days, I hope you don't mind." Mrs. Weatherford swept her hand to shoo the cat, but it remained stubbornly at Grace's side.

"The rascal won't leave my kitchen anytime he smells food." Mrs. Weatherford cast a chagrined look down at the little animal who regarded her without guilt or shame. "Colin is a wonder with animals. If I allowed him to keep every wounded creature he brought home, we would have quite the menagerie." Her chuckle interrupted the steam rising from her tea.

The cat rolled onto his back, revealing a small white star on his chest. Grace scratched at the spot, and his rhythmic purr rumbled under her fingertips. "What do you call him?"

"Tabby." Mrs. Weatherford playfully rolled her eyes. "My son is far better at rescuing animals than naming them."

As though summoned, Colin entered the room at that

very moment. Tabby leapt to his feet and trotted over to his savior. Colin lifted the kitten into his large hands, his touch gentle with the small creature who nuzzled affectionately against him.

This time, it was Colin Mrs. Weatherford shooed away. "Out of the kitchen with him."

"Sorry, Mum." Colin gave a quick, apologetic smile to Grace and Viv, then ducked from the room with the cat cradled to his chest.

Mrs. Weatherford shook her head with affectionate amusement as she watched him depart. "I'll visit Mr. Evans to see about getting you secured in that position at his shop." She settled back into her chair and gazed out to the garden with a sigh.

Grace glanced out the window where a gaping hole showed in the earth alongside a sad pile of uprooted flowers and a stack of what appeared to be sheets of aluminum. Most likely the beginnings of an Anderson shelter.

Grace hadn't seen any in Drayton where the chances of being bombed weren't high, but she'd heard of several cities where the Andys had been distributed. The small shelters were to be buried in the garden as a refuge if Hitler attacked Britain.

A tremor of unease rippled down Grace's spine. Of all the times to finally make their way to London, it was at the start of a war. Now they were in the prime target for bombings.

Not that returning to Drayton was an option. She would rather face the possibility of danger where she was wanted than contend with her uncle's hostility.

Viv peered out the window curiously and promptly looked away. After a lifetime of farming, she was—as she put it— "jolly well done with dirt."

Mrs. Weatherford sighed again and took a sip of tea. "It was a fine garden once."

"It will be again," Grace reassured her with more confidence than she felt. For if there were bombings, would any garden ever be the same again? Would any of them for that matter?

Such thoughts nipped at the back of her mind and cast them in an eerie shadow. "Mrs. Weatherford," she said abruptly, no longer wanting to think of war or bombings. "May I inquire as to what sort of shop Mr. Evans runs?"

"Of course, dear." Mrs. Weatherford set her teacup in its saucer with a clink, her eyes lighting up with enthusiasm. "It's a book shop."

Grace masked a twinge of disappointment. After all, she knew very little about books. Any attempts at reading had been quashed by countless interruptions. She'd been far too busy at her uncle's store, trying to earn enough money for her and her mother's survival, to bother with reading. Then her mother had become ill...

Uncle Horace's store had been easy enough to manage, especially as the household wares were items she personally used. Selling tea kettles, towels, vases and other goods she was familiar with came naturally. But she knew nothing about literature.

Well, that wasn't entirely true.

She could still recall her mother's copy of *Grimm's Fairy Tales* with an elegant princess painted on its front. How she'd loved letting her gaze wander over the colorful illustrations while her mother's voice spun magic with those fanciful tales. But outside of *Grimm's Fairy Tales*, she'd never had time to read.

"Brilliant." Grace smiled brightly to hide her apprehension. After all, she would make do. Anything would be better than working at her uncle's store.

But how was she possibly supposed to sell something she knew so little about?

TWO

GRACE'S FIRST ATTEMPT WITH PRIMROSE HILL BOOKS did not go as planned.

Not that she'd harbored lofty expectations for success, but she had anticipated the owner would at least be prepared for her arrival.

She found the shop without issue, yet another testament to Mrs. Weatherford's fine directional abilities. The narrow shopfront was not located on Primrose Hill as the name suggested, but rather was one of many in a line that ran along Hosier Lane, each with windows reflecting the dullness of the clouded afternoon sun. The bookshop's first two floors had been painted black with a yellow stuccoed facade rising above it, cracked and faded with age. A white sign proclaimed Primrose Hill Books in a glossy black looping text. The effect was clearly meant to be elegant, but seemed to Grace as rather flat and cheerless.

The sentiment was echoed in the shop's dingy windows, which were layered with lopsided strips of white scrim rather than displaying a purposefully set, enticing display. The tape wasn't uncommon; many had adhered it to their glass windows in shops and at home for prevention against shattering in case of a bombing. Usually, however, it was done neatly and with care.

A pull of trepidation dragged at Grace once more. What if Mr. Evans asked after the last book she'd read? She drew in a deep breath to fortify herself and pushed into the shop. A little bell rang overhead, far too happy for a place so dreary.

There was a mustiness in the air, mingled with a scent reminiscent of wet wool. Layers of dust on the shelves indicated most of the stock had not been touched in some time, and piles of books on the scuffed wooden floors lent it all a sense of disarray. This effect was heightened by a counter off to the right, which was cluttered with what appeared to be haphazardly stacked accounts amid a chaotic sea of pencil nubs and various other bits of rubbish.

It was no wonder Mr. Evans required assistance.

"Call out if you need something." The unseen voice was as dry and disused as the books.

"Mr. Evans?" Grace made her way deeper into the small shop.

Rows of unmarked shelves stretched high above her head, pressed so closely together she wondered how anyone might fit between them to peruse their contents. A second story balcony curled around the perimeter of the first floor, visible above the towering shelves and just as overcrowded and messy. Despite its external size, the shop's interior had been rendered far too small and tight.

Footsteps shuffled toward her as a portly man with white

hair and bushy brows squeezed from a narrow aisle with an open book framed between his hands. He lifted his head from the pages and regarded her for a long moment without speaking.

"Mr. Evans?" Grace stepped carefully around a knee-high stack of books.

His eyebrows crawled up over his glasses. "Who are you?"

Grace wanted nothing more than to navigate her way through the forest of shelves, back to the store's exit. But she'd arrived with purpose and put an edge of steel in her spine as her mother had always encouraged. "Good afternoon, Mr. Evans. I'm Grace Bennett. Mrs. Weatherford sent me here to speak with you about a position for a shop assistant."

His blue eyes narrowed behind his spectacles. "I told that meddlesome woman I didn't need help."

"I beg your pardon?" Grace asked, taken aback.

He looked down at his book and turned away. "There's nothing for you here, Miss Bennett."

Grace instinctively took a step toward the door. "I…I see," she stammered. "Thank you for your time."

He didn't acknowledge her as he scooted between the bookshelves once more in a clear sign of dismissal.

She stared after him in shock. If he wouldn't hire her, would there be more options without a letter of recommendation? She knew no one outside of Mrs. Weatherford, Colin and Viv. She was in a foreign city, away from a home where she no longer felt welcome. What else was she going to do?

A panicked urgency ran through her veins and left her palms prickling with heat. She should stay and fight for the job. After all, she needed it.

What if she couldn't afford the reduced rent on the room

in two months' time? Certainly she couldn't bring herself to ask Mrs. Weatherford for more assistance on top of what she had already given. Nor would Grace rely on Viv's aid.

All at once the stuffiness of the shop became stifling, the towering shelves too pressing. She should stay and fight, but her emotions were too tumultuous. God how she missed her mother's strength, her counsel and love.

Without another word, Grace found her way to the front door around tightly packed shelves and piles of books and left the shop.

She returned to Britton Street with brisk steps, wanting nothing more than to be alone. Solitude, however, was not to be had. Viv was in the parlor with Mrs. Weatherford, cooing over Tabby. Colin, who had worked all night at the Pet Kingdom in Harrods with a new baby elephant, was crouched beside the kitten with a bit of meat at the end of a spoon. Which meant all eyes turned to Grace the moment she closed the front door.

Though she knew her friends meant well, she wanted to slink from their stares rather than divulge how she'd run from the first sign of difficulty.

"How did it go with Mr. Evans?" Mrs. Weatherford sat forward in the burgundy armchair.

Grace's cheeks burned, but she managed to force a smile and act nonchalant. "I believe he is not looking to hire an assistant."

"Why ever would you assume such a thing?" Mrs. Weatherford asked.

Grace shifted her weight from one foot to the other. The gas mask box on its slender string bounced against her hip. "He told me as much."

Mrs. Weatherford pushed upright with a harrumph. "Colin, put the kettle on."

He looked up at his mother from where he sat on the floor beside Tabby with a spoon perched between his large fingers. "Will you take your tea out here?"

"It's not for me." She hastened to the stairs. "It's for Grace, who is no doubt in sore need of a cuppa while I go have a word with Mr. Evans."

"Wait." Viv put a hand to Colin's shoulder before he could leave.

She gave Tabby a scratch on the head and popped up from where she sat on the floor beside them. "Better than tea, let us go explore London." She fanned her hands toward Grace. "You're already dressed so nicely and I don't have my appointment until tomorrow afternoon. Let's go have a look about the city."

Viv's appointment was an interview at Harrods, secured in part by Colin with his influence of having worked there for several years, and also by her recommendation letter. While her position was indeed enviable, Grace would never begrudge her friend's happiness.

And as much as Grace didn't want to leave the cool quiet of the house, Viv's smile was so wide with excitement, Grace found she could not say no.

Viv readied herself with such haste, she descended the stairs the same time as Mrs. Weatherford, both with their hats pinned into place and neat heels clicking over the polished wood surface.

"You mark my words." Mrs. Weatherford glanced in a small mirror hanging beside the front door and adjusted the brim of her angular black hat. "Mr. Evans will hire you if he knows what's good for him."

Grace wished she could protest, to stoutly deny her need for a job or the kind help Mrs. Weatherford offered. But, alas, she could not refuse her charity. Uncle Horace had seen to that with his refusal to write a proper letter of recommendation. After so many years of restoring his shop, it seemed painfully unfair. Unfair and cruel.

Before she could even try to stop Mrs. Weatherford, the older woman disappeared out the front door, huffing with determination.

Viv took Grace's hand. "Let us go see the gem that is London, darling," she said in her finest "high society" inflection.

Grace couldn't help but smile at that and allowed her friend to pull her off to explore, leaving Colin with Tabby.

The women were soon swept up in the fast-moving city, amid tall buildings plastered with brightly colored adverts and the rumbles and honks of traffic. They darted and dashed through it all, keeping to the quick pace of city life with each hastened step.

But London was not the gem they had anticipated. Her sparkle had been dulled by the effects of an oncoming war, glued together with scrim tape and apprehension. Her shine was masked behind walls of sandbags and her soul unearthed to make way for shelters and trenches.

Such warnings were impossible to ignore.

In Drayton, where an attack was less likely, some preparations had been apparent. But there, the tape lining the windows had been idle amusement, and the greatest lurking fear was rationing rather than bombing. In London, such actions were done with blood-chilling necessity.

The evidence could be pushed aside temporarily, of course. Like when Grace and Viv entered Harrods for the first time and encountered the elaborate scrollwork along the ceilings, the Egyptian painted columns and exquisite fanning lights. The store went on as far as the fields in Drayton, each new department more exciting and elaborate than the last. There were silk scarves so fine, it felt like Grace was touching air, and perfumes set behind glittering glass counters that scented the air with an expensive musk.

The most fascinating by far was Pet Kingdom where Colin worked. The baby elephant he'd spent the night soothing now frolicked about in a pile of clean hay while a leopard cub raked its textured pink tongue over its pelt and watched them with curious green eyes.

"Imagine," Grace said dreamily as they left the animals and drifted through the other departments. "You will soon work here as a shopper's assistant."

"And you'd be with me," Viv whispered. "If you'd let me write you a letter of recommendation as well."

Grace's excitement wilted somewhat at the reminder of where she'd end up instead if Mr. Evans caved to Mrs. Weatherford. He seemed a brusque man in a store filled with wares she knew little about.

And yet she could not bring herself to present a false letter of recommendation. She'd never been good at lying, going all red about the face and tripping over her words. No doubt she'd fumble falsified information just as greatly. Still, she knew Viv wouldn't let it drop unless given some sort of concession.

"Perhaps if no further opportunities are presented, I may reconsider," Grace said slowly.

Viv's face lit up. "Consider it done."

"Only if no further opportunities are presented," Grace repeated, suddenly hopeful Mrs. Weatherford might get her way with Mr. Evans.

But Viv had turned away to examine a pair of stockings and merely acknowledged Grace's careful statement with a hum. Viv set the item aside, her hand splayed over its crinkly pink package.

"You know what we haven't done yet?" She spun toward Grace with such enthusiasm, her green skirt flared out around her knees. "We haven't gone to Hyde Park."

Grace grinned. How many countless summer days had they lain in the sun-warmed grass, breathing in its sweet scent as they pretended to be in Hyde Park? "It's only just up the road," she said with a lift of her brows.

Viv glanced around the brightly lit rows of endless elegant displays. "If we can find the way out."

Grace craned her neck, searching without success. It took longer than either cared to admit, and they became lost somewhere between the bedding department and braziers, but they were finally able to locate the exit and went up the street into Hyde Park.

What they had been expecting were clusters of deck chairs filled with extravagantly dressed people, the expanse of the Serpentine catching the sunlight like winking diamonds, and a lawn of endless green grass so soft it would tempt them to remove their shoes. They had not anticipated the trenches gouged into the soil like open wounds, or—worse still—the massive guns.

The hulking metal bodies rose taller than a man, supported by wheels so large, they came up to Grace's waist. A long barrel protruded from each beast, jutting toward the sky, ready to take down any threat.

Grace looked up into the heavy gray clouds, half expecting to see a fleet of aircraft in its murky depths.

"Don't trouble yourself worrying about Germany, ladies."

An older man paused before them. "Those anti-aircraft guns will shoot them out of the sky before they can touch us." He nodded with self-satisfied assurance. "You'll be safe."

Grace's stomach clenched and robbed her of any words. Viv seemed similarly affected and merely offered a weak smile. The man touched the brim of his hat and resumed his path across the park with a newspaper under his elbow.

"The war really is coming, isn't it?" Viv said softly.

It was. They all knew as much, even if they didn't want to admit it.

Already holidays had been cut short when teachers were asked to return home early to begin preparation for the likelihood of the evacuation of thousands of children from London. If they were planning to remove the children to the country, war would surely be soon upon them.

Still, there was a resignation in Viv's statement that plucked at a guilty string in Grace's chest.

"You don't need to be here, Viv. It isn't safe. You only came to help me. Because I was too scared to come on my own. You could—"

"Go back to Drayton?" Viv's lips curled up with mirth. "I'd rather die than go back and bury myself up to the elbows in dirt again."

We just might, even still. Grace didn't verbalize the macabre thought, but she did glance back once more at an anti-aircraft gun, dark and ominous where it rose against the afternoon sky.

"War hasn't even been declared yet." Viv adjusted the balance of her purse strap and the string of her gas mask box on her shoulder. "Come, let's return to Mrs. Weatherford's and see if she was able to talk some sense into Mr. Evans."

Grace made a sour face at her friend. "He doesn't want

me there any more than I want to be there. The shop is old and dusty and filled with books whose titles I've never even heard of."

A sparkle lit Viv's eyes. "That's why it's perfect for you, Duckie."

Grace couldn't help but smile at the endearment. Her mother had first called her that as a toddler when her blond curls flipped out at the base of her neck. Like a little duck's tail, Mum used to say. The moniker stuck. With her mother now dead, Viv was the only one who still remembered, and used, the nickname.

"Your uncle's shop was a dusty bit of nothing before you stepped up." Viv put her hands on her hips. "And something tells me Mrs. Weatherford will strong-arm Mr. Evans into a letter of recommendation in six months if he dares to refuse."

The image of Mrs. Weatherford haranguing Mr. Evans into submission was almost laughable. "Now there would be a battle of wills."

"I know who I'd put my money on." Viv winked. "Let's go see what she's accomplished."

By the time they returned to Britton Street, Mrs. Weatherford was already in the parlor with a cup of tea as the scent of roasting meat filled the air. Yet another delicious meal, no doubt. Mrs. Weatherford had quite the talent in the kitchen, the same as Grace's mother.

Mrs. Weatherford looked up from her teacup and waved the fog of steam from her glasses. "Ah, there you are. Mr. Evans will pay you a fair wage and would like you to start tomorrow morning promptly at eight."

Grace slid her low heels off and, without bothering with her slippers, padded onto the thick pile carpet in the parlor. "You mean…?"

A victorious smirk touched Mrs. Weatherford's lips. "Yes, dear. You are the new assistant at Primrose Hill Books."

Relief wrestled with trepidation. It was a job, one that would guarantee Grace a livelihood in London. With it, perhaps she could finally put Drayton and her uncle successfully behind her.

"Thank you for speaking with him, Mrs. Weatherford," Grace said gratefully. "It was so considerate of you."

"It was my pleasure, dear." The slight puff to the older woman's chest indicated that it had indeed been her pleasure to do so.

Grace paused. "Might I ask why it's called Primrose Hill Books when it isn't on Primrose Hill?"

Mrs. Weatherford gave a dreamy smile that told Grace the reason was a good one. "Mr. Evans and his wife, God rest her soul, met on Primrose Hill. They propped their backs against the same tree and discovered the other reading the very same book. Can you imagine?" She took a tea cake from the tray and held it pinched between her fingers. "When they opened the shop, they said it was the perfect name for a bookshop they shared. Quite romantic, isn't it?"

It was almost impossible to imagine the stodgy old shop owner as a young man in love, but the shop name was indeed charming. As was the story. Perhaps working at the store would not be so terrible.

And anyway, it would only be for six months.

THREE

GRACE ARRIVED AT PRIMROSE HILL BOOKS AT TEN
minutes to eight the next morning with perfect curls and
jangling nerves. Viv had helped set her hair the night before
and rose early to wish her luck despite her own interview
with Harrods not being until that afternoon.

Grace would need all the luck she could get.

Mr. Evans was behind the cluttered counter when Grace
entered. He wore a tweed jacket with a collared shirt underneath and didn't bother to look up at the ding of the bell.
"Good morning, Miss Bennett," he said in a bored drawl.

Grace smiled at him, determined for a fresh start with
her best foot forward. Or her other cheek turned, depend-
ing on how one looked at it. "Good morning, Mr. Evans.
I truly appreciate you giving me the opportunity to work
in your shop."

He lifted his head and regarded her through the thick

glass of his spectacles. His wispy white hair and overgrown eyebrows appeared as tamed down as they might ever be. "I don't need help, but that woman wouldn't let me be until I finally agreed." He wagged a stubby finger at her. "And don't you be locking your heart into this task, Miss Bennett. It's only for six months."

Grace's shoulders relaxed somewhat with her relief. At least he wouldn't expect her to be at the shop for the rest of her life.

"I won't become attached," she answered truthfully. How could she possibly with a place so dusty and desolate?

She scanned the shop and was struck anew with how cramped the space seemed. Shelves were crowded against one another like big teeth in a small mouth amid errant piles of scattered books. All without any sense of rhyme or reason.

At least when Grace had begun at her uncle's shop, there had been some semblance of order. What was she do with this haphazard chaos?

A sense of hopelessness crept in. After all, where was she even to start? Did Mr. Evans already have expectations he wanted her to meet?

She stood awkwardly in a state of uncertainty with her purse and gas mask box on her shoulder, still wearing her hat. Mr. Evans did not appear to notice as he scrawled a series of numbers into a ledger. The pencil tip was carefully pinched between the pads of his fingertips. One more sharpening and the thing would be nonexistent.

Grace cleared her throat. "Where am I to set my belongings?"

"Back room," he muttered as his hand continued to move against the paper.

She glanced to the rear of the store and saw a door, presumably where she was being directed. "Then what would you like me to do?"

The lead of the pencil snapped, and Mr. Evans hissed out an exhale of frustration. He leveled a stare at her. "I told you, I don't need help. You can sit in the back room and sew or settle into a corner with a book to read or file your nails. I don't care."

Grace nodded and slipped down the misaligned aisle of shelving toward the door he'd indicated. Above it was a dingy brass placard with "Primrose Hill Books" engraved at its top and a small line of words beneath—"where readers find love." Hopefully it was an omen that her six months might not be all bad.

The room was narrow and dimly lit by an uncovered bulb, with a flimsy table and chair. Boxes lined every wall, sometimes layered two and three deep, minimizing the space so that one could barely move. It was far less welcoming than the shop itself, which Grace hadn't thought possible. She located several hooks on the wall where she hung her effects and went back to the main area of the shop.

She'd never been one for sewing—that was Viv's area of expertise—and wouldn't know where to start with which book to read, let alone how to shelve them. A glance at her nails, however, had her lamenting having forgotten her nail file at home.

There was nothing for it but to find something to do. The thick layers of dust on the shelves begged to be wiped clean. Granted, dusting the shop hadn't been on the list Mr. Evans had recommended, but the shop was in sore need.

Three hours later, nearly choking on dust motes in the air, she regretted her choice. Her white shirtdress with sprigs of pink flowers, one of her favorites, was streaked with grime, and Mr. Evans glared in her direction every time he coughed. Which was quite often.

Through it all, several customers had come and gone. She'd tried to linger near them as she worked, employing considerable care to not send dust clouds in their direction, but still close enough should they require help.

Not that she would know what to do if they asked her a question. Fortunately no one did, at least not until five minutes after Mr. Evans departed to a nearby café for tea.

An older woman in a checked pinafore housedress approached with her gaze fixed on Grace. "Excuse me, do you have *The Black Spectacles*?"

Grace smiled easily. At least this was a question she could answer. "We don't carry spectacles here, I'm terribly sorry."

The woman blinked her wide blue eyes. "It's a book. By John Dickson Carr. I finished *The Crooked Hinge* last night and just had to find the next edition in the Gideon Falls series."

If the earth were to open up at that moment and swallow Grace whole, she'd offer no protest.

She had two book names and a series to work with and no idea where any of them might belong. While cleaning, she'd tried to find some order to the layout of the books, to no avail.

"Oh, of course." Grace waved for the woman to follow her in the hopes she might somehow have the dumb luck of stumbling upon the book by happenstance. Or be struck by lightning on the way. She'd accept either at that point.

"Did you find *The Crooked Hinge* exciting?" Grace asked tentatively in an effort to glean what type of book she was seeking.

The woman pressed her palm to her chest. "Oh, it was

the best kind of mystery. I locked myself in my bedroom for the last chapter so I could finish it without the children interrupting."

Ah, yes, a mystery. Maybe there were some located near the back where she was currently leading the woman. "I believe it will be somewhere on this wall." Grace's gaze skimmed over the spines of multiple books. None of which were in any order, not by title or name or even color of the book jacket.

"If I may…" A masculine voice spoke from behind Grace.

She leapt in surprise to find a tall man in a finely tailored gray jacket with his black hair combed neatly to the side. She'd noticed him earlier. After all, what woman would not when he was so handsome? But it had been rather a while ago, and she'd assumed he'd already departed.

"I believe it's on the shelf on the far wall." He glanced toward the opposite side of the shop.

"Yes, thank you." Grace's cheeks burned. No, her whole body burned, flaming with an embarrassment made all the more scorching by the man's gaze on her. She indicated the woman follow once more. "If you'll come this way, please."

"If you don't mind, miss…" The woman looked pointedly at the handsome man and blushed. "I'd rather he show me."

His eyebrows went up with surprise, and he gave a rich chuckle. "By all means." He offered his elbow to the older woman, who took it with a beaming smile.

Grace watched the two with amusement as the gentleman took down a black book with bold red type on the front. The woman thanked him and met Grace at the cash register on the cluttered counter.

"What a gentleman." The woman patted her reddened cheeks before removing the payment from her purse. "If I were as young and pretty as you, I don't think I'd let him leave without finding out his name."

Grace flicked an anxious glance at the man to ensure he hadn't heard the woman's statement. He remained facing a shelf several paces away, apparently oblivious. Thank goodness.

The tension in Grace's shoulders eased somewhat. She counted out the woman's change, thanked her and handed her the purchased book. The housewife gave her a quick wink and exited the shop, sending the little bell chiming.

When its ring cut off, a heavy silence filled the cramped space. While Grace had been oblivious to the man's lingering presence in the store earlier, she was keenly aware of it now. If this had been the shop in Drayton, she could offer to assist him, perhaps make a few suggestions. As it was, he appeared to know the store better than she.

She discreetly brushed as much of the lingering dust from her dress as possible and vowed not to wear anything white again until the shop had been thoroughly cleaned. In the end, she opted to tidy the bits and bobs scattered over the counter as she waited for him to make his selections. She found an old cup in one of the cabinets below, where she gathered the pencil nubs, each worn nearly to its end. Next she disposed of the scraps of rubbish, but only after confirming they were not in fact account slips, as the two often looked similar.

The gentleman was standing before the partially cleared off counter when Grace looked up. He smiled at her and met her gaze with the most striking green eyes. There was a slight cleft in his chin, which complemented the sharpness of his jaw nicely and made him as alluring as one of the actors in a cinema production.

Grace's mind tripped over itself for something fascinating to say and quickly came up empty. "Is there something I can help you with?"

He nudged the stack of books on the counter toward her, books she'd been too lost in his beautiful eyes to notice.

"I'd like to purchase these, please." He put his hands casually in his pockets and settled into the wide-legged stance of a man intent on conversation. "I've never known Mr. Evans to have a shop assistant."

Grace punched a button on the old National cash register, and its accompanying thwack resounded in the empty shop. "It's my first day." She cast him a sheepish glance as she reached for the next book. "It was kind of you to help earlier. Thank you."

His smile widened and made the smooth skin around his eyes crinkle at the corners. "It's the least I could do. I've been coming regularly since I was a boy. I noticed you've cleaned the place up a bit. That's quite the task to take on."

"I'm looking forward to the challenge," Grace replied, realizing the truth behind her words. If nothing else, putting the shop in order would help fill her time over the next six months.

"It will be a challenge indeed." The man glanced behind him with an exaggerated grimace. "Especially if you're a book lover. Mysteries could easily be thrillers, classics could easily be love stories, and on and on with all that."

"I'm not," she confessed. "A book lover, I mean. I haven't had much time for books."

He drew up slightly, almost as though affronted by her admission, though his smile did not waver. "Well, if you were to start with any of them, I'd suggest *The Count of Monte*

Cristo. It's a classic I've always enjoyed." He tilted his head. "Though it could also be a love story."

"I'll take it into consideration." Grace lifted the last book to ring up. "Thank you for the recommendation."

He took out his wallet and paid for the books. "May I be so bold as to ask your name?"

"Miss Grace Bennett," she replied.

"Miss Bennett." He nodded politely. "I'm George Anderson. I look forward to seeing what you do to the shop."

She nodded mutely and Mr. Anderson departed, walking backward as he did so to cast her one last devestating grin.

Heavens!

She put her hand to her chest as though she could slow its rapid beat. Just then the chime sounded at the door once more and Mr. Evans filled the shop with his cranky disposition.

His gaze scoured the organized countertop and his furry eyebrows wriggled with apparent consternation. "What the devil happened here? Have we been robbed?"

"I tidied up," Grace replied.

Mr. Evans scowled and glared around the shop. "That's why it's so dusty in here." He waved in front of him with a folded newspaper as though the air itself issued great offense.

She tensed, waiting for cutting words such as those her uncle had so often thrown at her. In all the years she'd worked for him, from the first day she'd completed the final year offered at the schoolhouse in Drayton until when she'd left for London, he had pointed out, in great detail, all of her many failures. Her work ethic was not on par with what he expected. She wasted product that could still be used. She could have sold more items with her suggestions if she'd been smarter, more intuitive, more driven. Less incompetent.

She clenched her hands into fists and squeezed, bracing herself for the emotional blows on her personal deficiencies.

"I suppose it does need a good scrubbing down," Mr. Evans grumbled in begrudging acquiescence.

Her fists relaxed. "I beg your pardon?"

"The place is a bit dusty, and I haven't the time to muddle with it." He slapped the paper on the countertop and took the stack of receipts, ignoring several that fluttered free. "I'd thank you not to go looking through my accounts."

"I'd never presume." Grace bent to retrieve the scraps of receipts and handed them to Mr. Evans, taking care to keep her gaze averted from the neat print.

He tucked them into the pile of papers and disappeared into the little room at the back of the shop. He did not emerge for some time, and when he did, he remained at the rear, sifting through the books, more like a customer than the shop's owner.

Grace spent the remainder of the afternoon finishing her dusting and polishing the counter. It was really quite nice underneath years of grime, with carved scrollwork at its corners and a lovely chestnut hue. Fortunately, no other patrons sought her help with their selections and her only task with the customers involved gathering their payment.

When at last it was time to take her leave, her announcement to Mr. Evans was met with a grunt of acknowledgment and little else.

Though dirty, exhausted and feeling like she hadn't done nearly enough, Grace eagerly rushed home in anticipation of hearing how Viv's interview went.

She flung open the front door upon her arrival. "Viv, did you—?"

The wireless was turned to full volume and a voice crackled throughout the parlor, informing listeners that a fleet had been mobilized.

A fleet of what?

Mrs. Weatherford and Viv sat before the radio, listening intently. Viv shot her a distracted glance and waved her over.

Grace quickly joined her friend on the blue mohair sofa. "What's going on?" she whispered. "Why is the broadcast on? It's not six."

Viv cast her a nervous glance. "News came this afternoon. The reserves have been called. We were informed earlier that we shouldn't conclude war is inevitable. But how can we not when they're telling us that fleets are mobilized and all naval reservists and remaining Royal Air Force personnel should report for duty?"

Grace fell back against the couch in stunned shock. How had she heard nothing about this? But then, she'd been in her own world busily cleaning, her mind set to task with determination and her customers few and far between.

The anticipation vibrating in the air now hummed in Grace's veins. This was it.

War.

Mrs. Weatherford said nothing, her face a stoic mask. She stood abruptly and snapped off the wireless. "That's about enough for one day." She drew in a deep breath and turned to Grace. "I trust your first day went well?"

"Yes, thank you," Grace replied softly.

"Good." Mrs. Weatherford gave a perfunctory nod. "If you'll excuse me, I have a kidney pie to prepare or we won't have a thing for supper."

Without waiting for another reply, she marched out of the room, her back unnaturally straight.

Viv lowered her voice. "They're evacuating the children tomorrow. All of them to the country. At least, the ones whose parents signed them up to go."

The news struck Grace in the chest. Viv was right; how could they not expect war when such measures were being implemented?

Grace thought of the housewife who had been in the store earlier, selecting a book without the knowledge that her children would be leaving the following day. All the mothers of London would be losing their children due to the evacuation. And many of them would also be sending their husbands to war.

If not enough men volunteered, they might be conscripted. Grace's stomach gave a slight flip.

Colin might be called up.

It was no wonder Mrs. Weatherford had been so disinclined to hear more.

Viv stared down at the carpet, solemn. A knot of fear tightened in Grace's chest and she fought for some levity, lest they both give in to hopelessness. "The children will be fine as long as they don't end up with my uncle and his family."

Viv offered a sad smile as she played along. "Not that he'd offer them a place anyway."

It was then Grace realized Viv was still wearing her smart navy suit. "Did you have your interview?"

Viv nodded. "I was offered a position as a shopper's assistant. I start tomorrow, for however long it will last now."

"It will last quite a while, I'm sure." Grace squeezed her friend's hand. "Everyone always needs a pair of stockings or a new blouse to make them feel fine."

"Or an elephant?" Viv tilted her head.

"Perhaps a wombat?" Grace shrugged.

Viv's mouth stretched in a ghost of a smile. "Maybe even a cheetah?"

"Don't forget its lead," Grace cautioned.

Viv's expression turned serious. "We'll make it through this, Grace Bennett. Just you see."

She clasped her hand over Grace's, a reminder of the camaraderie they'd shared since childhood. That solidarity had helped them survive the pain of Grace's mother's death, the drudgery of life in Drayton, Viv's overbearing parents and even the incessant teasing of Geoffrey Simmons, the dolt.

Together, they would be able to take on anything thrown at them—whether it be a curmudgeonly shop owner or a coming war.

FOUR

THE QUEUE OF CHILDREN WAS TRAGICALLY ENDLESS.

In truth, Grace hadn't had much chance to think of the evacuation. There had been too much activity the evening before as they prepared for the first night of the government mandated blackout while Colin put the final touches on the Anderson shelter in Mrs. Weatherford's poor torn-up garden.

The ruined flower beds had been mentioned several times by Mrs. Weatherford, despite her sniffed remarks that she didn't care a whit.

Through it all, Grace was ashamed to admit she hadn't remembered about the children. Not when she'd left Britton Street to make her way to Primrose Hill Books. Especially not when she caught sight of strange silver balloons in the sky, as large as townhouses and suspended above the city like bloated silver fish. Odd things that no doubt served some purpose of war.

She stared up at one so intently as she turned down Albion Place, that she nearly crashed into a man in a blue wool Royal Air Force uniform with his full kit slung over one shoulder.

"Forgive me," Grace said. "I didn't—"

Whatever else she meant to say died on her tongue, for that was when she caught sight of the children. The queue ran down the length of the street, heading in the direction of Farringdon Station.

The RAF officer replied, but she didn't hear him as he strode briskly past. She couldn't take in anything more than the endless stream of children with their small gas masks hanging from strings at their sides, their information pinned on their jackets and their bags of belongings. Such small bags for what might be a long absence. For who knew when the children would return?

Some were eager, their faces bright in anticipation for an adventure. Others were tearstained as they clung to their mothers. As for the women accompanying them, each one was pale, their expressions steeled against the agony of their task.

No mother should suffer a choice such as theirs: to send their child to live with a stranger in the country or allow them to stay in the city where it was dangerous.

Despite the pain of separation, there must truly be considerable risk if they were going to the effort to remove so many children. Certainly it was far better than keeping them here, where they were under the constant threat of being bombed.

Though Grace was not a mother, she hoped to become one someday. So it was that every stricken visage drove into her heart the sacrifice these women were making to ensure their children remained safe.

As Grace walked on in her stunned state, she came upon the mass of them congregated at the entrance to Farringdon Station where another stream of children came from the opposite direction. Hundreds, if not thousands.

Many mothers would have empty arms this night.

A heaviness lay in Grace's chest for those women and the little ones they had to send off to another's care. She quickened her pace, unable to endure the sight any longer.

She all but threw herself into the bookshop, earning her a sharp look from Mr. Evans upon her arrival. "Has the war already started?" he asked dryly and returned his focus to the book in front of him.

"It might as well have." Grace glanced out to the street as a mother hastened her two young children in the direction of the tube station. "The children are all being sent away."

He hummed in distracted agreement.

She peered up to the sky, seeking the large silver objects. "And those balloons—"

"Barrage balloons."

She turned back to him. "What on earth are those?"

Mr. Evans sighed without patience and set his book down. "They're affixed to steel cables and prevent aircraft from flying too low. They're there for our protection."

"So they can't bomb us then?" Grace asked hopefully.

Mr. Evans snorted. "Oh, they can bomb us well enough. The balloons prevented it in the Great War when planes couldn't fly as high, but now at least it forces them up into the range of the anti-aircraft guns."

Chills prickled over Grace's skin. She wanted to ask more questions, but he'd already lifted his book and resumed reading. Few customers entered the store that day. It was easy to see why when the children were being shipped off, the men were leaving for war and all the mothers were left behind with their heavy sorrow.

Grace had thought to try organizing the books, but could not clear the image of those children from her mind. Not when there had been so very many of them. Not when their mothers had been so strong in the face of what they must do to have their children protected.

She recalled the time her mother had gone to visit Mrs. Weatherford once when she was a child. Though Grace had stayed with Viv's family for the week, she still remembered how missing her mother had left her feeling bereft. And that had been only a week.

Those poor children.

In the end, Grace applied herself to the messily placed scrim on the windows, peeling away first the tape, then picking at the adhesive that remained in sticky patches along the glass. The task was mindless, which suited her well, for her mind was entirely overfull already.

When there were only two strips left and she was debating whether or not she had time to reapply more tape with proper care, Mr. Evans came to her. "Go home, Miss Bennett. There's not enough business to even bother staying open. Not today. Besides, I haven't anything to black out the windows when it grows dark." He folded his arms over his chest, and his inhale whistled through his nostrils as he looked about his shop. "War is coming and books aren't what people will be shopping for."

Grace gathered the discarded tape and stood. "But surely they need entertainment."

He nodded to the windows. "I'll bring in newspaper tomorrow."

Grace hid her grimace of distaste at the thought of layering the wide windows with plastered news sheets. "I can make curtains. Mrs. Weatherford has quite a bit of fabric on hand already. We've some to spare."

Indeed, Mrs. Weatherford had been quite elated to crow over her victory at getting so many yards of heavy black sateen at only two shillings a yard.

Grace didn't know why she was offering to help Mr. Evans. Especially when he was implying he soon may not have the business to support hiring an assistant. But they had the fabric to spare, and anything she could do to remain useful enough to glean a letter of recommendation would work in her favor.

Grace quickly gathered her purse, hat and gas mask, eager for the extra time off.

Mr. Evans met her at the entrance and flipped the sign from Open to Closed. "Good afternoon, Miss Bennett."

He closed the door behind her and locked it. The children were gone from the streets by that point, almost as if their organized departure hadn't happened. On her walk home, Grace pushed her thoughts from the painful recollection and instead considered how to draw more customers into Primrose Hill Books.

She'd done it with her uncle's shop. Several signs in the window and a few items placed strategically on sale had made all the difference. Soon customers had come with regularity.

Of course, there were fewer patrons at Primrose Hill Books, and the ones remaining perched on tightly strung nerves. But books served a purpose. Distractions were always needed. Most certainly in times of strife.

If she made one store successful once, by God, she could do it again. And this time, she'd jolly well make sure she recieved a glowing recommendation for her efforts.

She met Mrs. Weatherford just outside the townhouse, the older woman's arms laden with bags.

Mrs. Weatherford waved her over with half of a finger, which appeared the only appendage she had to spare. "Your timing is impeccable, Grace. Come here, child."

Grace rushed over and pulled several totes from Mrs. Weatherford's arm. An unexpected weight tugged at Grace's hand with such force, she nearly dropped the parcel. "What do you have in here? Sandbags?"

Mrs. Weatherford cast a conspiratorial glance around before leaning in and whispering, "Tea." She lifted one shoulder to heft another sack. "And sugar. Now come, let's get this inside quickly."

She didn't speak again until they spirited the packages into the house and safely tucked them in the kitchen. The heavy dark curtains hung from the windows in the otherwise cheerful kitchen, a reminder of the blackout starting that evening. There had been several test runs the previous month, but this time would be in earnest.

Mrs. Weatherford dropped her burden with great care and issued forth a relieved sigh. "Heavens, but that was heavy."

"This is all tea and sugar?" Grace surveyed the bags, which were stuffed to the seams.

"Some of it is flour too." Mrs. Weatherford wagged a finger. "Don't you go looking at me like that, Grace Bennett. The war is coming and you mark my words, there will be rationing. I had to get to these items before the hoarders."

Grace regarded the trove of dry goods. "The hoarders?"

Mrs. Weatherford set to work, unpacking her wares. "Mrs. Nesbitt had at least twice as much, and she's a woman on her own." Mrs. Weatherford bent over the counter to rearrange objects in the cabinet, making space for her new purchases.

"You know her, the proprietress of Nesbitt's Fine Reads, one of the many illustrious bookshops along Paternoster Row." She glanced at Grace for confirmation.

Grace shook her head.

Mrs. Weatherford's brows furrowed. "Surely Mr. Evans has mentioned Paternoster Row?"

"He hasn't." Grace stacked several bags of sugar in a cleared spot in the open cabinet.

Mrs. Weatherford shifted aside some boxes and replaced them with tins of tea. "Well, that street is where most book-lovers with good money go. I've told Mr. Evans a dozen times he should relocate." She took a step back and inspected the stacked cabinet with a satisfied nod. "You should go sometime. See what a proper bookshop looks like. I can give you directions."

A proper bookshop. It was exactly what Grace needed to study to see how to improve Primrose Hill Books. "That would be wonderful," she said. "While we're on the topic, would you mind if I took some of the black sateen to make curtains for the shop?"

Mrs. Weatherford cast a proud smile at her, the kind her own mother once gave. It touched a wounded place inside Grace, somewhere buried deep, and soothed it in the gentlest way.

"Of course, you may, dear," the older woman said. "Mind that you do at least three layers or it won't block out a bit of light. I'm sure he's very appreciative of your efforts." She filled the kettle with water from the tap. "Even if he doesn't say as much."

Colin came into the kitchen with Tabby following at his heels, mewing insistently. "Hullo, Grace." His cheeks colored with a slight blush, as always happened when he entered a room Viv or Grace were in. "We received a baby cheetah this morning. There's almost nothing to him, just a bit of fluff and a fierce personality." He made the shape of a ball with his fingers to indicate the animal's size.

"I imagine he must be darling."

"You'll have to come by and see him next time you're at Harrods." He glanced to his mother. "Can you hand me a tin of tuna, Mum?"

Mrs. Weatherford's mouth pinched, but she handed him the tin regardless. "I think Tabby is large enough to find a home. Soon we'll be sore pressed to feed ourselves, let alone a cat."

Colin took the can with a rueful smile.

"You both think I'm mad, but I tell you, everything will be rationed." Mrs. Weatherford folded the now empty totes and put the full kettle on the stove while Colin peeled the top off the tin with a can opener.

A pungent fish odor filled the small space and sent Tabby in a frenzy of emphatic cries. Mrs. Weatherford waved at the air. "Save yourself, Grace. Put the wireless on while I fetch our tea."

Grace didn't need a second offer and quickly fled the odiferous room. However, when she snapped on the set, the news greeting her was far worse than the smell of fish.

Lionel Marson's rich voice emanated from the speakers. "Germany has invaded Poland and bombed many towns..."

Grace stood stock-still, her hand hovering over the metal knob. On he went, detailing how Poland had been attacked that morning, how major Polish cities had been bombed and France was mobilizing. With the Agreement of Mutual Assistance being signed with Poland only days before, there would be nothing for it: Great Britain and France would have to intervene.

The rest of the afternoon and evening were spent in the parlor as each new bulletin aired, everyone perched in a desperate bid for more information. Much of what was said they already knew, but listened intently regardless.

Through it all, Grace made curtains for the shop with Viv's help once her friend came home from a successful first day at Harrods. With nerves on high alert, they picked at Mrs. Weatherford's pork pie and prepared for the blackout before the sun had fully set.

Hitler could do to England what he'd done to Poland. Any sliver of light at a window could tell his planes where to drop their bombs.

A chill of anticipation squeezed down Grace's spine. She'd been dreading the blackout and its strict rules. Now, she was grateful for the government's foresight in keeping them from being a blatant target in the dark night.

Likewise, she was appreciative for the Anderson shelter in the back garden. Knowing they had protection in such proximity lent her a calming sense of security.

Amid the pure darkness of their first blackout, Grace had difficulty finding sleep. Especially when her mind was filled with talk of war and her thoughts kept returning to the children from that morning.

Apparently, the heavy curtains did their job too well. Grace did eventually fall asleep, but the next morning, she awoke nearly half an hour later than intended. Despite her rushed attempt to get ready, she still made it to the bookshop several minutes late.

Mr. Evans glanced up at her arrival, his face dour. No doubt a rebuke was coming.

Grace clutched her bag, the triple layer blackout curtains within.

"And here I thought you might have abandoned the place as a lost cause." A smirk lifted the corners of Mr. Evans's mouth as he wandered back toward the rear of the shop. "Not that I'd have blamed you."

"I'm sorry for being late." She called to his back and exhaled slowly. "I brought the curtains."

He looked over his shoulder toward her bag and nodded once.

It was as much of a thank you as she'd expected. She tidied the shop first, cleaning the piles of receipts and bits of rubbish he'd left on the counter. Though she knew little of the books they sold, she chose covers with appealing fronts and displayed them in a curved arrangement in the large windows.

It was a start, at least.

She had just located a small ladder and was preparing to hang the heavy curtains when the jingling bell announced a visitor. An old man entered and caught her with his sharp gaze. "Who are you?"

"Miss Bennett." She climbed down from the ladder. "The new shop assistant."

At eye level, it was impossible to ignore how very much the man resembled a bird set against the bitter wind on a cold day. His downy white head was set low into the shrug of his hunched shoulders, and his spindly legs jutted from the bulk of his dark jacket. He glanced at the curtains waiting to be hung and tutted. "No need for curtains when tar would work just as well."

Grace nearly cringed at the idea of smearing tar over the glass. "May I help you?"

"Where is Evans?"

"Pritchard, is that you?" Mr. Evans emerged from the forest of shelves, an ever-present book propped in his hands just over the paunch of his belly. He snapped it shut and pushed his glasses higher on the bridge of his nose.

"You hired an assistant?" The man looked around the shop, his beak of a nose exacerbating his birdlike appearance. "Are you doing all that well, then?"

"You never know what you'll need when a war is on," Mr. Evans answered wryly. "Comparing our bookshops again, Pritchard?"

The man clicked his tongue. "Bah! War hasn't even been declared yet. And if this mess with Poland pushes us toward it, we'll show Hitler and his 'Nastys' a battle that will send them scuttling back to Germany. Mark my words, this will all be over by Christmas."

"I'll still take my curtains." Mr. Evans nodded toward Grace, releasing her from the need to be party to the conversation. "If nothing else, it'll keep the bloody ARP warden from knocking at my door."

Grace gathered the slippery fabric in her arms, climbed the ladder, and proceeded to hang the curtains while the men discussed book sales and politics.

"How the devil do you keep mice from your store?" Mr. Pritchard asked abruptly as Grace finished her task. "I've had issues with the buggers from the first."

"It's never been a problem." Mr. Evans's tone was becoming distracted, a clear indication he was finished with the chat. A social cue Mr. Pritchard had failed to grasp.

The man tucked his head deeper into his shoulders and

scowled. "Most likely because you're not as close to the Thames all the way out here. Not like I am at Paternoster Row."

"You need a cat," Grace said as she climbed down from the ladder and examined her handiwork. "Mrs. Weatherford's son has a tabby cat who needs a home."

Mr. Pritchard scoffed. "That meddlesome woman?"

Grace busied herself folding the ladder to hide her frown at his unkind assessment of the woman who had done so much for her. "A cat should help with the mice. I have it on good authority Mrs. Weatherford has no plans this morning and would likely appreciate the call."

At least to the point of finding a new home for Tabby.

Mr. Pritchard nodded slowly to himself. "I see. Well, it appears I might as well see about a cat. Good day to you, Evans."

Mr. Evans muttered some form of farewell, and Mr. Pritchard left the shop. With the curtains properly hung and a decent display in the windows, Grace turned to her next project: finding places to relocate the piles of books scattered about the floor.

The task was far larger than she'd anticipated. Whatever shelving system Mr. Evans had once incorporated was now nearly nonexistent, which meant Grace needed to create her own. Eventually. For now, she simply found places to put the discarded tomes.

She'd become so engrossed in her task, Mr. Evans had to remind her on several occasions that she had stayed beyond her allotted hours. Each time she'd put him off, saying she was nearly done. And each time she thought she truly was, only to discover more stacks.

A low rumble of thunder caught her attention, and Mr.

Evans appeared before her with an umbrella in hand. "Miss Bennett, go home. The shop is closing and it's begun to rain."

She looked up from a row of spines pressed so tightly together, no book could possibly fit between them despite the twenty or so more she still had to put away. They weren't in any order. Yet. But at least they were off the floor.

She glanced toward the window and found the curtains drawn. The blackout was clearly in effect.

Had it really become so late?

"Stay home tomorrow," Mr. Evans said. "You've put in far too much work for one day."

"But yesterday—"

"You were supposed to leave this afternoon, and it is now night." Mr. Evans pressed the brolly toward her once more. "If Mrs. Weatherford calls one more time for you, she'll have my head."

Ah, there it was then. Mrs. Weatherford. No doubt Grace's delay had caused her to worry.

Grace accepted the umbrella and quickly gathered her things. Mr. Evans followed her to the front and opened the door.

Blackness met her on the other side, as stark as it was deep—an endless sea of nothing.

Grace blinked as if to clear her vision, but it did no good against the true and complete darkness. She hadn't realized the blackout would be this all-consuming.

"I should walk you home," Mr. Evans said, more to himself than to her.

"Think nothing of it." Grace notched her chin a little higher, the way Viv did when putting her confidence on full display. Though in Grace's case, it was mere bravado.

"It will take me less than ten minutes. We needn't both end up drenched."

He frowned and opened his mouth to say something when a sharp whistle pierced the air.

"Put out that light," someone called from the distance. The self-important authority to the tone suggested an Air Raid Precautions warden, the volunteer service made up of neighbors who monitored blackout compliance.

"Good night, Mr. Evans." Grace slipped out of the shop as she snapped open the brolly.

Still Mr. Evans waited, holding the door open for her.

"Put it out, Mr. Evans," the ARP warden shouted again, this time closer.

Finally, he let the door fall closed and a thick blanket of darkness fell over Grace. It seemed to press against her eyes, making her strain to see something—anything—and failing miserably.

Usually there were people about, cars with bright headlights slicing through the pitch-black and lampposts with a golden glow in a radius beneath. But not now. Not during a blackout.

She hesitated where she stood in an attempt to gain her bearings which didn't seem quite able to sort themselves out. Rain pattered on her umbrella while she remained in place.

She would have to move based on memory in the absence of sight. It was fascinating how only a week of being in London resulted in her being able to picture the path to Britton Street with such ease. Except that had been when she could properly make out her surroundings.

She took a cautious step forward, the scuff of her shoe loud in the empty street. She half expected an obstruction to trip her up. It didn't. Nor was the next step impacted, or the one after that. She continued with the strange, hesitant shuffle of her feet on pavement that rasped against the bottom of her shoes.

How many steps was it to the street? Her pace faltered and she found herself stretching her free hand in front of her, patting at air.

Maybe she should go back and take Mr. Evans up on his offer to walk her home. But then, how would he return to the shop?

Her nerves felt as though they were uncoiling with each blind step, her senses on wild alert. A rumbling filled the silence of night. It came with such haste, she drew back quickly, stumbling in the process. The whoosh of a car with its headlamps off sped by, dragging her skirt in a gust of powerful wind as it splashed what must have been a bucketful of puddle water on her.

Her dress clung to her, ice cold and drenched with filthy rainwater. She wrapped her arms about herself as she clutched the brolly handle, not that it mattered if rain fell on her now.

Lightning flickered overhead, casting the world in a brilliant wash of light. It was enough to make out what direction she needed to go, as well as confirm there were no more cars making their way toward her.

Drenched, blind and freezing, Grace stumbled her way back to Britton Street one careful footstep and flash of lightning at a time. The usual ten-minute journey took an eternity. Who knew how much time she'd wasted repeatedly walking past Mrs. Weatherford's townhouse in a fruitless bid to identify the right door.

Finally, she managed to ascertain which was indeed the correct home and carefully climbed up the stairs. Her shoes were so thoroughly soaked, they seemed to weigh several pounds each and squished with each footfall, causing water to well up around her toes. Her free hand patted at the door for the handle. Cool metal met her palm, and she curled her fingers around it. The door clicked open, unlocked, and swung inward.

The light from inside was like an explosion against her eyes, almost as blinding as the complete darkness. She staggered inside, nearly collapsing.

"Grace," Mrs. Weatherford exclaimed from the parlor. "Goodness, child, what's happened to you? We've been worried sick."

It was in extreme times such as this that Mrs. Weatherford's bossy nature held great benefit. Within the short side of an hour, Grace was dry with a fresh change of clothes and a hot cup of tea in her hand before tucking herself into bed.

Safe and warm beneath her quilt, she snuggled deep into her bed and made friends with the dark once more as it pulled her into slumber. But before sleep claimed her, she made a plan to use her time off from the shop to visit Paternoster Row the following morning. If she could see how the displays were set and the books shelved in those stores, she might have a stronger idea of how to properly direct her efforts.

Unfortunately, such well-laid plans dissolved with the news that met her the following day.

FIVE

BRITAIN HAD OFFICIALLY DECLARED WAR.

The prime minister made a special broadcast at 11:15 the next morning before Grace could leave.

She sat on the mohair sofa with Viv as Chamberlain's voice filled the small parlor. Colin was no longer on the floor as Tabby was now with Mr. Pritchard. Instead, the young man perched tensely at the edge of the Morris chair beside his mother's seat.

A tea tray sat on the center of the small table beside a vase of dahlias, untouched.

The prime minister relayed that Germany had ignored requests to pull free from Poland. Grace held her breath and prayed silently that Chamberlain wouldn't announce the news they had been dreading.

But all the listeners in London holding their breath

couldn't stop his next words. "…consequently, this country is at war with Germany."

Even though the declaration was expected, it hit Grace like a blow. How could something so expected carry such visceral impact?

She was not alone.

Viv dabbed at her eyes with a pretty lace-lined handkerchief she'd sewn before they left Drayton, and Mrs. Weatherford sucked in a breath. Colin immediately reached for his mother's hand.

They were at war.

But what did that mean? Would they be bombed? The men conscripted? Food rationed?

Grace remembered her mother's stories from the Great War and how difficult it had been. But those had simply been tales to Grace, ones without context for a life she could scarce imagine. And now that unfathomable world was about to become their new reality.

A shrill wail cut through the silence, the blaring of the air raid horn that had no end as its warbling cry rose and fell. The blood in Grace's veins froze. She couldn't breathe. Couldn't move.

They would be bombed. Like Poland. Overtaken by the Germans.

"Grace." Mrs. Weatherford said her name with an insistence that broke through the haze of her fear. "Go fill the tub and sinks with water. Viv, open all the windows. I'll fetch our masks and supplies while Colin turns off the gas at the mains."

"B-but the bombs," Viv stuttered, looking more terrified than Grace had ever seen her.

"They've only just seen the plane." Mrs. Weatherford

pushed to her feet and snapped off the wireless. "We have at least five minutes to get to the Andy if not more."

There was a calm authority to her tone as she spoke, and it pulled each one of them to the task she'd assigned. Though Grace didn't know why she had been told to fill the tub and sinks, she did as asked, letting the gush of water accompany the siren's wail.

Never had the taps run more slowly.

By the time the last sink filled, she ran to the Andy on legs that threatened to give out. There was little to the shelter, merely a curve of metal buried beneath a bit of dirt to form a submerged upside down U. How such a contraption could possibly keep them protected from a bombing was beyond her, a consideration that hadn't crossed her mind until that moment.

She stepped down through the small entrance, squeezing her way into the shelter. It smelled of dirt and damp metal, and blotted out the sun overhead, leaving the interior dim. Viv was already there, sitting in the near darkness on one of the small benches Colin had set on either side of the narrow space. Her arms were hugged around her middle and she looked up sharply, her long-lashed brown eyes wide with worry.

The siren cut off. An ominous silence replaced the warbling cry.

Grace sat beside Viv and took her friend's hand in hers. But she could offer no words of comfort. Not when every muscle in her own body was tensed for an explosion.

This was it. Like Poland. They would be bombed as surely as had Warsaw.

She didn't know what a bomb might sound like, or even

what to expect. Let alone what to do if they were struck in their tin of a shelter.

Colin joined them in the Andy and folded his large frame on the bench opposite them. His head bowed forward somewhat to accommodate the low arching ceiling. Mrs. Weatherford entered the shelter last with four gas masks dangling from one shoulder and a large box clasped in her hands. The clatter of her movements echoed against the steel frame and reverberated in their ears.

Colin immediately reached up to take the box from his mother. She smiled her gratitude and handed everyone their respective mask.

Grace accepted hers with hands that wouldn't stop shaking. "Should we put it on?"

"Only if you hear the wooden rattle outside." Mrs. Weatherford sat on the bench beside Colin. "The ARP wardens are all equipped with one for such a purpose. And I've purchased some Anti-Gas Ointment from the chemist. We have approximately one minute to smear it on our exposed skin, which is plenty of time. So you see, there's no need to worry."

She lifted the top from the plain box, revealing myriad supplies within. A yellow-topped tin of No. 2 Anti-Gas Ointment, a container of Smiths crisps, a couple bottles of what appeared to be lemonade and a bit of yarn and knitting needles.

"Did you turn off the gas, Colin?" Mrs. Weatherford's voice was smooth and calm, as if they were not all sitting about waiting to die.

He nodded.

"And the sinks and tub?" She looked to Grace.

Grace nodded also. Viv did likewise beside her before Mrs. Weatherford could ask if she'd completed her task.

"Brilliant." Mrs. Weatherford edged the box toward Grace and Viv. "Would you like some crisps?"

Grace's mouth was too dry to swallow her own saliva, let alone any food. Not that her knotted stomach would tolerate anything. She stared down at the teal tin of potato crisps and shook her head.

"Should we put the door into place?" Viv indicated the steel door set to the side of the gaping entrance.

Mrs. Weatherford didn't even bother to look back at it. "If we hear planes, we will. Otherwise it will be dark as the blackout in here."

"How can you be so calm?" Grace asked.

"This isn't the first time London has been bombed, my dear." Mrs. Weatherford extended the tin to Viv and received another silent no. "Having knowledge is the best way to fight off fear. I've spent quite a bit of time bending Mr. Stokes's ear about how to properly prepare."

"Mr. Stokes is our ARP warden." Colin popped the top off a bottle of lemonade and handed it to Grace, who accepted it with an automatic numbness. He did likewise for Viv and his mother before finally taking one himself.

Mrs. Weatherford settled the top back on the box and took a sip from her bottle. "We fill the tubs and sinks to have a means to put a fire out if the water lines are compromised. The windows are drawn open to ensure any fires within can be seen in the hopes they will be put out by authorities. The gas main, well, I'm quite sure that's self-explanatory."

Some of Grace's tension relaxed at Mrs. Weatherford's nonchalant demeanor. Grace didn't know that she could ever be as unperturbed about bombs as her mother's friend, but at least the woman's no-nonsense approach took the edge off her panic.

The bottle of lemonade was cool in Grace's hand. She put the glass to her lips and tilted her head. The sweet, tangy drink filled her mouth with a tartness that zinged at the back of her jaw. She hadn't realized how parched she'd been until the refreshing wash of liquid ran down her throat.

"What was it like in the Great War?" Viv asked.

They all looked to Mrs. Weatherford, including Colin. Grace knew her own mother's experiences, of course, but surely life had been far different in London.

"Well." Mrs. Weatherford glanced about at all their faces. "It wasn't pleasant. Are you sure you want to know when we'll likely be facing the same soon?"

"Having knowledge is the best way to fight off fear." Viv grinned at her. "As you said."

"How can I say no to such a cheeky reply?" Mrs. Weatherford smoothed her skirt, took a deep breath and told them how it had been years ago. How the rationing of food was so carefully monitored that people could be fined even for feeding pigeons at the park. She spoke of zeppelins and how the light aircraft soared over the city like balloons before dropping bombs, too high for the RAF to reach.

But she also spoke of victory, how the zeppelins were defeated with new planes that could climb to necessary heights, how women were accepted in roles for work and were allowed to vote and how the British people overcame the trying times with a mutual camaraderie.

"What was the worst part of it?" Viv cast a nervous look at Grace. "So we're prepared."

Mrs. Weatherford regarded Colin with a rare solemnity

before looking away with a blank stare. "The men who didn't come back," she said in a quiet voice.

The alarm's blaring wail pierced the air once more, startling them with its suddenness.

Even in Grace's jittery state, she noted the siren's call was different from the first, with a drone holding one long note rather than wavering up and down in inflection.

"That's the all clear." Mrs. Weatherford drank the last bit of her lemonade and set the empty bottle in the box. "You've all survived your first air raid warning. May there be no more after this." She gathered up the gas masks while Colin hefted the box, and they all removed themselves from the dismal, cramped little shelter.

It was announced later that evening on the wireless that the air raid warning had been a false alarm.

But what if the next one was not?

Such concerns edged to the forefront of Grace's mind as she tried to sleep, the silence luring fear from its darkest corners.

The unending string of news on the radio the following day didn't offer any more information before Grace had to make her way to the bookshop.

Mr. Evans didn't lift his head when she entered. She knew better than to expect as much at this point. Detritus littered the countertop, the blackout curtains were still drawn tight against the daylight and several new piles of books had sprung from the dingy floorboards like weeds.

"It appears we're at war," Grace said softly.

Mr. Evans looked up with an elevation of his brows. "It should be done by Christmas according to Mr. Pritchard."

"What do you think?" Grace asked.

"War is unpredictable, Miss Bennett." Mr. Evans nestled a strip of paper between the pages of his book and closed the ledger, leaving another scrap behind.

She picked up the errant bit of paper to return it to him.

Mr. Evans put a hand up to stop her. "Those are some of the books sold here and how they might be sorted according to topic."

She gave a little gasp of excitement and focused on the list. A neat row of handwritten titles with categories beside them. "Where might I find these books?"

He shrugged. "But once you've located them, it's as good a place as any to start sorting out this mess, is it not?" With that, he turned toward the back of the shop. "Make sure you leave by two," he said over his shoulder as he strode away. "I'll not have you staying until evening again and going home in the dark. And I'll certainly not be subjected to another call from Mrs. Weatherford on the matter."

Grace winced. She could only imagine how such a discussion had gone. Rather than ponder over it and allow herself to feel bad for Mr. Evans, she put her attention to the list.

There were twenty-five titles labeled as classic fiction at the top followed by groups of history, philosophy and mystery. By the afternoon, she'd managed to locate only four of the classic fiction when the chime of the bell interupted her task. She pulled herself from a shelf she was examining and took her search to the front of the store to be near the customer.

The patron was not just anyone, however. Mr. George Anderson greeted her with a handsome smile. "Good afternoon, Miss Bennett."

Grace's pulse quickened. "Good day, Mr. Anderson. May I help you?" She almost laughed at her offer in light of how things went last time. "Or perhaps at least keep you company while I look about for titles."

"Are you looking for something?" He glanced at the list in her hands.

She stuffed the paper behind her, realizing he meant to help, and shook her head. "It's nothing."

Those green eyes narrowed with playful suspicion and a smile teased at his mouth. "Nothing? I think not."

She opened her mouth to protest, but what was the point when he knew the store better than she? Slowly, she brought the bit of paper around. "I'm trying to organize the shop and have been given these titles with which to start."

He took the list and studied it. With his gray well-tailored three-piece suit, and his dark hair impeccably combed, he looked like a solicitor reading over an important case rather than a customer aiding a shop's assistant with a tally of misplaced books.

What did he do for employment?

Grace pressed her lips together to keep from asking.

"I've found *Wuthering Heights, Sense and Sensibility, A Tale of Two Cities* and *Frankenstein*," she said instead and came around beside him to point to the titles. He smelled clean, like shaving soap and something spicy she couldn't name. It was an appealing scent.

"That's a fine start." He winked at her. "Let's see what else we can locate."

They scanned through the shelves together. While they did, she confessed her intent to go to Paternoster Row to see how best to help advertise Primrose Hill Books.

"Paternoster Row is a prestigious location for publishing." His lashes lowered slightly as his gaze skimmed down the row of books before them. "There are printers and book binders and various publishing companies. Quite a few have a slant toward religion on account of its history."

"What history is that?" she asked.

"St. Paul's Cathedral is there." His index finger ran along a series of multicolored spines. "It's said that ages ago the clergymen would go on procession down the street while offering the Lord's Prayer, hence the name." He paused over a book with a maroon binding and gilt lettering along the top. "*Sense and Sensibility.* And if I may be so bold, an excellent story. A classic."

"But also a love story?" Grace took the book in her hand and added it to the pathetically small pile she'd excavated.

He gave that rich, warm chuckle she found she liked a great deal. "You aren't going to make this shop as pretentious as some of the others, are you?" He grimaced.

"I haven't seen them yet." Grace admitted. "But I don't think that's possible regardless. I would like to at least make this place appear more welcoming."

"There's an old world feel here I've always appreciated." He lifted a shoulder. "It would be a shame to have it be like another Nesbitt's Fine Reads, all crisp newness without any personality."

"I'll take it by your authority until I see for myself. I would like to do what I can to elevate Primrose Hill Books' appeal. To bring in more customers."

"It's good of you to care so much."

"My intentions aren't altogether altruistic," she admitted. She explained about not having a letter of recommendation and how she'd spent years improving her uncle's shop only to end up in London with no options. Sharing her story with others wasn't something she often did, but there was a kindness in Mr. Anderson that pulled at her and made him seem trustworthy.

He listened with a slight furrow of his brow, nodding periodically in understanding. "I'm sorry that's been the way of it. I'd love to be of assistance in your quest to better the shop in order to obtain the most glowing letter of recommendation to ever exist."

Heat rose in Grace's cheeks, and suddenly she found she didn't mind her predicament as thoroughly as she once did. "You can be, actually."

He lifted the list they'd been working off and raised a single brow in a terribly debonair manner. "By locating all these?"

"I don't even know if such a feat is possible." She glanced toward the front of the shop to ensure no one had entered. Their conversation had been so engrossing, she might have actually missed the bell's chime. "I wonder if I might ask you some questions about reading, to determine how best to advertise."

"Ah, you wish to tap into the mind of a reader." He lifted his pointer finger. "Brilliant."

Another wave of warmth suffused her face. "What do you like best about reading?"

His fingertips steepled together and tapped against one another as he thought. "That's quite the question, like asking me to describe all the colors in a spinning kaleidoscope."

"Is it truly that complicated?" She laughed.

"I'll try." He tilted his head and his gaze focused in the distance as he considered his response with apparent care. "Reading is…" His brows knit together and then his forehead smoothed as the right words appeared to dawn on him. "It's going somewhere without ever taking a train or ship, an unveiling of new, incredible worlds. It's living a life you weren't born into and a chance to see everything colored by someone else's perspective. It's learning without having to face consequences of failures, and how best to succeed." He hesitated. "I think within all of us, there is a void, a gap waiting to be filled by something. For me, that something is books and all their proffered experiences."

Grace's heart went soft at the poetic affection with which he spoke, finding herself both envious of the books as well as the fulfillment he found in them. Nothing in all of her years had ever inspired such passion.

"I see what you mean by trying to describe all the colors in a spinning kaleidoscope," she said. "That was beautiful."

He met her eyes once more and gave a sheepish smile. "Well, I don't know that it will help you with advertising." He cleared his throat.

"It absolutely does." Grace paused as she assembled the racing thoughts in her head. "Perhaps something about lighting a blackout with the enjoyment of reading or using it as a means of taking oneself away from the war with a new adventure."

He opened his hands as if presenting her as a masterpiece. "Those are perfect. You'll do a stellar job of this."

"Thank you." Heat flushed through Grace's cheeks and chest.

He glanced at his watch. "Forgive me, but I have an appointment I must run to. I should like to continue our discussion on how I might assist you in your efforts. Would you perhaps like to meet for tea some time?"

Her cheeks were so hot now that she was sorely tempted to press her cold hands to them for a bit of relief. She nodded. "I'd like that very much."

"Perhaps next Wednesday at noon?" he asked.

Grace was working that day, but Mr. Evans would give her the time off for tea if she asked. Or, at least, she hoped. "That would be lovely."

"Would the café around the corner suit you, P&V's?"

She nodded. "I've been wanting to try it."

He grinned. "I look forward to it." He gave her a little bow. "Good day, Miss Bennett."

Giddy excitement tickled up through her, but she tamped it down long enough to see him out of the shop properly. Only when he was gone did she allow herself to press her hands first to her chest to calm her frantic heartbeat, then to her cheeks to cool their blaze.

"You can go on Wednesday," Mr. Evans called from somewhere in the bookshop.

Grace froze, hands splayed on her cheeks, eyes wide. "I…I beg your pardon?" she stammered.

"I wasn't intending to listen, but the two of you were rather loud." Mr. Evans emerged from the other side of the shop, his arms folded over the chest of his dun-colored pullover.

She straightened quickly, dropping her hands.

Mr. Evans glanced at the pile of books they'd managed to accumulate. "You could do worse than the likes of George Anderson. He's an engineer and most likely won't be called up to war. But then again, he's also just the sort of bloke who will volunteer regardless."

The reminder of war was jarring. For that one brief moment, she had forgotten about it. As though the world had, for the span of a blink, been once more blissfully normal.

Except that it wasn't. There were barrage balloons in the air outside to ward off bombers and children who had been carted to the country to live with strangers. Men were leaving and may never return, and at any moment, Hitler could drop his bombs.

It was like waking from a dream and realizing you were in the onset of a nightmare.

Somewhere outside, a cloud passed over the sun and cast a shadow of gray over the shop.

"I only hope you won't be foolish about this nonsense with Mr. Anderson." Mr. Evans gave her a stern look, the way one's father might. "Every girl is rushing to marry before the men can be sent off to war." His mouth flattened in a chastising gesture. "Keep your head about you."

Grace suppressed the urge to squirm where she stood. Was he truly giving her relationship advice? "I don't plan to wed anytime soon," she replied slowly.

He grunted, though she couldn't tell if that meant he believed her or not, and disappeared down the aisle. As the afternoon went on, Grace found only two more books from the list he'd given her, a search that was decidedly less enjoyable without Mr. Anderson.

When it was finally time for her to leave for the day, it wasn't Britton Street she headed for. No, this time she was determined to find her way to Paternoster Row to see how the rest of London touted her bookshops.

SIX

ALL THROUGHOUT PATERNOSTER ROW, WIDE windows peeked out from multiple shops, showcasing the books being sold within. Gilt letters adorned the glass with store names while painted posters advertised sale prices meant to lure in customers with a bargain. The front displays varied from those that were artfully arranged to piles of books stacked in no particular order, all but blocking the interior. If nothing else, perhaps the latter didn't require blackout curtains. After all, who needed three layers of fabric when one had stacks of books five deep?

Grace strode along the raised pavement of the narrow street, pressing close to the tall buildings to avoid the black-painted bollards meant to keep vehicles from edging onto the walkway.

Between the shops, vendors were scattered about with their wheeled carts, selling everything from lemonade to

sandwiches, and the greasy scent of fish and chips lingered
in the air.

She had been admiring the artfully arranged display of F.
G. Longman's large square windows when a familiar face
caught her attention. Standing in the doorway of a store on
the opposite side of the street was a wide-shouldered, beak-
nosed man with skinny legs and a tabby cat close at his heels.

Mr. Pritchard.

Before she could worry that he might spot her, he turned
abruptly and disappeared inside a shop, Pritchard & Potts,
pausing only to hold the door for Tabby to slip in behind
him. The name of his establishment had been painted in a
bold hand on the window that had nothing but blackness
on the other side.

Tar.

Grace suddenly found herself grateful for Mrs. Weatherford's overabundance of dark fabric and the fine curtains
she'd been able to make for Primrose Hill Books.

Lining the front of Pritchard & Potts were large bins filled
with books so tossed about, they weren't even in proper
stacks. Grace could only imagine the interior of the shop
was just as bad.

Perhaps even worse than Mr. Evans's shop.

She suppressed a shudder and continued down Paternoster Row. One particular storefront was painted a beautiful
eye-catching red. Its large glass windows exhibited a neat
arrangement of only a few choice books. The name "Nesbitt's Fine Reads" was proudly presented in a curling script
of shimmering gold and glossy black.

While Primrose Hill Books may never reach the pinna-
cle of such grandeur, Grace was determined to glean what

she could. While bearing in mind what Mr. Anderson had said of it, of course.

She pushed into the store and immediately noted how easily the door gave on its well-oiled hinges. A delicate tinkle above her head welcomed her.

While Nesbitt's Fine Reads had several rows of shelving, there was by far more space as well as a definitive—and well-labeled—order. The taller shelves sat on the outside perimeter with tables at the room's center, enticing readers toward brightly colored books on small stands. A second floor above offered walls set with white imbedded shelves all filled with an array of books.

Everywhere Grace looked, the store seemed clean and new. Wood was sharp cornered and polished to a high shine, glass gleamed with the reflection of good lighting and there wasn't a speck of dust to be found. Even the jackets of the books appeared so crisp and clean, they might have just been removed from their packing boxes moments before.

Nesbitt's Fine Reads was exquisite.

"May I help you find something?"

Grace spun around to find a woman with a sharp nose and steel-gray hair raked back into a severe bun.

"I was simply looking," Grace replied. "Thank you."

The woman didn't move. Her neat charcoal suit made her appear painfully slender, and her dark eyes fixed on Grace with intent.

"You're one of the new tenants in Mrs. Weatherford's little rundown townhouse, are you not?" She enunciated the hard consonants as she spoke, as though biting them off along with her insult.

It was on the tip of Grace's tongue to stand up for the woman who had so graciously taken Grace in when she had nowhere else to go. But though Grace had only just met Mrs. Nesbitt, she knew the woman's kind. Her type was universal whether it be a small farm town or a big city. She would take any stalwart defense and laugh about it later.

Rather than give in to the need to protect Mrs. Weatherford, Grace edged her chin a bit higher and made her back squeeze upright a little straighter. "I am," she replied. "What of it?"

Her impudence was reflected in Mrs. Nesbitt's narrowed eyes. "Are you here to spy on me?" the woman demanded. "I know you work in that miserable hovel of a shop owned by Percival Evans."

"If it's so miserable, why do you find it such a threat that I'm here?" A thrill at her own audacity raced through Grace's veins. She'd never been one to stand up to others, but something about Mrs. Nesbitt's nastiness had her emboldened.

Mrs. Nesbitt sniffed and tossed her head dramatically. "Don't come in here with the intention to copy my shop."

"I don't intend to copy it," Grace answered indignantly. "I intend to do far better." With that, she swept from the shop.

Floating on her victory and eager to put some of her ideas to paper, she rushed back to the townhouse. Between what she'd seen in the large plate windows of Paternoster Row, the organization of Mrs. Nesbitt's Fine Reads and even the elaborate detail of a reader's mind Mr. Anderson had offered, Grace knew exactly what she wanted to do.

The thought of George Anderson sent excitement tickling through her. Viv would just die when she heard about the upcoming date.

Later that evening, Grace was in the middle of writing a meticulous catalog of what she wished to implement at Primrose Hill Books when the door to the room she shared with Viv opened and her friend swept in, bringing with her a new floral scent.

Viv had always been chic, but her sense of fashion had risen to grander levels during their brief time in London. Her blue pullover from Harrods paired beautifully with the tweed pencil skirt she'd sewn the day before, and her curls were artfully arranged so she looked like a woman on a magazine cover.

"Grace, darling. I hoped to find you in here." A small bag dangled from the crook of her elbow.

Grace sprang up from her seat. "And I was hoping you'd return home soon. I have news." She grinned at her friend.

Viv rubbed her hands in anticipation. "Oh, do go first."

Grace wriggled her shoulders coyly. "I've been asked on a date."

Viv gave a squeal of delight. "The gentleman from the bookshop?"

Grace had mentioned George Anderson in passing to Viv on one of their many evening chats as they fell asleep in their small separate beds. Leave it to Viv to hold on to that bit of information.

Grace nodded excitedly and went on about how he'd offered to come up with more ideas with her at the café.

"And you said yes?" Viv folded her hands over her chest, sending the bag at her arm spinning.

"Of course."

Viv clapped her hands, her pretty face alight with joy. However much Grace had been looking forward to her date, she was now doubly eager after Viv's jubilant display.

"And I have something for you too." Viv pulled the bag from her arm and took out a little box.

Grace accepted the parcel and drew off the top to reveal

a bracelet within. It was a simple thing of metal chain links with a flat white oval at its center on one side and a small medallion on the other. The card it was attached to declared it to be an ARP identification wristlet.

"I have one too." Viv held out her wrist, proudly displaying her matching jewelry. She'd written her name and their address on it, the same as the one she'd given Grace. "I found them at Woolworths."

Grace stared down at hers once more as a shroud of dread brushed over her. "An identification wristlet?"

"In case we get bombed." Viv's mouth twisted to the side and Grace knew she was biting the inside of her lip, a habit she'd had since she was a girl. "These are far sturdier than our identity cards. So they can know who we are."

In the last year, the National Registry issued each person in Britain an identity card to carry at all times. But Viv was right; the bit of paper, no matter how thick, was fragile.

"Viv…" Grace swallowed, uncertain what to say.

"If something happens, isn't it better that we know?" Viv set aside the bag on the table beside a pile of pale yellow chiffon she'd purchased the day before. "I can't bear the thought of never knowing what happened to you if you didn't come home. The other night when you became lost in the blackout…" Viv's smooth forehead puckered with concern. "I was so worried about you."

Grace stepped closer to her friend to embrace her, but Viv put her hand up. "No, you'll make me cry if you do that and my makeup will run all down my face." She pressed the back of her forefinger to the underside of her eyes to delicately dab away any moisture. "I know you probably think this is morbid."

Grace pressed her lips together to stifle her protest. After years of friendship, they knew one another all too well.

"That's Saint Christopher at the top, the patron saint of safe travel." Viv tapped the medallion. "You don't have to wear it, but I shall. I'm a mess with the fear of being bombed. A bus started up this afternoon and half the people on the street jumped, thinking it was a bomb." She gave a self-deprecating laugh. "Including me."

"It was considerate of you to buy this for me." The wristlet hung heavy in Grace's hand, weighted by the impact of its purpose—to identify someone who had been blasted beyond recognition by a bomb.

A finger of ice slid down Grace's spine. "Perhaps I'll wear it a bit later," she promised.

Viv nodded with understanding. "Later."

Grace put the wristlet in the drawer of the small table next to her bed.

Viv sniffed at a savory aroma in the air and drifted toward the bedroom door. "I heard Mrs. Weatherford is making toad in the hole tonight. With your mother's recipe. Do you think it's done yet?"

When Grace was a child, her mother made the meal with such regularity, Grace had grown tired of the stuff. It was a funny thought that she should crave it so much now after years of having gone without it and knowing her mother would never make it again.

"We can go down and see." Grace shared her friend's eagerness. "Thank you for my wristlet. And for thinking of me."

Viv squeezed her arms around Grace. "Always, darling." Her stomach gave a rumble, and she clapped a hand over it with a giggle.

Together, they left the room and descended the stairs, both breathing in the scent of Yorkshire pudding and browned sausage. Midway down, Mrs. Weatherford's hushed whisper filled the stairwell. "Good evening, Mr. Simons, it's Mrs. Weatherford."

Viv stopped in front of Grace and mouthed, "Colin's boss."

"I want to ensure you've had success in securing Colin as an essential employee," Mrs. Weatherford said in an uncharacteristically quiet voice. Clearly she did not want Colin to hear.

This was not a conversation they ought to be listening in on.

Grace shook her head to Viv, indicating they should move on. But Viv simply waved off Grace's concerns with her hand and stayed put.

"How long do you expect until you receive a response?" Mrs. Weatherford's question was followed by a long pause. "I see," she said at last. "I shall call again tomorrow to see if you've heard back." Another pause, this one shorter. "Yes, tomorrow," she said firmly. "Good evening."

A click of the receiver being set in its cradle indicated the call had ended. Viv breezed down the stairs as if they hadn't just been listening in on a clandestine chat they should never had heard.

"The toad in the hole smells divine," Viv exclaimed. "Is it nearly time to eat?"

"Is it seven in the evening?" Mrs. Weatherford smoothed the apron over her lavender housedress, as cool and collected as Viv. The prickly reply was paired with a line of worry across her brow. Clearly she had too much on her mind.

"It is exactly," Viv replied brightly.

"Then, yes, supper is indeed ready." Mrs. Weatherford waved them into the dining room with her.

Grace said nothing, not trusting herself to speak around the twist of guilt.

"Who were you on the phone with, Mum?" Colin asked as he set the last plate on the table. There was such innocence to his question, Grace was sure he did not suspect the call's nature.

His gaze flicked to Viv and Grace, and his cheeks flushed as he offered a shy smile. He was a quiet young man, given often to introspection that made you wonder what went on behind his sharp blue eyes.

Knowing Colin, he was most likely devising a new way to feed a lion or mend a bird's broken wing.

"Oh, it was just Miss Gibbons calling to complain about the grocer." Mrs. Weatherford picked up a long knife, sliding it through the suspended sausages in their pillowy bed of pudding. "Apparently there's nearly no sugar to be had. I tell you, these people out there buying up the shop…" She tsked. "They should be ashamed."

She set the knife aside and smiled brightly at the three of them. "Onion gravy, anyone?"

As they ate, Grace considered Colin once more. He was a good man, polite and genuinely kind.

He performed all the tasks around the house from replacing spent bulbs to doing minor repairs. Aside from caring for the animals at Harrods, his chief concern was ensuring they were all comfortable and safe.

But given the chance, would he want to go to war?

Most men did, it seemed.

Why anyone would eagerly put themselves in a war zone where one could be shot was beyond her. But then, she'd never been brave. Not like the men willing to trade their lives for the safety of those in Britain.

Thoughts of such courage filled her mind as she crawled into the brass bed that night and pulled the quilt over her shoulders amid the blackness of the room. Compared to such heroism, she was little more than a coward.

It was a deficiency she ought to face head-on, as her mother had always encouraged her to do, by speaking up for herself, by not allowing others to bully her. And she meant to. Eventually.

Just as soon as she set Primrose Hill Books to rights.

The next morning, she arrived at the bookshop nearly ten minutes early with the list of her ideas in hand. She burst through the front door, and the bell announced her arrival with its shrill cry.

Mr. Evans lifted his head and gave her a frown.

She winced. "Sorry. I didn't mean to open the door so abruptly."

He continued to frown at her.

"Truly," she said. "It's just that I'm so excited for the ideas I…have…"

He put his hand on a brown-wrapped parcel with a note atop it and slid it toward her. "This is for you," he said solemnly.

Grace glanced down at the envelope with "Miss Bennett" written in a scrolling hand over its cream-colored surface.

"I'm sorry." Mr. Evans shuffled away from the counter, leaving behind a few scattered bits of paper and the nub of an abandoned pencil.

What could he possibly be sorry for?

Grace opened the top of the envelope and reached for the

note within. The paper made a gentle shushing noise in the heavy silence of the shop as she removed it. She skimmed to the bottom and saw the letter had been signed by George. Not Mr. Anderson, but George.

Her pulse kicked up at the lack of formality. At least, until she read the letter where he confessed to having volunteered with the R.A.F. She was surprised to learn he was not just an engineer, but also had considerable flight experience. He hadn't expected to be called up so quickly, but received the notice two days after signing.

Not only did he regret having to cancel their date, he was apologetic at his inability to assist in improving the shop, though he went on to offer several suggestions for advertising slogans. That, and he left her something that he hoped to discuss next time he saw her, something that had a great impact on his own love of reading.

Grace's heart clenched with a mix of disappointment and alarm. Planes were often shot at in war. If he was going in as a pilot, his life would be in a constant state of danger.

She closed her eyes. No, she wouldn't think of that. She would see him again.

But when?

She gently laid the note aside and drew the gift closer to her. The parcel was wrapped in a plain brown paper and quite obviously a book, given its shape and weight. George's neat printing marked the center of the paper.

A classic, but also a love story.

Smiling to herself, she peeled away the wrap to reveal a leather-bound book. It had been well used, given its scuffed surface and how the once sharp corners were dulled and curled inward. She turned it to its side to reveal the spine.

The title had been nearly buffed away, but it was still there in a whisper of gold lettering. *The Count of Monte Cristo* by Alexandre Dumas.

Not only had he gifted her a book he thought she might enjoy, it appeared he'd given her the exact one he had read in his youth. Over and over, as indicated by how well the copy had been loved.

She ran her fingers over the worn cover and imagined George as a boy, letting his mind take him to a new place. Now she would experience the adventure that had led him into a lifetime of reading. She only hoped those pages might offer her a similar passion. And she hoped even more fervently for the possibility of seeing him again to return the volume and discuss its contents.

Still, the shop would not be the same without the possibility of seeing his handsome smile.

"I told you he'd likely volunteer," Mr. Evans called from behind the bookshelves.

Grace closed her eyes, fighting off a swell of worry. Staying busy would help get her through this. After all, she'd worked through concern and hurt before, when her mother was ill. Even after she'd died. Grace's tasks would keep her mind occupied. She blinked her eyes open and put on a bright smile for no one in particular.

"I knew I ought to have married him first," Grace said loudly and with a heavy flair of drama. Then waited.

Mr. Evans poked his head out from between the shelves and regarded her with waggling brows. "I do hope that was a joke."

"I had to do something to lure you from your work." Grace lifted the list she'd assembled. "I have some changes for the shop I'd like to discuss with you."

"No." He tucked himself away once more, like a turtle disinclined to face the world.

She carefully folded George's note back into its envelope, slipped it into her purse and settled the book on the counter. "We'll start small," she coaxed.

"You've already cleaned the place and upset my piles."

"Just have a look." She peeked around a shelf and found him scowling at her the way a sullen child might.

Regardless, she thrust the list at him and left him with it while she put her things in the back room. When she returned, he slid her a wary look.

He set the list on top of a row of books. "You can move things about to help properly organize. But mind you're not too heavy on your advertising. And I'll not be buying back books or hawking used wares like Foyle's."

"Of course not," Grace promised.

He issued a low mutter that might have been a yes.

"I beg your pardon?" she asked innocently. "Was that permission to make changes to Primrose Hill Books?"

He sighed. "Yes."

She snapped up her list, already knowing where to start. "You shan't regret this."

"I hope you're right," he grumbled and pulled a book from the shelf into his waiting palms.

Regardless of his trepidation, she was certain he would be happy with the results. Eventually. For it would all take a considerable amount of work to implement in the coming months. She only hoped it wouldn't take more than her allotted time at the bookshop, however, as she certainly had no plans to stay.

SEVEN

THE NEXT TWO MONTHS DRAGGED ON FOR LONDON
with unrealized anticipation of the war. All the preparation,
all the expectation and fraying nerves had been for naught.
There were no more air raid warnings, no rations put into
place, no gas attacks and the news on the wireless seemed
to report the same updates on a tiresome loop.

Grace had not heard from George. While she didn't have
an address to reach out to him, she'd hoped he might send
her a letter to the shop.

Nonetheless, for Grace that time had passed in a frenzy of
organizing books, shifting shelves and more cleaning than
she ever thought possible. The work had kept her so busy
for so long, one day she realized somehow it had become
November.

Primrose Hill Books was far from perfect, but Grace still
straightened with pride every time she walked into the store.

Her accomplishment showed itself in the open, welcome space she'd created. New tables were set in the middle of the shop with the books facing the entrance to greet patrons, their genres clearly marked in black print on white pasteboard.

In truth, only about a quarter of the books in Primrose Hill Books were on display, for those were all she'd been able to sort through. That amount, however, was still considerable in light of Mr. Evans's massive stock. The remaining inventory was piled in the back room, making it almost impossible to move in the already cramped space, and piled along the second floor, which had been blocked off while she sorted through the mess.

She carried a box down from the small spiral staircase one chilly morning when a ding announced a new customer. Quickly, she set the box aside in an alcove at the foot of the stairs, reattached the "Do Not Enter" sign to the railing and went to the front.

Mr. Pritchard skulked around the entryway, his head tucked low in his large jacket. Behind him, as had now become usual, was Tabby, trotting at his heels.

"Good day, Mr. Pritchard." Grace smiled at him. "If you're looking for Mr. Evans, he's in the back by the history section."

The older man scrunched his face as he read the signs. "These are new."

"I put them up a few weeks ago."

Mr. Pritchard scowled. "I hope they work better for you than this cat does for me." He slid a glance toward Tabby, who was contentedly cleaning his paws. "The cat would sooner catch a nap than a mouse."

In response to this, Tabby rubbed one tufted paw over his ear and face.

"I'm sorry to hear that," Grace said. "But he seems quite fond of you."

"Doesn't help my mouse problem." Mr. Pritchard tutted. "It appears you've been rather busy, Miss Basset."

She didn't bother to correct him on her name as he squinted intently at a sign on the counter. It was one of the suggestions she'd made when speaking to George, stating "Lighten Your Blackout with a Good Book."

She thought of him often, usually with a twinge of guilt at not having read more of *The Count of Monte Cristo*. In all of her wayward attempts, she had either been too distracted to concentrate, too tired to stay awake, or even a bit of both. And there it had remained on her bedside table, only several pages into the first chapter.

Except it was also next to a to-do list that seemingly had no end. She was either at the shop working or she was jotting down ideas for advertising or organizing at home. And when she finally did take a moment to catch her breath, it was to fall asleep and start over again the next day.

"I hear business has picked up for this place." Mr. Pritchard straightened from the sign and peered down at her from his beak of a nose. "Do you think it's these adverts?"

She lifted her shoulder in a noncommittal shrug, unsure if Mr. Evans would want any information divulged.

Mr. Pritchard stepped closer to her, bringing with him the scent of peppermint and mothballs. "I'll pay you a shilling more an hour than what you're currently earning if you come to Pritchard & Potts."

"Mr. Pritchard." Mr. Evans appeared behind them.

Before Grace could open her mouth to protest that she wouldn't work for Mr. Pritchard for a pound more an hour, Mr. Evans continued in an even tone. "If you want to come and look at my shop, you're welcome. Feel free even to tout your dissatisfaction with the world and make your radical claims about the war." His blue eyes narrowed behind the thick glass of his spectacles. "But if you mean to come in here to lure away Miss Bennett, I shall ask you to take your leave."

Elation prickled over Grace's skin. Her uncle would have never stood up for her in such a manner.

Mr. Pritchard drew upright and clicked his tongue in annoyance, making the white wisps of hair on the top of his head tremble. "She would be better used in a book shop on Paternoster Row, a place far more prestigious than Hosier Lane." He curled his lips at the last word. With that, he strode from the shop on his spindly legs with Tabby loping after him.

"I wasn't going to accept," Grace said.

"I imagine you wouldn't." Mr. Evans lowered his head to peer at her over the rims of his spectacles. "You're already more than two months into your allotted time here."

His dry wit was one of the things she'd come to appreciate about him over the last several months. She smiled in response. "Are you certain you won't want me to stay longer?"

He waved his hand dismissively and shuffled toward the counter where he proceeded to go through the ledger she'd assembled several weeks prior. Yet another bit of organizing and tracking of sales and popular titles she'd implimented. He tended to look at it often and comment on the comparison of day-to-day sales.

When he paid her later that week, she noticed he had

added a shilling more an hour to her wages. A kindness he took no thanks for, but merely reminded her of her six-month commitment. From which she would doubtless emerge with a brilliant letter of recommendation.

Viv was doing equally well at Harrods where her boss had commended her ability to help women find just the right clothes to complement them. Grace and Viv had fallen into a routine upon returning home from work, both around four in the afternoon, to meet in the kitchen for tea to discuss their day, sometimes with the company of Mrs. Weatherford when she wasn't off running errands.

They sat together one afternoon while rain pattered at the windows, a comfortable silence between them, when Viv gave a long, unexpected sigh. "Isn't it just driving you to distraction?"

Grace looked up from where she'd been mesmerized by the raindrops melting into one another before trickling down the windows. "Isn't what driving me to distraction?"

Viv looked longingly outside. "The boredom."

Grace could have laughed. She'd been anything but bored with how busy she stayed at the shop.

Viv rolled her eyes. "You're not bored, I know, but this war has been interminable."

"But nothing's happening," Grace protested. After all, there hadn't been any more air raid sirens. Nor had there been any attacks or rationing. There were rumors, of course. But there would always be rumors and so far all had been unfounded.

"Exactly." Viv's eyes widened with exasperation. "I thought London would be all glitz and glam with theater tickets and late nights out dancing."

"We could try to go to the cinema again," Grace offered hesitantly.

Viv pinned her with a sullen stare, no doubt recalling the failure of their last attempt. The building had been black as death's cloak, and they'd nearly fallen over several times as they tripped their way down the partition that formed something of a corridor leading to the paybox. It was so dark inside, they could scarce see the coins they counted out. Then on the way home, they'd nearly been struck by a car that was quite obviously exceeding the newly enforced speed limits.

The attempt to go to a theater had been an equal failure. They'd forgotten their gas masks, a common occurrence of late, and were turned away. While their return home had been uneventful, it had been met with a lecture from Mrs. Weatherford on the importance of gas masks and why they shouldn't have been left in the first place.

Besides, Grace had had enough of venturing into the blackout. Between her terrible experience the first week, nearly being run down together after the cinema and all the reports of muggings and assaults in the newly darkened city, they had decided against risking going out later.

Still, Grace hated the idea of Viv being so painfully bored.

"They've added white paint to the curbs." Viv smoothed the lapel on her suit, yet another new dress she'd sewn. There had been at least one every two weeks or so, not only for her, but for Grace and Mrs. Weatherford as well. "And I heard ARP wardens wear luminescent capes now."

Grace stirred her tea, and the silt at the bottom kicked up into a small whirlpool. "Yes, and still over a thousand people have been hit by cars. It's so dark at night, dock men are falling into the water and drowning."

A flicker of lightning flashed outside the windows. Two months ago, they might have both jumped for fear it was a bomb. Now, they remained as they were without even a stutter to their pulses.

Viv was right; there was nothing going on with the war—or rather, as it was now being called, the bore war.

"I think…" Viv tapped a glossy red nail against the curved lip of her teacup. "I'm considering joining the ATS."

Grace dropped her spoon where it clinked against the side of her cup. The Auxiliary Territorial Service was a women's branch in the British Army, one that would require Viv to attend training and most likely be assigned somewhere other than London. "Why would you do that?"

"Why wouldn't I?" Viv lifted a shoulder. "The women are being used as clerks and shopkeeps from what I hear. I'd be doing something similar to what I'm doing now, but at least I'd be helping end all of this." She waved her hands in the air to imply the entirety of their current situation. "I'm ready for the war to be done, so we can go to cinemas and dances without fear of being run over on our way home. And maybe meet a handsome stranger once all the men come back from war, perhaps even go on a date. I want to stop worrying about the idea that bombs may drop or that we'll be subject to rationing. I want life to be normal again."

"But you love Harrods," Grace protested.

"It's exciting." Viv dropped her hands to her lap. "Or at least it was in the beginning. So few women care about fashion right now. Those who do still come in tell me of their struggles. They're all so anxious about their men who have been sent off to war and their children being cared for by strangers in the country. Some of the letters these women receive are just terribly sad. Little ones wanting to come home, swearing to be good so they aren't sent away again." She looked down at her hands. "I just want it all to be done."

The quiet of the house on a rainy day was shattered suddenly by a choked cry.

Viv and Grace startled, met concerned gazes, then leapt up from the table to investigate what had caused such a sound. Mrs. Weatherford was by the front door with a cascade of envelopes scattered at her feet, her fingers pressed to her mouth. Colin stood in front of her with the sleeves of his white collared shirt pushed past his forearms, an open letter in his hands.

"What is it?" Viv asked.

"Are you all right?" Grace rushed to Mrs. Weatherford.

She didn't even acknowledge Grace as she continued staring at Colin with wide eyes behind her glasses.

Grace looked to Colin, who didn't flush at their entrance for the first time, his expression fierce where it remained fixed on the letter. He swallowed and his sharp Adam's apple bobbed at his slender throat. "It's finally happened."

He turned the correspondence toward them, showing the bold typeface at the top displaying "National Service (Armed Forces) Act, 1939" from the Ministry of Labour and National Service. Saturday, November 11th was stamped in blue ink for him to report to the Medical Board Centre for evaluation.

"I thought yours was to be deemed a reserved occupation." Mrs. Weatherford shook her head, her eyes falling on the orders with apparent disbelief.

"They only said they would try, Mum," Colin replied

patiently. "There was never a guarantee. I can't stay here while the other men are off fighting."

Mrs. Weatherford's eyes sharpened. "Did you volunteer?"

"No." He turned the letter toward himself once more and set his jaw. "I know you don't want me to go, Mum. And I know you were trying to keep me here. But I can't ignore it. I won't."

Grace studied Colin as he and his mother spoke, the paper in his large, gentle hands trembling ever so slightly, despite the way he'd squared his shoulders with determination to do what was right. And her heart broke.

Men like Colin were not meant for war.

"They're calling you up on Armistice Day." Mrs. Weatherford smoothed her hands down the blue flowered dress that Viv had sewn for her. The action was one Grace had seen before, when Mrs. Weatherford fought to control her emotions.

"Your father died to make that day possible," she continued. "How could they call you up then of all days?" Her voice pitched high with fear and hurt.

Grace reached for Mrs. Weatherford again, but the older woman brushed her off. "I must call Mr. Simons. He told me he submitted for you to be an essential employee. He'll be able to—"

Colin stepped toward his mother to stop her. Mrs. Weatherford finally stilled and looked at him with wide, wet eyes.

"I'll do my bit, Mum." He lifted his thin chest. "Our country needs me."

Emotion burned in Grace's throat. This young man who was so tenderhearted and kind, who still carried elements of his adolescence with his naive sweetness, displayed such bravery.

She couldn't imagine the townhouse without him any more than she could imagine Mrs. Weatherford existing without her son. Not when she doted on him with such adoration or how she watched him with eyes that shone with pride and love.

Mrs. Weatherford's chin trembled. She pressed her lips together, but it didn't stop, nor did the rapid blinking of her eyes. "Do excuse me," she choked out. "I..." She quickly fled up the stairs.

Her bedroom door on the second level clicked shut a moment later and a wail cut through the silence, sharp with raw pain.

Colin lowered his head, hiding his expression.

Grace put a hand to the soft cotton of his sleeve. "Go to her. I'll put a fresh kettle on."

He nodded without looking at her and went up the stairs with slow, heavy steps as Grace led Viv back into the kitchen. As soon as they were alone, Grace pressed her hands to her chest where a dull ache had begun.

Colin. At war.

First George. Now Colin.

Would all the men in London be gone soon?

She looked to Viv and the weight of sorrow settled over her. Viv would soon leave too.

As if hearing her thoughts, Viv shook her head emphatically, sending her red curls bobbing around her face. "I shouldn't have said what I did, Grace." She sucked in a hard inhale. "I won't join the ATS. Not with Colin gone."

Viv's arms wrapped around her and the sweet floral perfume of Viv's latest scent *It's You* joined their embrace.

"I won't leave," Viv promised. "Mrs. Weatherford will need us both now."

Grace nodded against her friend's shoulder, grateful to not lose Viv along with George and Colin. Truly, it would be too much to bear.

In the following days, Colin remained busy in his efforts to ensure the house was up to snuff before his departure. He immediately gave notice at his job at Pet Kingdom and spent his time fixing every creaking stair and squeaking hinge. He'd even gone so far as to show Grace and Viv how to perform minor repairs in his absence in case a faucet leaked, or a knob came loose.

Grace returned to the townhouse one day to find him crouched beside a window in the parlor, painstakingly applying scrim in an artful pattern to ensure any potential bomb blasts might keep the glass from shattering. Not that there appeared to be much likelihood of bombs anymore.

Viv had warned Grace she'd be late that day with an errand to run, so Grace set aside the list of potential advertising lines she'd been considering and knelt beside him. She didn't bother to ask if she could help, knowing he would decline. Instead, she cut a strip of the tape, moistened the back and slicked it onto the glass, following his same careful pattern.

He looked at her, studying her a moment with his tender blue eyes, then gave a grateful smile.

"I thought your mum couldn't abide taped windows?" Grace cut off another length of scrim.

"It will ensure you all remain safe." Colin smoothed his

large hand over the piece Grace had attached, pressing out the tiny bubbles of air. "You should see what I've done to her remaining flowers."

Grace's mouth fell open. "You don't mean you've…dug for victory?"

Ever since October, the government had been announcing the need for flower beds to be torn up and replaced with vegetable patches in their bid for "digging for victory." Though the rationing Mrs. Weatherford had sworn would come had not been implemented as yet, the call for an abundance of home-grown vegetables was indicative of its impending announcement.

That didn't mean Mrs. Weatherford was ready to have her few thriving roses and hyacinths plucked from her beloved garden.

Colin nodded slowly, his gaze skimming over his handiwork. "I'm not familiar with vegetables, but I read the manual and tried as best I could." He lifted his shoulders in a helpless shrug.

"You could have asked Viv," Grace said. "She lived on a farm before coming here."

"That's exactly why I did it when she wasn't here." Colin got to his feet and started on the upper portion of the window. "She's always so put together. I couldn't have her out in the garden, buried in dirt and ruining her nails."

Grace rose from the ground alongside Colin. Her head came only to his chest, making her far too short to reach the windows stretching high up the wall.

"And you know she's too stubborn to take no for an answer." Rather than try to attach a piece herself, she cut and moistened a length before handing it to Colin.

He grinned as he accepted the scrim. "You said it, not me."

"Has your mother seen the garden yet?" Grace uncurled another piece of the adhesive paper from its roll.

He shook his head. "She's joined the local Women's Voluntary Service and has gone to her first meeting. No doubt we'll know when she sees it."

He looked out the window, studying the street below, and the mirth faded from his expression. "She's going to need help while I'm gone, Grace."

"I'll be here," she vowed.

He lowered his head. "I hate that I have to leave her. What if Germany does bomb London? The three of you won't be safe."

He could scarcely stop bombs from falling from the sky, but Grace didn't say as much. "We have the Andy you buried in the backyard to protect us, as well as the taped windows. You've even secured us with a garden. And you know your mother is well stocked on goods."

He lifted his head and gave a small laugh. "Ah, yes. To keep the hoarders from buying it all first." He winked at Grace.

"Exactly." Grace leveled a gaze at him. "We'll be fine here, Colin. You see to yourself, and we'll have the grandest welcome party you've ever seen when you return."

His responding smile was so sweet, it made Grace's heart splinter.

"I'd like that," he replied.

The front door opened and closed, followed by the light bump and clatter of shoes being removed and a purse and gas mask hung.

Colin grimaced and glanced around the wall.

"Is it your mother?" Grace mouthed.

Colin nodded with a wince.

"Should we tell her?" Grace asked.

He shook his head so vigorously, Grace had to press her hands to her mouth to keep from laughing.

A door swung open at the rear of the house and clicked closed. That was when they both realized there was no need to tell Mrs. Weatherford about the sacrifice of her flower beds. Her discovery was announced in the form of a shrill scream.

The devastation of Mrs. Weatherford's flower beds and the taped windows, which she referred to as "unsightly," were hardly their greatest loss. That came in the form of Colin's departure.

On the morning of Armistice Day, Colin left for his medical examination. Two days later, he had orders to report for duty.

It all flew by far too quickly, and they found themselves waking to the day of Colin's departure in stunned shock.

He accepted a hug from Viv first, who could scarcely summon a smile to see him off.

Next, he embraced Grace. "Please take care of Mum," he whispered.

Grace nodded against his chest. "I promise."

When at last he said goodbye to Mrs. Weatherford, his eyes filled with tears. He blinked with a hard sniff and swiftly left the house with an unnaturally straight back. His mother had wanted to accompany him, of course, but in the end, Colin told her he needed to do it alone.

The door closed behind him and the house fell unnaturally silent, as though it too immediately mourned the loss of his presence. Mrs. Weatherford went to the front window of the parlor and watched him as he made his way down the street.

She didn't leave from that spot for the remainder of the day, as if she could still see him walking away, continuing to bid him farewell.

Only days before, the war had been a true bore—a buildup to nothing. Yet now, its reality struck them where it caused the most hurt.

Already the sacrifice had been great. Yet it was only the start of so much more to come.

EIGHT

DESPITE MORE YOUNG MEN DISAPPEARING FROM THE streets of London, patrons continued to frequent Primrose Hill Books. The housewives seeking a new novel, the elderly men who considered the rows of political books with shrewd expressions, the men and women too young for war and too old to be sent away to the country for safety, all of them occupied the shop and Grace was all too happy to lose herself in the aiding of their selections. What's more, she found the customers who arrived in the newly organized store stayed twice as long and purchased three times more books than before.

What a difference it made when they could find what it was they sought. All except a retired professor who groused at the overly clean shelves, remarking that it lacked the authenticity of the haphazard chaos of their previous sorting system. His obvious appreciation for the shop's former state brought a smile to Grace's lips as it made her recall George's affection for the old, dusty shop.

She'd even managed to convince Mr. Evans to engage in the National Book token system. It was a marvelous advertising opportunity where one could purchase the card as a gift and the recipient could redeem it for any book of their choosing. Grace had learned of the ingenious system from a trip to Foyle's, the six-story bookseller who touted secondhand books and notable teas with celebrity guests. Once she'd seen the tokens there, she realized they were everywhere, which put Mr. Evans's shop at a severe disadvantage.

Until now.

With Christmas soon upon them, Primrose Hill Books sold several dozen the first day Grace put out the advert announcing they had book tokens.

"I'll give it to you, Miss Bennett," Mr. Evans admitted in a grudging tone after the customer he'd rung up had departed. "That was a jolly good idea you had with those book tickets."

She bit back a grin at his habit of calling them tickets rather than tokens.

"I'm pleased they've worked so well." She tied a piece of twine around a bit of folded silver tissue and pulled it apart to make a decorative ball. Perfect for the new winter scene she'd assembled in the window.

"December is nearly over." He made a note in the small ledger Grace kept beside the register, marking the sales with the same efficiency she'd begun. When he finished, he set the pencil—a proper one he didn't need to pinch between his fingertips—neatly to the side and tossed a torn piece of paper into the dust bin near the counter.

"I hope 1940 brings us an end to the war." She bound together another bundle of silver tissue. One more and she'd have all she needed.

"You're two-thirds of the way through your six months here." He regarded the ledger before letting it fall closed.

"I am." She studied him and found his face impassive.

He opened his mouth as if he meant to say something further when a tall, slender man with a heavy mustache entered the shop and set the small bell jingling. Mr. Evans gave a soul-deep exhale. "Good afternoon, Mr. Stokes. Have we suffered an infraction?"

The man's name was familiar, but Grace couldn't place it.

"I'm not on duty." There was an authority to his tone that tugged harder at Grace's memory, and it struck her at once.

Mr. Stokes was the local ARP warden.

"I confess, it's been rather dull of late." Mr. Stokes scanned the rows of books, his brow furrowed. The lines creased his forehead, indicating it was an expression he wore often. "I could use a book to get me through the night. My partner is little more than a lad and not much of a conversationalist. You would think with Christmas festivities, there would be more lights visible, but…nothing." The corner of his lip tucked downward in apparent disappointment at not having more opportunities for rebuke.

"Perhaps a nice mystery, eh?" Mr. Evans waved the other man to follow him.

That was where Mr. Evans excelled. And where Grace failed. She had focused for so long on the setup of the store that she had not had time to read its wares, especially not to the point of being able to recommend a book. Was that what Mr. Evans had planned to tell her when he mentioned her time at Primrose Hill Books would soon come to an end?

She never had the opportunity to find out. The rest of

that afternoon became impossibly busy, and Mr. Evans hadn't brought it up again. With the new year soon upon them, she had it set in her mind that she would take the time to read the books they sold. Then perhaps she could finally offer proper recommendations rather than merely suggesting books based on what seemed most popular.

Christmas was a solemn affair without Colin. Mrs. Weatherford had put together a feast in light of the impending ration, which was rumored to begin in January. She'd found a plump turkey to roast for their dinner along with parsnips, potatoes and brussels sprouts. They'd exchanged gifts in an attempt to lighten the heavy mood, though it only helped a little. The house was not the same without Colin's goodness to make it glow with warmth.

Grace had given book tokens to Mrs. Weatherford—they truly were handy gifts—and a fashionable new hat for Viv who had sewn new dresses for Mrs. Weatherford and Grace. Mrs. Weatherford had purchased both girls a handbag fitted for gas masks.

It was a curious thing with a rounded bottom for the canister to go inside and a pocket to fit the bulk of the mask. The handbags were fashionable black leather with gold snaps at their tops. Certainly a handbag any lady would carry proudly.

"So you won't be leaving them behind when you go out." Mrs. Weatherford had made the declaration with a note of finality that told them she'd take no more excuses at leaving their masks home going forward.

Not only did Christmas passing not bring an end to the war as many had optimistically predicted, but it brought the implementation of the threatened ration. The limits to bacon, butter and sugar only served to make one of the coldest winters in London all the more bitter.

Each person in England, including the king and queen, were given a small book of stamps to limit the amount of rationed goods they could purchase. Somehow, even with Mrs. Weatherford's stockpile of sugar she'd held under lock and key in the previous months, Grace and Viv found the sugar caddy often sparse.

It was in that dull gray world where Grace discovered an unexpected ray of sunshine.

One afternoon, on a particularly icy day after she'd been given leave from Primrose Hill Books, she found herself in the very peculiar position of having free time. And she knew exactly how to spend it. She made herself a cup of tea, snuggled into the Morris chair with a thick blanket over her legs and settled under the weight of *The Count of Monte Cristo* on her lap.

She ran her fingers over the worn cover and thought of George Anderson. Not only him, but all the men who had been called up.

Where were they? Was it as drearily dull for them?

She truly hoped so. Better to be bored than in danger.

Slowly, she opened the book, noting how the old spine didn't bother to creak, as though it had been oiled by age, and began to read.

What she found within was nothing like the texts she'd read in school that offered dry accounts of maths or broken down sentence structures and word formation. No, this book, when finally given the proper attention it deserved, somehow locked her in its grasp and did not once let go.

What started as an accusation in the beginning spiraled into treachery before tailspinning into the greatest betrayal.

Word after word, page after page, she was pulled deeper into a place she had never experienced and walked in the footsteps of a person she'd never been.

She was emotionally invested in the tale, her eyes darting faster and faster across the page to devour every word, desperate to know what would become of Edmond—

"Grace?" Mrs. Weatherford's voice broke into the story, shattering the scene playing out in Grace's mind.

She startled and looked up at Mrs. Weatherford.

"Supper is nearly ready." The older woman glanced about and tsked before rushing to the window. "You didn't draw the curtains. I'm certain we'll hear of it from Mr. Stokes later."

Grace blinked, caught in a momentary state of confusion. It had grown rather dark. She'd recalled noticing it briefly and meaning to put on a light, but that had been when Mercédès and Edmond had their engagement party and the nefarious plotting had truly begun to unfold.

A light snapped on, a flash of brilliance that made the page bloom white in front of Grace's eyes and rendered the stark black letters so much easier to see.

"What are you reading?" Mrs. Weatherford angled her face at the cover as she stepped closer.

"*The Count of Monte Cristo.*" Grace's cheeks warmed. "It was the book Mr. Anderson left for me before he was called up."

Mrs. Weatherford's eyes dimmed. "That has always been one of Colin's favorite books as well."

"Have you heard from him?" Grace asked.

Mrs. Weatherford wandered aimlessly around the room, straightening an immaculate pile of magazines and plumping pillows that could truly not possibly fluff anymore. "I haven't, though I expect I soon shall. You know how they train those boys so thoroughly before…" Her voice caught.

Before they're sent into battle.

The words hung unsaid in the air, as well as the implication of danger.

"If you'd like to read it when I'm done, you may borrow it," Grace offered in an attempt to change the subject.

"Thank you, but I have a lovely novel by Jane Austen from one of the book tokens you gave me. I haven't read *Emma* yet." She fidgeted with the blackout curtain, making sure it fell just so. "And I stay quite busy with the other women of the WVS, of course. Now come along before supper cools."

The Women's Voluntary Service had done Mrs. Weatherford a world of good in Colin's absence. Not only did it keep her busy so she didn't scrub the floors of the house into a carbolic oblivion, but she was in the company of other mothers in similar situations, whose sons were also at war.

Grace obediently set the book aside and went to the kitchen where they'd taken to eating their meals. The formal dining area felt far too large without Colin sitting opposite his mother.

Viv grinned at Grace as she entered. "I figured you wanted to skip our tea today considering how involved you were with George's book."

It was as though Grace had tipped fully into another world and was just now finding her way back into reality. She laughed, feeling somewhat foolish. "I'm so sorry I didn't hear you come in. I didn't even notice the room had grown dark."

Yet even as she chatted through supper and ate the tender chicken Mrs. Weatherford roasted for their meal, Grace found her thoughts turning back to Edmond Dantés. More than that, she recalled his experiences with the same poignancy as if she herself had lived through them rather than the character in the book.

This was clearly what George had meant when he described how he felt about reading.

That night, she stayed up with the blanket covering her head and a torch illuminating the pages as she fell back into Edmond's story. After every chapter, she swore to herself it would be the last until her eyes finally fell closed, blending the images in her mind with those of her dreams.

The next morning, she startled awake, bleary-eyed and nearly late. After a particularly unsweetened cup of tea and bite of toast with barely a scrape of butter, Grace bundled up against the harsh cold for the trek to Primrose Hill Books.

The quick walk that had seemed so brief and pleasant in the summer and fall had become grueling in the winter. The wind pushed at her, making her forward progress all the more difficult as a deep wet cold sank into her bones.

She was nearly to Farringdon Station, lost in reliving what she'd read in *The Count of Monte Cristo*, when a peal of laughter pulled her attention to a side street. Two children bundled against the dismal weather raced back and forth in what appeared to be a game of tag, their cheeks red from the nip in the air and their laughter fogging in front of their mouths.

Once those giggles had been ubiquitous, blending into the roar of traffic and chatter of passing people. It struck Grace suddenly how the sound of children had become foreign.

Not all mothers had sent their children away to the country, of course, but with so many who had, there were few left to be seen.

And yet, the children playing were not the only ones she spotted that morning. As she continued on toward the bookshop, she came upon several little girls whispering together with a toy pram holding their dolls.

Were children returning?

Buoyed by the possibility this might mean an end to the war, Grace pushed into the store and immediately addressed Mr. Evans. "Have you seen the children? It looks as though they're returning."

Mr. Evans waved emphatically, nearly upsetting a jar of sharpened pencils. "Shut the door, Miss Bennett. It's cold as brass monkeys out there."

Grace did as she was asked, pushing the door against a gust of wind trying to curl its icy fingers inside. Once the chill was thoroughly blocked out, the warmth of the shop tingled at her cheeks and hands, making her almost hot in the bundle of her winter clothes.

"The children have been coming back since Christmas." Mr. Evans squinted at something in the ledger. "What does this say?" He turned it toward her.

She looked down at his jerky script and ignored the ache pounding in her head from lack of sleep. "It says five copies."

He hummed in acknowledgment and wrote something beside the note. "I don't know how you've come to read my writing better than I do."

"I think we ought to order children's books and create a new section." Grace set her handbag on the counter with a thunk, its weight considerable with the combination of her gas mask and book.

"They'll all be sent back now that Christmas is over, I wager." Mr. Evans lifted his generous brows as he wrote, as though doing so made it easier to see.

"A small section then." Grace unbelted her coat and

tugged the muffler from her neck as she scanned the shop, envisioning where a space for children's books might go.

A center table had been prepared for the newest popular book, *What Hitler Wants*. The attention-grabbing orange banded dust jacket promised to delve beyond Hitler's manifesto, *Mein Kampf*, to offer insight into what drove Hitler's decisions and what he might be motivated to do going forward. It was an atrocious publication in Grace's opinion, but the masses clearly disagreed and wanted to know more.

Maybe there was something to Mrs. Weatherford's claim that having knowledge truly was the best way to fight off fear.

Grace indicated the table set aside for the book on Hitler. "Here." The space would be better used for a children's section.

Mr. Evans grunted, which she'd come to take as his form of agreement. Or at least, it wasn't ever a no.

She set to work that afternoon, putting together a list of books for Simpkin Marshalls to fill. The wholesale book distributor was located on Paternoster Row and had an uncanny knack of prompt delivery from its massively stocked warehouse.

Yet through it all, she couldn't dislodge *The Count of Monte Cristo* from her head. Edmond had only just crawled through the tunnel toward the abbé's prison cell.

What would he find in there? What if they were caught? The very thought sent her pulse racing.

After ordering new stock for the returning children, she slipped the thick book from her handbag and snuck between two large shelves near the rear of the store. Immediately, she fell into the story and the fog of exhaustion in her brain cleared away.

"Miss Bennett." Mr. Evans's voice cut into the stone-walled dungeon cell and slammed her right back in the middle of the bookshop.

She leapt and slapped the book closed, immediately regretting not having noted the page number first. Never in all her time at her uncle's shop had she taken even a moment from her tasks for herself in such a way. She slowly looked at Mr. Evans, tense with guilt.

His heavy brows crawled together as he bent to study the title on the spine. "Are you reading *The Count of Monte Cristo*?"

She nodded. "Yes, I..." It was on the edge of her tongue to offer a justification, but she stopped herself. Nothing could excuse what she'd done. "I'm sorry."

The corners of his mouth lifted. "I see you took Mr. Anderson's recommendation." He nodded to the book. "Carry on, Miss Bennett. I expect if it has captivated you so thoroughly, we can anticipate selling quite a few copies based on your recommendation."

Relief eased the tension from her shoulders. "I'll order more from Simpkin Marshalls."

"See that you do." He picked a bit of yellow lint from his tweed jacket. "And you may want to consider Jane Austen for your next book. Women seem to enjoy her protagonists."

Curiosity piqued, she made a mental note to purchase one of Miss Austen's books. Maybe *Emma*. Mrs. Weatherford appeared to have found it enjoyable.

"I'm pleased to see you've become a reader in your time here." Mr. Evans drew his spectacles off to examine them. Without the magnifying effect of the glass, his eyes appeared rather small. "Even if you do have only one more month remaining in our agreement."

Was there truly only one more month to go? How was it even a dismal Christmas season had passed with such swiftness?

Grace nodded, unsure of what to say, and realized belatedly he most likely couldn't see her.

He drew out a handkerchief, wiped at a spot on the lens, then replaced the glasses on his face and blinked owlishly at her. "You haven't become attached to Primrose Hill Books now, have you?"

The question took her aback, but not nearly as much as her immediate awareness that indeed, she had become attached.

She liked how customers could easily find their books in the newly organized store, she enjoyed the book jackets and how creative some publishers were with their designs. She even relished the dusty scent that lingered in the shop no matter how often she cleaned, and had come to appreciate Mr. Evans, dry humor and all.

Before she could formulate a reply, the bell dinged, announcing an incoming customer.

"Evans?" Mr. Pritchard's voice chirped from the front of the shop. "Are you here?"

Mr. Evans rolled his eyes heavenward and shuffled out to greet the man who Grace could never tell was a friend or foe. "Good afternoon, Pritchard."

"Have you tried the fish and chips at Warrington's recently?" Mr. Pritchard asked. "I just had some and they're bloody awful. It's a shame what's become of London when you cannot even find a decent meal of fish and chips. I know they don't have the same fat to fry them in, but after the queue I stood in and the price I paid…"

The men continued on discussing how the ration had affected their enjoyment of food and how margarine could never fully replace butter. While they did so, Grace grappled with the dismal realization that soon she would no longer be employed at the bookshop.

After all the times she'd dreamed of being alongside Viv at Harrods, amid the colorful, stylish clothes and the air scented with costly perfume, never once had she considered how much she genuinely enjoyed her current position.

Her stomach clenched and she clutched George's book more tightly in her hands, as though it could somehow help ground her spiraling emotions.

In only one month, she would have her letter of recommendation, and her employment at Primrose Hill Books would be done.

Mr. Evans had told her from the start not to get attached. Though she hadn't meant to, somehow she had.

And now she didn't want it to end.

NINE

GRACE HAD NOT BEEN ABLE TO DISLODGE HER
melancholy at the idea of no longer working for Primrose Hill Books. Yet in the three weeks that followed, she
couldn't summon the temerity to speak to Mr. Evans about
the possibility of staying on. Not when he'd been so insistent that she not become attached.

She did, however, finish *The Count of Monte Cristo* and
so thoroughly enjoyed it, she couldn't stop recommending
it to customers. So much that she'd had to order more than
the five they had stocked, something Mr. Evans had commented on with enthusiasm.

She couldn't wait to get to the last page to find out if Edmond had his revenge and if his life finally settled into happiness. But as much as she loved reading the story, no one had
prepared her for the end being so bittersweet. No one told
her finishing the book would leave her so bereft. It was as

though she'd said goodbye for the last time to a close friend. When she mentioned it to Mr. Evans, he simply smiled and recommended she try another book. And so, she consoled herself with *Emma*, which was a most marvelous distraction.

Through it all, however, Grace couldn't help but notice Viv had been rather out of sorts. It became most apparent during one of their afternoon teas in the sunny yellow and white kitchen at the townhouse. First Viv forgot to turn the stovetop on, which left the kettle sitting cold on its surface, and then she brought the tea over without any teacups.

All of it was very unlike Viv, who loved to add fanfare to any event, even something as common as afternoon tea.

Grace quickly acquired two cups and studied her friend. "Something is weighing on you. What is it?"

Viv sank into the opposite chair and sighed. Her gaze wandered to the barren garden outside where Colin's planting efforts for Dig for Victory had been frozen over by the winter's brutality. A mound humped up from the middle of the desiccated flower beds where the Andy was buried. Normally a garden would have been locked in winter dormancy, but now there was only bare earth, stripped to stark desolation.

"Do you ever feel like you don't do enough?" Viv took a sip of her tea and left a red half-moon on the cup's rim from her lipstick.

Grace wrapped her hands around the heat of her teacup. The last week had been cold enough to freeze a mix of snow and ice on the ground. Though the kitchen was the warmest room in the townhouse, Grace's hands never seemed to thoroughly thaw.

"This war will continue until we do something." Viv's large brown eyes were apprehensive.

Whatever she had to say, she knew Grace would not like it.

Nervousness tightened in Grace's stomach. "What are you going on about?"

Viv's mouth twisted slightly, indicating she was biting her lip, a confirmation that she was indeed anxious. "I can't do it any longer. You know I've never been one to sit around waiting for things to happen."

Grace set aside her teacup. She did know. Viv had always run headfirst into life, ready for whatever she might face. "The ATS?" Grace surmised.

Viv nodded. "The uniforms are ghastly, I know, but the service suits my talents. And it's far better than becoming a Land Girl."

The Land Girls were part of the Women's Land Army, a group of women who assisted with growing crops. While the service was voluntary, it didn't mean people wouldn't pressure Viv to join if they knew anything of her history with her parents' farm.

She'd heard from her parents only once in the time since they'd arrived in London. In the letter, her mother had expressed her displeasure at Viv's abrupt departure and told her to not bother returning. Viv had passed it off indifferently with a light jest, but Grace knew it had cut her deeply.

"You'd make a fine Land Girl," Grace protested as she bit back a smile.

Viv's mouth fell open in exaggerated offense. "You're so wicked, Grace Bennett." She nudged Grace's toe with hers in a mock kick. "You could come with me, you know." Viv's auburn brows were finely arched, plucked each day to perfection. They rose now in invitation. "Imagine it, the two of us in the ATS, commiserating in those atrocious brown uniforms that make our bums look long and rectangular, sacrificing youth and fashion to do our bit for England."

"Well, when you sell it like that…" Grace laughed. Despite her mirth, she knew she ought to do something for her country. The men were being called up, mothers had sacrificed their children to the country to remain safe, strangers were caring for those children, women were volunteering. And what was she doing?

Nothing.

"Come with me, Duckie." Viv winked, turning on the full effect of her charm. "We can do this together."

Grace's chest squeezed at what joining the ATS would mean, aside from the duty of aiding her country, of course. She would be leaving behind Primrose Hill Books and the disappointment of no longer working there. She wouldn't have to work at Harrods without Viv. Best of all, she would still be at her friend's side, the way they'd always been since they were girls.

But it would also mean leaving Mrs. Weatherford alone.

The WVS offered her mother's friend only so much of a reprieve, and the threads of Mrs. Weatherford's life were beginning to unravel. Mrs. Weatherford preferred to be in charge, but had to yield to the woman heading her local WVS, who had no intention of relinquishing the leadership role. Instead, Mrs. Weatherford shifted her need for control to the house.

The tar-like odor of carbolic soap permeated every surface from her daily scouring. Towels were adjusted neatly to the exact center of their racks, food tins were lined with their labels facing out like rows of soldiers and even the teacups were put away with their handles pointed in the same direction.

If Grace were to leave, Mrs. Weatherford would have no one. And Grace had promised Colin she would look after his mother.

Grace shook her head. "I can't."

"Mrs. Weatherford," Viv guessed.

Grace stared into the depths of her tea, just able to make out the bottom in the dark liquid. "I can't leave her alone here. And you know I've never been daring like you. I'm not cut out for the ATS or any of the other lines of service."

"You're more daring than you think." Viv lifted the rose-painted teacup to her lips and took a small sip.

There it was again—a pinch of guilt.

Not that Viv had intended to cause such a reaction, but Grace knew she wasn't doing enough for the war effort. And the more they all helped, the sooner it would be over.

A curl of steam rose up in front of Viv as she lowered her cup. "I understand, Grace. Besides, imagine having our room to yourself so you can keep the light on to read at night, instead of having to constantly purchase new torches."

Grace had to laugh at that. No. 8 size batteries were nearly impossible to locate anymore. It was far easier to purchase a new torch than find the batteries to put in it. After Viv's confession to being hopelessly bored, Grace had dedicated her afternoons and evenings to her friend. There had been teas, cafés, cinemas and shopping during the day and the programs on the wireless in the evening.

But even as she listened to the broadcasts, Grace's mind always crept back to whatever story she was in the middle of reading. It made for late nights buried under her covers with her newest book.

Mr. Evans had been correct. Grace had loved Jane Austen and was currently making her way through the author's entire collection.

"It won't be the same here without you," Grace said to her friend.

Viv reached across the table and took Grace's hand. "I'll come back here every time I'm on leave."

"What of your parents?"

"They'll disapprove, I'm sure." Viv rolled her eyes and drew her hand back to her teacup. "They've already told me I don't need to bother returning home, and I won't. I'd much prefer to come here to see you rather than find myself trapped in an eternal lecture on my disappointments."

"The ATS will be all the better for having you." Grace sat back in her chair and regarded her friend in a new, proud light. "You've always been so brave."

Viv scoffed humbly at the praise and took a sip of her tea. "I'm only sorry we won't get to work at Harrods together. I'll ensure I put in a good word for you before I leave. How delightful would it be if they gave you my position?"

Grace simply nodded and offered what she hoped was a convincing smile. She didn't want to work at Harrods. Especially not without Viv.

More than ever, Grace knew without a doubt that she would prefer to continue her employment at the bookshop. Now she need only convince Mr. Evans.

When Grace entered Primrose Hill Books the next morning, she found a large box sitting on the counter. Mr. Evans greeted her as he lifted a stack of books from its depths and set them aside in a neat pile.

In the time it took Grace to deposit her belongings in the

back room and return to the front, he'd nearly unpacked the entire container.

"Is that the new shipment from Simpkin's?" She kept her tone mild, but her nerves made her feel as though she was rattling inside.

He nodded and pulled out three more books.

"There's less than a week left in my employment here," she ventured.

"I'm already working on your letter of recommendation," he said gruffly. "You needn't worry after it."

Disappointment punched into her gut. His preparation of the letter made everything so much more solid, real.

Too real.

Before she attempted a different angle, he reached into the box and withdrew a book bound in a length of canvas. He laid it on the counter with reverence and carefully withdrew the cloth.

The book inside was filthy. Dirt left brown smears over the golden yellow cover, and a rust-colored stain seeped from its worn face down into the pages beneath. Grace tilted her head to read the spine.

Quantentheorie des einatomigen idealen Gases by Albert Einstein.

She straightened as a chill prickled over her skin. "Is that German?"

"It is." Mr. Evans lips tucked together, his brows edging together. "It was saved from the book burning the Nazis did around seven years ago. Foyle has been determined to get his hands on all of them and even made a bid to Hitler himself. Who knows why?" Mr. Evans put his hands over the cover, hovering without touching. "Knowing Foyle, he'd probably stuff them into the sandbags around his shop like he does with the rest of the old books he's used so callously."

Grace had seen the squared off sandbags in front of Foyles and had wondered at their shape. Never had she dreamed he would have filled them with old books. Her gaze wandered to the reddish-brown stain on the cover of the battered tome. It was fascinating and yet disconcerting.

"What is that?" She indicated the book.

Mr. Evans drew in a long inhale and slowly let it out. "Blood." He lifted the book free of the cloth. "Old blood. Hitler didn't take kindly to the books he meant to burn being hidden."

His unspoken suggestion dropped on her with horror. "Do you mean someone may have died to save it?"

She followed him into the back room where he moved around several boxes to reveal a safe embedded in the wall. She blinked in surprise, having never even known of its existence.

"Most likely." He spun at the knob, ignoring the keyhole an inch below it, and the door swung open with a heavy, metallic groan. Inside were nearly a dozen more books with German titles along their spines. While not new, none were in the same poor condition as the one by Albert Einstein.

"There are many voices Hitler would quiet, especially those who are Jewish." Mr. Evans slid the new book reverently beside the others. "It is the duty of the rest of the world to ensure they will never be silenced." He tapped a yellow spine with *Almansor* in gilt at its top. "'Where they burn books, they will ultimately burn people as well.' Heinrich Heine isn't Jewish, but his ideals go against what Hitler believes." Mr. Evans pushed the safe door closed with an ominous bang. "This war is about far more than blackouts and food rationing, Miss Bennett."

She swallowed.

People were dying to save books, to prevent ideas and people from being snuffed out.

Grace wasn't doing nearly enough.

"I think I may join the ATS," she said abruptly.

His large eyes blinked behind his spectacles. "I do not think that is a wise decision, Miss Bennett. Why not join the ARP as a warden instead?"

Grace frowned at the idea of being like Mr. Stokes, noting every amount of light emanating from households and gleefully telling them to be put out.

The bell at the front of the shop jangled, announcing a customer. Wordlessly, Grace left Mr. Evans with the safe as she went to the front of the store. It was no patron who awaited her, but Mrs. Nesbitt.

She wore a beige mackintosh belted at her narrow waist and a black hat set perfectly in the center of her hair, which was pulled back as severely as before. Her mouth was an angry slash of red in her hard-set features.

"You are just the wretch I came to see," Mrs. Nesbitt said, her words nipped out with arrogant precision.

The aggression of her demeanor was like a slap and rendered Grace momentarily at a loss for words. "I...I beg your pardon?" she stammered.

"Don't play innocent with me, you minx." Mrs. Nesbitt stormed into the shop, her hard, black heels striking the floor like jackboots. "Look how organized this is. How clean. How perfectly laid out by section." She jabbed a finger at a sign marked History by way of demonstration. "And displayed." She slid a side glare at the children's table set artfully with a colorful array of books.

She didn't bother to hide the accusation icing over her words. "How curious that your orders at Simpkin Marshalls are increasing as the rest of us struggle to sell our usual stock?"

Grace's boldness in dealing with the sharp-tongued woman previously was gone, washed away by the open hostility and cemented by the need to uphold the face of Primrose Hill Books within its walls.

Grace dug her nails into her patience and clung on. "With all due respect, Mrs. Nesbitt," she replied levelly, "you are not the only shop to use displays in such a fashion, nor are you the only one to label the sections."

"Your display is quite purposefully styled," Mrs. Nesbitt snapped.

Grace knew the exhibit in the front window was eye-catching, a blend of popular mysteries with a sprinkle of children's books to entice a housewife with a child in tow to enter. It was purposefully styled, as Mrs. Nesbitt said, but then many displays on Paternoster Row had been.

"Thank you," Mr. Evans replied. "Grace has worked hard on it, as well as everything else in the shop."

Mrs. Nesbitt spun around and faced Mr. Evans, tall and skinny to his short and plump. "I mean it looks very much like my display. How dare you?"

He gave her a bored look. "Do not blame your flagging sales on our prosper."

"How could I not?" Mrs. Nesbitt declared. "To what else do you attribute your success aside from organizing your shop like mine?"

"Competition," Grace interjected, bolstered by Mr. Evans's support. "You are amid many other booksellers on Paternoster Row, yet we're alone here on Hosier Lane."

"And offer friendly service." Mr. Evans gave what appeared to be a kind smile in Grace's direction. "On that note, Mrs. Nesbitt, I'd like you to take your leave lest you scare off my customers."

Her mouth fell open with apparent offense. "I've never..."

"Heard of such a thing?" Mr. Evans's brows lifted. "Well, if you haven't, then I wager it's far overdue." He indicated the door.

Mrs. Nesbitt sniffed, lifted her head so high she most likely couldn't see properly and swept from the bookshop.

Mr. Evans frowned at Grace.

She flinched inwardly, anticipating a rebuke for having caused such a row in the store where they might have been heard by customers.

"Don't join the ATS, Miss Bennett. Stay here."

"In London?"

"At Primrose Hill Books." He put his hands in his pockets and lowered his head. "I know you've a mind to go to Harrods and it's not fair of me to ask." He glanced up at her, his expression hesitant. "I'm grateful for what you've done with the shop and would like you to at least consider staying on."

Grace stared at him, unable to believe her ears. Surely she was dreaming.

"With a raise, of course," he added.

She grinned at him. "Who could say no to such an offer?"

"I'm glad to hear it." He nodded, more to himself. "Quite glad indeed."

That afternoon at tea with Viv, Grace happily shared she

wouldn't need the good word put in for her at Harrods after all. With Viv having gathered all the information required to begin her application for the ATS, the two had much to celebrate.

As it turned out, women who volunteered for service were not sent away for training with the same haste as the men. Between the time it took Viv to finally fill out the application, complete her medical test and wait for her paperwork informing her where she would report, January melted into late February and the icy chill in the air softened the ground enough for a new season of planting to begin.

It was a Wednesday morning when Mrs. Weatherford appeared in the sunny kitchen, wearing a baggy pair of brown trousers belted under her bosom with the legs rolled several times to flop over her ankles. This was matched with an old moss-colored pullover whose neckline had begun to unravel.

The attire was sloppy and large, clearly belonging to Colin. It was far from Mrs. Weatherford's usually neat attire comprised of floral, pastel prints.

Both Grace and Viv paused in eating their morning meal of toast and greasy margarine, which they could never fully get used to, and gaped at Mrs. Weatherford.

"Colin tore up my flowers for this garden of his, and I'm going to make certain it grows." She nodded toward the window where the earth outside was still blank and bare. "I intend to plant my own vegetables since the ones he sowed froze over with this wretched winter."

"Do you know how to plant?" Grace asked.

"I know flowers." Mrs. Weatherford tugged the trousers

up a little higher with a confident air. "And Colin always did the planting. But truly, how hard could it possibly be?"

Viv choked on her tea.

Mrs. Weatherford thrust out a leaflet, with images of brightly colored plants alongside what appeared to be a chart. "According to this, I ought to plant onions, parsnips, turnips and beans in February."

"Not turnips," Viv said reluctantly. "Those do better when planted in the summer. And truly, you ought to wait until March."

Mrs. Weatherford flipped the leaflet back to her face and squinted at its small script.

Grace lifted her eyebrows at Viv, curious to see if her friend would help Mrs. Weatherford. Viv shook her head firmly once. No.

"Ah, yes, you're quite right on the turnips." Mrs. Weatherford set the paper aside and slapped a wilting straw hat on her head. "Well then. I'm off to plant. Proper this time. Or at the very least, my level best."

She marched out the door with the determination of a soldier.

"You're truly going to let her go about it on her own?" Grace scolded.

Viv's face crumpled into a petulant pout. "You know I'm bloody well done messing about in the dirt." She glanced out the window where Mrs. Weatherford set aside a stack of materials for planting before assuming her task.

The older woman started in the middle of the yard and poked a hole into the earth with a gloved finger.

"Do you think she knows what she's doing?" Grace asked.

Viv sipped her tea, her gaze fixed on Mrs. Weatherford

who was now making holes in a circular pattern. "She does not."

Grace tilted her head imploringly at Viv.

Her friend settled back in her seat, teacup stubbornly locked in her hands. "I'm not helping."

Outside, Mrs. Weatherford inspected three pouches of seeds before putting a little of each into the poked earth.

"Is she planting them all together?" Grace leaned on the thin-cushioned seat for a better view.

"I'm not going out there." Viv crossed her legs and sipped her tea.

Mrs. Weatherford brushed the dirt back over the holes where the seeds had been deposited and scooted over two feet. She punched her finger into the soil and began with a second spiral.

Grace frowned. "She didn't even mark the plants."

Viv set the cup on the table with such a firm hand, a few droplets sloshed over the rim. "I can't take it. I'm going upstairs to put on old clothes to help her."

Grace hid her smile and gathered up the tea. "I'll clean up here then put on a set of trousers to join you."

It took them the better part of the morning to section off an area of the garden for planting, ensuring to leave space for future seeds that could be sown in warmer months.

"I think you may be even better at this than Colin," Mrs. Weatherford said to Viv when they'd finished. "I know you're eager to join the ATS, but I dare say I believe you would make a fine Land Girl."

Viv simply offered a tight smile to the compliment.

While the work had been hard and terribly messy, it had been enjoyable with the three of them chatting as they toiled. Little did they know it was the last time such joy would be had together, for that afternoon, Viv's orders came with the post and she was to leave the following day for a training facility in Devon.

For the first time in her life, Grace would be without her dearest friend to face the wild unknown of London at war.

TEN

LIFE WITHOUT VIV WAS LONELY. NOT ONLY HAD GRACE lost the companionship of her best friend, but she felt as though she'd missed out on something larger than herself by declining to join the ATS.

Rather than sign on as an ARP warden, Grace allowed Mrs. Weatherford to convince her to attend several WVS meetings.

There, Grace found herself among housewives, some older than her, but many her own age, with husbands and children. She helped them roll bandages while they lamented the toils of dirty nappies, the excruciating delay of the mail with the war on and the difficulties of getting by on their own. Through it all, they offered encouragement and swapped recipes to get through the ration any way they could. Especially after meat was added to the restrictions in March.

After all, there was only so much one could do with four ounces of meat.

Viv had always been the outgoing, carefree one in their friendship. It had never bothered Grace before that she was more reserved. At least, not until Viv wasn't there and Grace found herself in a room full of strangers who remained as such week after week.

And so it was that as April rolled in, Grace began making excuses for being unable to attend the WVS meetings—which Mrs. Weatherford thankfully never protested—and instead curled up in her bed with a book propped in front of her.

When she wasn't assisting Mrs. Weatherford in their fledgling garden, Grace devoured the rest of Jane Austen's works before moving on to several novels by Charles Dickens. Then came Mary Shelley's *Frankenstein* and finally something more current by Daphne du Maurier.

Each and every book Grace enjoyed, she passionately recommended to the customers of Primrose Hill Books. The increase in sales was stunning. So much so that Mr. Evans began loaning Grace books to read. She'd resisted the suggestion at first, until she realized the financial impact of her newfound reading habit, then gratefully accepted Mr. Evans's generous offer.

Grace had just recommended *Rebecca*, the latest Daphne du Maurier book she'd read, to a woman she recognized from the WVS—a woman who did not appear to remember her—when Mr. Stokes walked in. Mr. Evans no longer worried about blackout infractions when they saw the middle-aged man with his perpetually furrowed brow, not when he'd become a regular fixture at the store and had a propensity to go through books almost as quickly as Grace.

"We haven't seen you in nearly three days," she commented after she'd completed the WVS woman's purchase of the book she'd recommended. "I assume *The Count of Monte Cristo* took some time to read?"

Grace didn't bother to hide her smile. He had asked for a book that would last more than one night. The exhaustion shadowing the skin under his eyes indicated he had likely tried to get through the massive book with haste.

She knew what she'd been doing when she recommended the book to Mr. Stokes. No doubt George also had known what he was doing when he gave her his old copy of *The Count of Monte Cristo*. A sudden yearning to have another conversation with him struck her. How she longed to share how impactful his gift had been. If nothing else, she wished she had his address, to write her appreciation for the book.

"You were right about the story occupying a good portion of my time." Mr. Stokes rubbed at the back of his neck. "It was far longer than others and equally as riveting." He sighed. "The lad I was working with was conscripted so I've been carrying the load of two men in his absence. Do you happen to know of anyone who would be interested in joining the ARP as a warden?"

"Grace has been considering it," Mr. Evans offered from somewhere in the history section.

Now that the store had been properly organized, it was easier to see the types of books that drew the shop owner's attention. History and philosophy. A majority of Mr. Evans's days were spent poring through his own stock, ensuring there were no printing inaccuracies, as he put it.

Grace grimaced at having been volunteered and busied herself at the counter, organizing the neat surface with such unnecessary effort, she reminded herself briefly of Mrs. Weatherford. Regardless, it was better than looking directly at Mr. Stokes and encouraging his entreaty that she join up.

After all, her attempt to help with the WVS had felt pointless. Worse than pointless, it made her feel awkward and socially inept. Would being an ARP Warden be any better? Air raids still came on occasion, all resulting in nothing more than a few hours in windowless, stuffy places until the all clear sounded. People seldom even bothered to seek shelter anymore.

She'd eventually received two letters from Viv in the time her friend had been gone. With Viv being stationed in England, they came with more frequency than those from Colin, who was stationed abroad. Though given the backed up postal service, that wasn't saying much. At least the correspondence had let Grace know Viv appeared to be happily adjusting to her new tasks. Certainly with more ease than Grace had with the Women's Volunteer Service.

"Miss Bennett, is that true you wish to join on as an ARP warden?" Mr. Stokes asked.

Grace straightened a copy of *Bobby Bear's Annual* where the children's book was on display by the register to attract housewives for one last impulsive purchase. "I've considered it."

Mr. Stokes's mustache twitched. "But you're a woman."

Grace stiffened, affronted by the blatancy of his demeaning implication.

"If you mean to imply she couldn't do it, you're daft." Mr. Evans emerged from the history aisle, shooting a glare at Mr. Stokes from over his thick glasses. "Miss Bennett could do the job of any man, and far better at that."

Mr. Stokes scoffed.

His dubious response, as much as Mr. Evans's commendation of her abilities, notched her chin a little higher. "I'll do it."

Mr. Stokes's forehead creases deepened. "You will?"

"Don't act as though you've competition for the position, Mr. Stokes." Mr. Evans smiled at Grace and melted back among his books.

"Very well," Mr. Stokes said. "Go to the warden's post this afternoon and inquire within." He cleared his throat. "And I'd like another book if you would recommend one."

Later that day, after Grace's shift had ended, she did as Mr. Stokes said and inquired within the warden's post. Several days later, she was awarded a tin hat with a white W painted on it to denote her role as a warden, a whistle, a gas rattle to alert the public in the event of a gas attack, an orange bound copy of the *Air Raid Warden's Training Manual* as well as a CD mask. It was the latter that dismayed her the most, for the professional grade gas mask was far larger than her current one, having large glass eyes and a filter that was made to accommodate a microphone. How would such a monstrosity ever fit neatly in her handbag?

So it was that she ended up on her first shift four nights later alongside Mr. Stokes with her mask strung about her shoulder in its ungainly box rather than with a smart handbag at her side. She wore a light coat against the chill April carried in, and the blasted string refused to remain set against her shoulder. If nothing else, the metal ARP badge she'd pinned to her lapel helped tether the string into place.

By the time they stepped out of the immaculate office-like interior of the warden's post, the blackout was in full effect. The moon's face was nearly completely hidden, and any light it might have offered was rendered opaque with a veil of heavy clouds.

It was far too dark to see anything.

Grace's palms prickled with sweat despite the night chill.

"Come on then." Mr. Stokes's steps strode confidently ahead.

Grace cautiously inched forward.

"Miss Bennett, we can't linger in front of the post all night." Impatience edged Mr. Stokes's tone.

Regret lanced through her. She never ought to have signed on with the Air Raid Precautions unit. How could she face every night in pitch-darkness?

She shuffled closer to the sound of Mr. Stokes's voice.

His laughter rang out. "You new wardens are all the same, blind as moles in the daylight. Find the white lines on the curbs, Miss Bennett, your eyes will adjust and you can follow them with ease."

The direction was given with more condescension than instruction, but still Grace did as he suggested. True to his words, her vision did adjust to identify the thickly painted lines.

She and the veteran warden carefully made their way through the blackened streets of their allotted sector, once so familiar by day and completely unrecognizable in the dark. As they did so, he showed her where the shelters were located as well as any areas that might cause public issue if bombed.

As they passed people's homes, he rattled off their names. In the event of a bombing, they'd need to mark each resident down as they entered the shelters.

Between names and locations, Mr. Stokes reiterated all the details that had already been presented to Grace in the Air Raid Warden's Training Manual, albeit the passages on the effects of gas were not as vivid, nor were the descriptions of injuries anywhere near as gratuitous with gore.

If Mr. Stokes had been able to see her face, he would know his words had left her disgusted. But perhaps that was the point. She wouldn't put it past him to encourage her to quit.

"The Taylors," he muttered with hostility under his breath. "Do you see that?" he asked, more loudly this time, clearly put out.

Grace searched the darkness in front of them, trying to ignore how the heaviness of it seemed to press into her eyes. There, in the distance, a glow of golden light framed the square of a distant window.

Grace almost laughed. The light was barely visible. "Surely that can't be seen by German planes."

Mr. Stokes's footsteps resumed at a clipped pace. "The RAF has already tested infractions such as this and confirmed they can indeed be seen from the skies at night. The Germans invaded Norway and Denmark only yesterday. We could be next. Do you want your house bombed because the Taylors didn't cover their windows properly?"

The question jarred Grace. "Of course not."

"Missed the bus indeed," Mr. Stokes groused, referencing Chamberlain's recent claim. "If we lose this war, it's because our government is too bloody slow to act."

Grace had heard the broadcast as well, where Chamberlain claimed Hitler had "missed the bus" in that he should have attacked earlier in the war when he was prepared and Britain was not. The boast was ill-timed when days later, Hitler attacked Norway and Denmark. The latter fell in a matter of hours.

All of England had soured on Chamberlain's response to the war.

Mr. Stokes darted up the front stairs at a pace Grace doubted she could ever grow used to in such pitch-blackness. "Mr. Taylor, put that light out. You know I told you there'd be a fine next time..."

Grace did her best to slink into the shadows. Certainly they felt great enough to swallow her up. She would be at the ready should they be attacked by Germany, but she refused to take such pleasure in fining the people of London for not tightly drawing their curtains.

Over the next month, Grace donned her tin warden's hat three nights a week to grudgingly accompany Mr. Stokes as he terrorized the well-meaning citizens of London whose blackout efforts weren't up to snuff.

In that time, Mrs. Weatherford had heard from Colin, who offered multiple assurances he was doing well and succeeding in his training. Grace had also received another letter from Viv. Her friend's exuberance poured from the page with such vivacity that Grace had the comforting sensation of her friend's voice in her head as she read. Whatever it was Viv had been assigned was noted in the letter and run through with the thick black band of a censor's blot. Regardless, everything was right and tight with Viv, and that brought Grace incredible relief.

Through all the letters from Viv, Grace couldn't help but wonder about George Anderson. In truth, she'd hoped to have received something from him and had been somewhat disappointed when nothing had arrived. Still, she never ceased to peruse the letters received at Primrose Hill Books from the post in the off chance that he might have written.

She was going through the most recent post delivery one afternoon when Mr. Pritchard pushed into the shop with a newspaper clutched in his bony hands. Tabby wound anxious circles around his ankles as he shouted his news into the store. "Evans! The Nastys are in France. Also Holland and Belgium. But, France, Evans—France!"

Fear shivered up Grace's spine. Hitler hadn't been so bold as to attack France yet, but now he was in all the countries bordering England. If France fell, there would be nothing but the Channel to keep Hitler away.

A chill crept over her skin and her thoughts immediately went to her friends in the war. Only later did she realize she ought to be equally terrified for herself and everyone else in London.

Mr. Evans came to the front of the store with more haste than Grace had ever seen. He didn't bother to mark his place in his book as he closed it and set it aside on the counter. "Has Chamberlain resigned yet?"

Mr. Pritchard shook his head. "I can't say." He looked helplessly at the paper. It was half the pages now than it'd been in the previous year, another indication of the ration on paper.

"Heaven help us all if he hasn't." Mr. Evans took off his glasses and pinched the bridge of his nose where the weight of his eyewear had left permanent indents in his aged skin.

The door chimed the merry announcement of a new visitor, a shrill, overly bright sound in the ominous quiet that had descended. A delivery boy from Simpkin Marshalls came in, a large box held in skinny arms.

It was the recent order of *Pigeon Pie*, the political satire of the "bore war" by Nancy Mitford.

Grace could have groaned.

Such a book would be in terribly poor taste now.

She'd wanted to order the book before its release several

days prior, but Mr. Evans had vacillated on the idea, stating he was more of a classic book seller than a trend follower. Finally he'd relented, and now that risk was about to explode in Grace's face.

The state of war escalated in the following days, and as expected, the book was a flop. Sales went down as people found themselves plastered to their sofas at home before their wireless sets, desperate for any news.

And little of it was anything good.

The only bright spot was when Chamberlain stepped down as prime minister, his perpetually defensive tactics tiring and now dangerous, and the First Lord of the Admiralty, Winston Churchill, assumed his place. Much to the profound relief of all of Great Britain.

War was on everyone's lips, weighing heavily on all their minds, consuming conversation and occupying every aspect of their lives. The details carried on the threads of such gossip were horrifying. The worst of which was the bombing of Rotterdam, Holland, which had been rumored to have killed over thirty thousand people.

Mr. Stokes had informed Grace of that terrible figure with an edge of awed glee in his voice. Something was finally happening in the unending stretch of an actionless war, and it lit a fire inside him. His approach to people's misdemeanors became practically militant, and he constantly reminded Grace of her duties should they be bombed.

The curious thing to all of it, however, was how delightful the weather had been. It was an odd thing to note, of course, but never had Grace seen such a beautiful May. The sun shone, the skies were clear and brilliantly blue and the garden's sprouted shoots unfurled into healthy, broad leaves and flowers that promised vegetables soon.

The sandbags bricking up public shelters and call-up adverts had long since faded into the background of her awareness. Now, there was only birdsong and sunny days. It was surreal to imagine that nearby, allied countries were under attack with lives being lost daily to bombs and battle.

But that lovely May was a mirage, a pretty, fragile shell waiting to shatter the reality of their world. Hitler's troops had torn through France and were poised on the opposite side of the Channel.

Britain was next.

Already rumors swirled of coastline evacuations as the children of London were once more removed to the country.

While the presentation of *Pigeon Pie* at Primrose Hill Books was an enormous failure, copies of *What Hitler Wants* were nearly impossible to keep on the shelves. But people desperate for information on Hitler's logic were not the only patrons who still managed to trickle through their belled door. Housewives came in periodically too, anxious over their husbands who fought in France and melancholic at having to once more send their children away. They were women desperate for distraction, a way to occupy their minds so they could forget their heavy hearts.

One particular woman, a young brunette around Grace's age, lingered in the shop for well over an hour. Initially she'd declined assistance, but when she remained in a corner by the classic fiction for a considerable amount of time, Grace was compelled to go to her once more.

"Are you certain there's nothing I can offer assistance with?" Grace asked.

The woman startled and sniffed hard, turning her head

away. "I'm sorry. I...I shouldn't..." A sob burst from her, abrupt and unexpected.

Mr. Evans, who had been in the next aisle over, scuttled quickly to the opposite side of the store, leaving Grace with the crying customer.

Most of the housewives who came into Evans's seeking books were stony-faced, hiding their hurt behind a mask of decorum. None had shown their feelings so openly.

It was a painful thing to behold and tugged at a deep place in Grace's chest.

"Don't trouble yourself over it." She reached into her pocket and withdrew a handkerchief, which she offered to the woman. "These are hard times for us all."

The brunette accepted the handkerchief with an apologetic smile, the flush of her face nearly as red as her lipstick. "Forgive me." She dabbed at her eyes. "My husband is in France and I..." She swallowed hard and pressed her lips together in an apparent effort to squelch a new wave of despair. "I sent my daughter away two days ago." Her large brown eyes met Grace's, her lashes spiky with tears. "Do you have children?"

"No," Grace said softly.

The woman looked miserably at the handkerchief, now stained with mascara, lipstick and the dampness of her sorrow. "I didn't send her away with the first round. It was selfish, I know, but I couldn't bear to. But with what is happening with France...and Hitler being so close..."

She put her hands to her chest and her face crumpled. "I cannot stand the pain of missing her. I keep expecting to hear her little voice calling for me, or singing those silly songs she makes up. I did laundry today and made the mistake of smelling her pillow." Tears welled in her eyes. "She always has this scent about her, like powder and honey. It smelled just like that. Like her." She lowered her face to her hands where she cradled the wadded handkerchief and wept.

Grace's throat drew tight with the force of her own emotions. She was no mother, but she did know loss, how powerful and visceral it could be. Wordlessly, she embraced the woman.

"I miss her so much," the woman sobbed.

"I know." Grace held her gently as the woman gave in to her grief. "This will get better. You've done what is best to keep your daughter safe."

The brunette nodded and straightened as she wiped at her streaked makeup. "I probably shouldn't have come out in such a state. Do forgive me." She sniffed and dabbed under her eyes where the skin had gone gray with her running mascara. "A friend recommended I get a book to lose myself in. I thought I could find one, but can scarce concentrate to even decide."

Grace discreetly exhaled a relieved breath. This was her area of expertise. "Then let me help you." She led her to a shelf and withdrew *Emma*, whose humor made it a particular favorite of Grace's. "This will have you laughing one minute and sighing wistfully the next."

The woman's hand closed around the volume. "It's a classic fiction?"

"And also a romance." No sooner were the words out of Grace's mouth than George emerged in her thoughts.

The housewife's thanks and further apologies were profuse as she purchased the book and quickly departed, clutching it to her like a treasured possession.

Several days later, Grace noted a battered envelope addressed to her atop a pile of mail at the edge of the counter. Her pulse missed a beat.

Surely it couldn't be George. She shouldn't dare to hope after all this time. Yet her hand trembled with it as she reached for the piece of mail and read the return address with Flight Lieutenant George Anderson written in neat script.

She sucked in a hard gasp and opened the envelope, trying to keep from tearing it in her haste.

George had written to her.

After all this time, he truly had sent her a letter. Was he in France? Was he safe? When would he be home?

She unfolded the correspondence and stopped. Gaps in the page showed where pieces had been cut out. What remained was a ravaged note with nearly half the text removed. The date at the top indicated the letter had been drafted back in February.

The thing could scarcely be held, it'd been so pruned of its contents. Grace lay the fragile paper upon the smooth counter surface to keep it intact and read.

George apologized for his delay in writing to her for a reason she couldn't read. He hoped she'd enjoyed *The Count of Monte Cristo* and bemoaned his lack of access to books where he was. He had a copy of something which he'd read time and again, though its name had been cut from the paper. He hoped to eventually be back in London sometime that year and asked if she might still be free for a date.

Her pulse kicked up its heels at the last bit. He hadn't even bothered to hide the invitation behind a suggestion of being available to help her with advertising the shop.

A date.

Grace had been on a few when she lived in Drayton, all of which had not ended well. Tom Fisher had been a terrible bore, Simon Jones had pushed too hard to kiss her and Harry Hull was just trying to get to Viv.

And not a one of them had made her heart skip like George Anderson.

She floated through the rest of the day on thoughts of that shredded letter. The smile was still hovering on her lips when she entered the townhouse and found Mrs. Weatherford in the parlor amid bandages in various states of being rolled and packaged.

"They're coming back home," she said excitedly from where she sat on the floor before a box of bundled bandages.

Grace lifted a strip of linen and began to roll, the way she'd done with countless others at the WVS meetings. "Who is coming home?"

"Our men." Mrs. Weatherford beamed so brightly, even Mr. Stokes wouldn't have been able to dim her brilliance. "The BEF is returning home from France, and we at the WVS have been informed to prepare for their arrival. We're to offer aid where we can and present refreshment and comfort." She huffed as though trying to catch her breath. "Grace, Colin will be coming home."

If the British Expeditionary Force was returning from France already, that could mean only one of two things: either France was victorious in ousting the Germans, or France had fallen and the British were fleeing. From the official reports Grace had heard, as well as the unofficial rumors, she was more inclined to believe the latter.

She hid her distress at the news, for an uncomfortable gnawing in her gut told her the BEF's return was not a good sign. If their men were coming back to English soil, it was because they were retreating from the enemy, and that Hitler was winning.

But what would that mean for Britain?

ELEVEN

THE CONFIRMATION OF GRACE'S SUSPICION WAS AS
swift as it was bitter. But it didn't come from the BBC or
any newspaper. It came from the saddest source of all: Mrs.
Weatherford.

The blackout curtains were closed before the older woman
finally arrived home the first night of her assistance with the
WVS for the men returning from Dunkirk. Grace wished
that she might have joined the ladies of the WVS, at least
this once in their aid of the returning soldiers, but only those
who were members were allowed to help the men. Instead,
she waited in the parlor with *Pigeon Pie* cradled in her lap.
If nothing else, her purchase was one more sale out of their
unmoving stock. The story held humor to be sure, if one
took into consideration it was written prior to Hitler's attack on France.

Never had there been a book with such poor timing.

The click of the front door alerted Grace to Mrs. Weatherford's return. She all but leapt out of the Morris chair and ran to the foyer.

Mrs. Weatherford's gaze was stuck in the distance, her hands feeling for the doorframe, which she leaned heavily upon as she stepped out of her short heels.

"Mrs. Weatherford?" Grace reached for the older woman.

To her surprise, Mrs. Weatherford did not protest when Grace's hand closed around her soft forearm. In fact, she offered no reaction whatsoever.

"Mrs. Weatherford?" Grace said again, this time slightly louder. "How was it?"

But even as she asked the question, the tension squeezing at Grace's chest told her she wouldn't want to hear the answer.

"Hmm?" Mrs. Weatherford's brows lifted with great exaggeration.

"Did you see the men?" Grace asked, unable to stop herself. "Of the BEF?"

Mrs. Weatherford nodded slowly. "I did." She drew in a deep breath and lifted her head, her vision going distant once more. "It was…it was…it…" She swallowed hard. "It was awful. Those men looked near death." Her voice quavered. "Their eyes were filled with horror, and all of them were so tired they were falling asleep as they chewed the boiled eggs and apples we brought for them. I've never in all my life seen such defeat."

Grace had been anticipating bad news, but the details hit her hard. Colin was stationed in France. Had he been at Dunkirk as well?

But she didn't voice such concerns, not when they matched the worry carved on his mother's face.

Every day thereafter, Mrs. Weatherford went with the other WVS ladies to aid the BEF returning to London, and every night she returned depleted of all her energy and spirit.

The few times she was home, the phone rang seemingly without end as women with sons and husbands in Colin's division in France exchanged horror stories and gossip from some of the few men who had returned.

The accounts were grisly with soldiers being stranded on the beach without cover as Nazi planes sprayed bullets. Men swam miles to boats, only to find them bombed and their salvation lost. They were fleeing in retreat—or as Mr. Stokes had called it, a bloodbath.

Yet through it all, Mrs. Weatherford clung to hope with a white-knuckled grip.

Despite the other woman's forcedly happy demeanor, Grace could only guess what Mrs. Weatherford was going through when Grace herself couldn't stop imagining Colin amid such violent chaos.

Gentle Colin, who wanted only to help animals, whose heart was as golden as they came. If it so happened that he had to kill someone to save himself, it would be him taking the bullet. And if a man needed help, Colin would never leave him behind.

War was not meant for tender souls.

Most especially not ones such as Colin's.

All over Britain, telegrams were being delivered to front doors, sharing painful messages of men who had been killed or taken prisoner.

As more soldiers swept into London on the trains, no telegram was presented to the townhouse door on Britton Street. The silence was a blessing as much as it stretched out their expectation, so much so that every pop or creak of the house settling made Grace and Mrs. Weatherford jump.

It wasn't until two days later that Churchill addressed the enormity of their loss. Over 335,000 men had been saved from the Germans with casualties expected to be around 30,000 including those missing, dead or wounded. A staggering number to every mother and wife and sister waiting anxiously for news of her loved one.

But it was not only men Britain lost; equipment had been abandoned, given up to spare lives. A worthy sacrifice, as Grace saw it, but still costly and dangerous.

Even such dismal numbers, however, were met with a positive slant by the newspapers and radio, for the civilians with fishing vessels and personal watercraft who helped bring thousands of BEF over the Channel to safety were touted as heroes. A symbolic gesture that declared Britain would never surrender.

There was power to Churchill's voice as he spoke that made determination pound in Grace's chest and brought tears to Mrs. Weatherford's eyes as she nodded to the new prime minister's message.

Yes, there had been a great defeat, but they would carry on.

The spirit of his words charged through London like lightning, crackling with power.

Days continued to tick by. It was on a rare quiet afternoon that Mrs. Weatherford appeared in the parlor where Grace was reading her latest book, *Of Human Bondage*, an incredible tale of a man who grew up at the mercy of life's worst cruelties. It pulled at a wounded part of Grace that had been buried deep, a place she suspected everyone kept inside themselves, that remained tender despite one's victories and strengths.

Grace looked up to find Mrs. Weatherford wearing Colin's old clothing, now dirt-stained from their many toils in the garden as they dug for victory. "Have you seen the gloves?"

"They're in the Andy with the trowel and watering can." They really ought not use the Anderson shelter for a gardening shed, but setting gardening tools on the bench inside was quite convenient, especially when the floor was practically flooded by the recent rain and no use for anything else at that point. And with only the two of them in the townhouse, there was plenty of room for a few tools inside.

There had been air raids from time to time, yes, but they all had been without cause. A friendly aircraft mistaken for a German plane or something of that ilk. Most people didn't even go to their shelters anymore. What was the point?

Grace pulled the quilt from her lap in preparation to join the older woman in the garden. "Let me change and I'll help."

"Don't trouble yourself, love." Mrs. Weatherford waved her off. "You've done more than your fair share lately, and I only need to do a bit of weeding and watering."

Grace gave her a grateful smile and settled the blanket back over her legs, nestling deeper into the cushioned seat of the sofa to resume her reading. However, she did not get far into the next page when a horrendous shriek came from outside. In the rear garden.

Mrs. Weatherford.

Grace darted from the chair in a tangle of quilt, nearly tripping over the book she dropped in her haste, and bolted toward the kitchen's back door.

Had the Germans arrived?

There were rumors of how parachutists had dropped into the Netherlands dressed like nuns and policemen before shooting citizens where they stood, using trust as their greatest weapon. Granted, the rumor had been told by Mr. Stokes, but Grace would take no chances. She paused on her way out the kitchen door to grab a large knife.

Mrs. Weatherford stood several paces from the lettuce bed with her gloved hands curled in front of her as she stared in horror at the plants.

"What is it?" Grace rushed to her side, blade extended toward the garden.

Mrs. Weatherford let out a long, slow breath, closed her eyes and shuddered. "Worms."

"Worms?" Grace asked, incredulous. She had been expecting Nazis in the garden, machine guns at the ready to do their worst to the people of London.

"I went to see why the lettuce was wilting…" A shiver racked through Mrs. Weatherford. "I'll go fetch the leaflet on pests," she said weakly and turned back toward the Anderson shelter where the public informationals to encourage Dig for Victory were neatly organized in a blue painted tin.

With great apprehension, Grace crept toward the nearest head of limp lettuce and lifted a leaf with the point of her knife. Thick, brown things wriggled and coiled among the base of the plant like plump sausages, near bursting from their gluttony. An especially fat one dropped from the leaf above and landed with a plop on the flat of the blade.

Grace gasped in horror and leapt backward, dropping the knife.

Some hero she was.

Mrs. Weatherford ducked out from the Andy with a leaflet in hand. "It's right here. They're called…" She squinted at the page. "Cutworms. Heavens, that sounds terrifying." Her gaze darted over the page. As she read, her mouth slid down her face in a disgusted grimace.

"What is it?" Grace tried to peer at the leaflet. "How are we rid of them?"

Mrs. Weatherford grimaced. "We're to cut them in half, squish them or rip them apart."

They both scowled in horror and turned toward the lettuce. The knife lay before the plant Grace had been inspecting, its blade glinting in the sun.

"Maybe we ought to stick to beans?" Grace suggested.

"I've never been partial to lettuce myself," Mrs. Weatherford replied. "I'll go to the chemist to see if he can suggest something to kill those foul creatures and we can be done with the lot of it."

The chemist did indeed have something, a white powdery substance he warned must be washed thoroughly from the leaves before consumption, not that there was anything left of it after the cutworms finally succumbed to the poison.

In the second week of June, Italy joined the war in support of Germany, and the unspent energy crackling over London found a source to exact its potency. Grace and Mr. Stokes were patrolling the darkened streets of London later that night when an efficient clip of footsteps was heard across the street followed by a scuffle and a cry.

Adrenaline shot through her and drew her attention toward the scene. Her eyes searched the dark. She withdrew the hooded lamp from her pocket, a bell-shaped thing that cast a muted light on the ground. They didn't use it often, however, as Mr. Stokes insisted they maintain their night vision.

The blackout sadly brought out the worst in people, presenting too many temptations for theft and assault by the sinister sort. Mr. Stokes put himself between Grace and the sound as they waited to see if they might be required to intervene with their limited authority and sharp whistles.

During her time in the ARP, Grace had learned to read movement in the darkness by the subtle shadows cast by the moon. Though it was only a sliver that night, she could make out two police officers and a man with a suitcase beside a woman.

It was no robbery at all, but an arrest.

The man's words were spoken rapidly, not in English, but what sounded like Italian.

"We don't wish to use violence," one of the officers declared in a dull tone. "Come along at once."

The man turned from the woman toward the police as if he intended to go with them. She reached for him, letting out a broken sob.

"What's happened?" Grace asked.

"It's none of our concern." Mr. Stokes indicated she ought to walk onward.

She did not. "They are arresting him?"

"Of course they are," Mr. Stokes replied with an impatient whine. "The men at least for now. They're taking all the Tallies out of England so they can't spy on us for Hitler."

A crash came from down the street, followed by the tinkling of glass. Together, they rushed toward the sound and found a group of more than twenty men climbing through the shattered window of an Italian café, shouting hostile slurs against the Italians for having sided with the Nazis.

Grace was frozen in stunned shock. She had eaten at the café several times with Viv. The owner and his wife had always been kind, expressing their own fears for London and offering extra biscuits for their tea, even with the ration on. And now the establishment the immigrants had run for more than twenty years was being ransacked.

A man exited the broken window with a chair in his hands.

"A robbery." She lifted her whistle to her lips.

Mr. Stokes settled his hand over hers and pushed the metal from her mouth. "A retaliation."

She jerked a sharp look at him, making out his glittering eyes in the semidarkness. "I beg your pardon."

"Italy staked its loyalty," Mr. Stokes replied dryly. "And it was not with us."

She stared at him, appalled. "These are British citizens."

"They're Italians." He lifted his head higher as another man exited with a sack of what might have been flour. "Most likely spies."

"These are store owners who worked hard to build a business for themselves in London, who love this city as much as we do." Grace's voice pitched higher with vehemence even as her thoughts swirled at the madness of it all.

"We must put a stop to this." She marched forward, but Mr. Stokes caught her arm again and gently pulled her back.

"Miss Bennett, be sensible," he hissed. "There are more than a dozen men and you are only one warden."

She glared up at him with tears burning in her eyes. "Only one?"

He slid his gaze from hers.

Another crash sounded from the café, followed by a glow of light as a fire erupted within the building.

"Cease this at once," she shouted into the night.

Her order was met with laughter and jeers.

"Mind yourself, lest you be seen as a Nazi supporter."
Mr. Stokes's voice was low and filled with enough caution
to give her pause.

She clenched her fists as tears leaked hot down her cheeks
in anger for her crippling helplessness. She shoved Mr. Stokes
away from her. "How can you stand this?"

"Put that light out," Mr. Stokes called to the men in a
dispassionate, grating voice. "You don't want bombs dropping on us."

He didn't look at her again as the fire was doused and a
startling blackness took the place of those brilliant flames
so fueled by hate.

After her shift, she could not find sleep. Not only in her
worry over Colin, who had still not been heard from, but
for her own impotence.

She'd joined the ARP to help. But that night, she had not
helped. By not being able to stop the men from looting the
café, she had been part of the problem.

She tried to read, but found that even books could not
ease the burden on her soul.

The following day she was off from the bookshop, and
Mrs. Weatherford had remained home as the BEF had ceased
trickling in from Dunkirk. Her hope had begun to fade with
the number of arrivals, especially considering how few had
returned from Colin's division.

Grace spent most of the morning in the garden, pulling
weeds and inspecting the plants. Yellow blossoms had sprung
on the tomato plants while those of the squash had begun
to swell with yellow-green orbs. She had hoped the activity with the plants and the fresh air might take her mind

from things, but she found herself continuing to prod at her wounded thoughts, leaving them raw and angry.

Upon completing her task, she tugged off her gloves and stepped out of her clogs before going into the kitchen to wash the residual grit from her hands. She was just finishing when a knock at the door sounded over the gush of the tap. Her blood went cold.

They were expecting no visitors.

The post would be pushed through the mail slot at the door.

There would be no reason for someone to be knocking, unless…

Grace flicked the water from her fingers and hastily dried her hands. Her pulse whooshed in her ears, but was not loud enough to quiet the sound of Mrs. Weatherford's tentative footsteps heading toward the front door. Grace pushed out of the kitchen as Mrs. Weatherford accepted something from the delivery boy in a rectangular orange envelope.

A post office telegram.

The breath pushed painfully from Grace's lungs.

There were few reasons why Mrs. Weatherford would receive a telegram, and none were good.

Mrs. Weatherford closed the door with an automatic movement, her gaze fixed on the orange envelope. Grace approached carefully, but the older woman didn't acknowledge her presence.

They both waited a long moment, neither one of them speaking. Neither one of them even breathing, locked in a suspended moment that might change the rest of their lives.

Grace should offer to read it, and yet there was a part of her that was too much of a coward to see the print on the telegram within.

Mrs. Weatherford took a deep breath and slowly let it out so the envelope fluttered in her shivering grip. Guilt pinched at Grace, a whisper of an emotion by comparison to her fear, but enough to nudge her response. After all, to expect Mrs. Weatherford to face the task was cruel.

Grace braced herself for what she was offering and whispered, "Do you want me to open it?"

Mrs. Weatherford shook her head. "I should—" Her voice caught. "We have to know."

Her hands quivered with such force, it was a wonder she could slide a nail under the flap and draw open the envelope. Before she even realized what she was doing, Grace held on to Mrs. Weatherford's arm, clinging as the message inched out to reveal the words "Deeply regret to inform you..."

Mrs. Weatherford sucked in a sharp inhale and slowly unveiled the remainder of the telegram.

The message was written in a strip of white, the letters in bold capitalization as it declared the words that would change their lives irrevocably.

"Deeply regret to inform you that your son Pte Colin Weatherford is now reported to have lost his life in the attack at Dunkirk—"

The envelope and telegram dropped from Mrs. Weatherford's hand and swirled to the floor. It didn't matter. Grace didn't need to see anything else.

Colin was dead.

"My son," Mrs. Weatherford whimpered. "My son. My son. My sweet gentle boy." She looked at her trembling hands, now empty of the letter, as if in disbelief it had ever been there.

The aching knot at the back of Grace's throat balled tight, choking her with bitter tears.

The enormity of his loss gaped like a chasm inside her. Anger and sorrow and helplessness, all overwhelmed her. Colin shouldn't have died in such a manner. He was too extraordinary to merely be one of the 30,000 lost.

Never again would he bring home another wounded animal to heal or greet her with a shy blush. Their dark, dark world needed his light, and now it was forever snuffed out.

A low keening filled the room as Mrs. Weatherford fell to her knees, blindly grabbing the envelope and crumpling it in her fist as if it could somehow keep the earth from flying out beneath her.

All around Britain, thousands more women were getting similar telegrams where a few typefaced words would rip into the tenderest places in their chest, forever altering their lives with gaping loss.

More so now than ever before, Grace found herself wishing to hear from Viv and George, to know they were safe in the face of such uncertainty and sorrow.

Grace was the only one moving about the townhouse the following morning as Mrs. Weatherford remained in bed. The older woman's freshly washed teacup was absent from the strainer where it usually was drying by the time Grace rose. After an attempt to bring Mrs. Weatherford tea went unanswered, Grace set a small tray by her door in the hopes it would be of some comfort.

Perhaps Grace ought to have telephoned Mr. Evans and begged off work that day, but she didn't want to be trapped at home under the weight of her own thoughts and grief. They had been poor company through the night, burning in her chest like the fire inside the Italian café and heavy with the crushing blow of Colin's death.

She wanted her day to be filled with ordering new books and engaging in conversation with the customers of Primrose Hill Books. The day was already warm, the air dry against her gritty eyes, which still appeared red-rimmed and swollen despite an extra swipe of mascara and a pat more face powder.

Mr. Evans looked up when she entered and immediately straightened from where he was bent over his ledger. "What is it?"

"A telegraph." It was all Grace could muster.

His mouth set in a hard line. "Colin?"

Grace nodded.

Mr. Evans's eyes closed behind his spectacles and stayed closed for a long time before he blinked them open. "He was too good for the likes of this bloody war."

Grace's throat went tight with the familiar ache of mourning.

"Go home, Miss Bennett." The tip of his nose had gone pink. "I'll cover your wages for the next week."

She shook her head vehemently. "I'd like to work. Please." Even she could hear the desperate tremble in her voice.

He studied her a long time and finally nodded. "But if you want to go, you need only ask."

She nodded, grateful for a chance for a reprieve from her grief.

As it turned out, such melancholy could not be outrun. It followed her like a shadow, slinking at her back and creeping through her thoughts every moment her mind was not occupied. It reminded her of Colin cradling a wounded creature in his big, tender hands and how the shattering of the Italian café's window had crashed through the damp night air. It had reminded her again and again how she could stop none of it, that she was utterly and helplessly ineffectual.

She was in the small back room for a spell, giving in to a cry when Mr. Evans came in. He stopped abruptly and stared at her, his eyes wide with uncertainty. Grace turned her face from him, wishing he would slip away as he had done the other day with the sobbing mother.

Instead, his footsteps shuffled closer and a handkerchief appeared in front of her. She accepted it, having already soaked through her own, and wiped at her eyes. "I'm sorry—"

"Don't apologize for feeling." He leaned against a stack of books nearest her. "Never apologize for feeling. Do you want to"—he opened his hands in an uncertain gesture—"talk about it?"

She studied him to gauge his sincerity. He regarded her, unblinking, his expression earnest. He was serious.

She nearly declined. For no amount of talking could possibly bring back Colin. Indeed, she didn't even know if the grip around her throat could relax enough to put voice to such agony.

But then, she recalled the Italian café, her silence, and the guilt lashed like fire at her insides. "Have you ever done something you're ashamed of?"

His furry brows lifted, suggesting of all the things she might say, he had not been anticipating that. "Yes," he replied after a moment's thought. "I think most people have." He crossed his arms. "If this pertains to Colin, I know he would have forgiven you. He was that kind of man."

There was that ache at the back of her throat again. She swallowed and shook her head. Before she could stop herself, she told him about the night at the Italian café, the details tearing at her conscience and leaving her raw.

He remained propped against the wall as she spoke, his arms folded in a relaxed state against his chest. When she was done, he slowly pushed to standing, scooted a large box of books toward the table and sat on it so he was nearly level with her.

His eyes were clear and sharp, more fixed with intent than she'd ever seen them. "There's a war going on, Miss Bennett. You are but one person, so sometimes that means a café is looted, yes, but that it didn't burn. You can't save the world, but keep trying in any small way you can."

His mouth lifted at the corners in an almost embarrassed smile. "Such as an old man collecting battered and singed books to keep voices alive." He set his age-spotted hand on hers, its warmth comforting. "Or finding a story to help a young mother forget her pain." He removed his hand and straightened. "It doesn't matter how you fight, but that you never, never stop."

Grace nodded. "I won't." The determination inside her sent chills coursing over her skin. "I'll never stop."

"That's the young woman I know." He rose from the box. "Speaking of which, I've been winning my own battle with a strategy I borrowed from you. Would you like to see?"

Curious, Grace wiped self-consciously at her eyes to clear away any makeup that might have been smeared and followed Mr. Evans out to the store.

"You may have seen it already." He indicated the small table with *Pigeon Pie* set in the back corner.

In truth, she'd avoided the table of her failure until that moment. What she beheld left her stunned.

What had once contained a neat stack of one hundred books had only a handful remaining. The pasteboard propped in the center of the table proclaimed: "Written while Chamberlain was still prime minister."

Mr. Evans grinned at her. "They've been selling like butter ever since."

Grace laughed in spite of herself. "That was quite genius of you."

Mr. Evans's old cheeks went red beneath his glasses as he tilted his head humbly. "I was rather proud of it. Nonetheless, it's your idea. I only added my own stodgy twist."

As the march of time pressed on, they sold the remainder of their stock of the ill-fated *Pigeon Pie*, and Mr. Evans's advice became all the more poignant.

For those coming weeks brought the fall of France. And then, what they all had feared the most: the bombing of Britain.

TWELVE

GERMAN BOMBERS DESCENDED ON CARDIFF AND Plymouth first, targeting docks and prompting aerial battles with the RAF. London had not been hit as yet, but the expectation that it might happen hung forefront in everyone's mind.

The BBC broadcasts were listened to fastidiously and clung to every tongue, with people repeating what had been heard to analyze the potential for their own bombing.

While Grace didn't know where George was stationed, she was well aware being a fighter pilot would place him directly in the middle of danger.

She'd received another letter from him, this one equally as sliced through for censorship as the last, leaving only half his message visible, but enough to be assured he was doing well. Viv's letters only had periodic items run through with a black marker, but it was easy to make out that regardless of where she was, she appeared to be safe.

The person she worried most over, however, was Mrs. Weatherford. For the entire time Grace had known the older woman, she had been one to push the world into action with her immeasurable energy. There wasn't a solution she didn't find, a problem she couldn't fix.

Now, she shuffled through the house with eyes that focused on nothing. No longer that bright, cheerful person with a bit of advice for everyone—whether they wanted it or not. She was a husk of herself, with her flat gray hair falling around her pallid face. Lifeless.

No longer did Mrs. Weatherford attend the WVS or meticulously clean the house. Grace never thought she'd see the day when the foyer lost the residual scent of carbolic. And when Mrs. Weatherford found out about tea and margarine being added to the ration booklet, she didn't crow with delight at her stockpiled trove, she simply replied with a resigned nod.

The rest of London, however, hummed with energy in anticipation of a war that now seemed certain to strike their soil. It seemed a strange thing, to hope for action even after Dunkirk, but the "bore war" had seemed much like a freshly wound watch with no hands.

Now something was finally going to happen.

It was a sunny Saturday when Grace finally brought herself to remove the children's book display from the front of the shop. With so many little ones relocated once more to the country, the prime window location would be best spent on more enticing reads for the adults who had remained behind. After she left the shop that afternoon, however, she didn't immediately return home.

Instead, she basked in the brilliant sun beaming down on her and enjoyed a seat outside at a café for tea and a confection. Restaurants followed different rations than the citizens of Britain and were allowed slightly more, meaning the tea was richer and sweeter, as was the pastry, nearly masking the margarine. Nearly.

But the effort didn't offer her the cheer that she'd hoped. Instead, it made her miss having Viv opposite her, laughing and sharing the latest gossip from Harrods. And it made her ache for Mrs. Weatherford, who couldn't bring herself to enjoy such a fine afternoon, let alone any of life's other pleasures.

And how could she when Colin was dead?

Determined not to fall prey to sadness on such a fine day, Grace found herself at King Square Gardens. Vendors stood by their wheeled carts painted in glossy, bright colors to attract patrons to their goods, and people lounged about on benches and canvas sling chairs set alongside the emerald green grass.

All around the park were patches of vegetables as part of the Dig for Victory campaign, clusters of climbing sweet peas replacing the jasmine, and cabbages where roses had once bloomed.

Grace settled into an available sling chair, the thick fabric warm from the sun, and tilted her head back indulgently. The air smelled sweetly of grass mixed with a spice of sausage from a nearby vendor, and the shuffles of footsteps and light conversation melted into the background in a soothing ambience.

All at once, the peaceful quiet was interrupted by the nagging wail of the air raid siren.

She remained where she was, reconciled to endure the blaring annoyance, as commonplace as sandbags at that point.

At the beginning of the war, the warbling cry had made her heart leap into her throat. Now, it was simply a nuisance.

Several people grudgingly rose from their chairs to seek shelter, though they were indeed the minority. Most remained where they were, luxuriating in the sunshine.

After so many false air raids, the warning had become like the little boy crying wolf.

It cut off eventually, leaving a lazy drone in the background of Grace's awareness, like a bumblebee drunk on nectar as it bobbed its way through the air. Except the drone seemed to grow louder, more insistent.

She peeked an eye open, squinting at the sky with its tufts of cottony white clouds.

"What is it?" someone beside her asked, craning their neck to look at the sky.

Grace blinked against the brightness of the sun. Dots of black flecked the cerulean blue. A distant whump echoed in the distance, followed by several others as puffs of black smoke somewhere in the city billowed upward.

It took a stunned moment for her to realize those specks were planes. And they were dropping bombs on what appeared to be the East End.

Ice frosted in Grace's veins despite the hot day, prickling her skin so the tiny hairs along her arms stood on end.

London was being bombed.

She pushed up from her chair, her movements as slow as if in water. She ought to have run, to encourage others to a nearby shelter, take their names to ensure they were accounted for to notify their ARP warden. Something.

Anything.

After all, she'd trained the last several months for this very moment.

But she was rooted to the ground as the thumping of bombs continued. On and on and on.

A hand clasped on her shoulder. "You should get to shelter, miss."

Grace nodded, not bothering to look at the man who'd spoken. How could she when the horrific scene kept her gaze locked on the bombing planes?

A woman screamed nearby, an ugly shriek pitched with fear. It was then Grace found her legs. But she didn't go to the shelter. Not when Mrs. Weatherford would be home, most likely ignoring the warning as they all had.

The man, a fellow warden with a limp that must have kept him from conscription, was already directing people toward the nearest shelter. He turned to Grace, his eyes wide in his pallid face, and indicated she should follow.

She shook her head. "I'll be home in minutes. We have an Anderson shelter."

His gaze slid to the swarm of planes still unleashing a merciless assault on the East End and turned away in silent assent. She wasted no time making the short trek back to Britton Street.

By the time she arrived, the sky had turned from gray and black to an angry orange red, as if that part of London had become a roiling inferno. Grace pushed through the door of the townhouse, crying out for Mrs. Weatherford.

Grace stepped over a pile of mail in the doorway, not bothering to pick it up and add it to the growing stack on the table as she normally did.

The older woman's feet were visible just beyond the wall

of the parlor where she was most likely perched in the Morris chair.

"London is being bombed." Grace tried to keep the fear from her voice as she went to her mother's friend. "We must go to the shelter at once."

But Mrs. Weatherford wouldn't go, preferring to stay where she sat, her stare distant with despondency. After several failed attempts to nudge her to safety, Grace left her in the parlor and stood on the front steps of the townhouse, watching the German planes. If they drew closer, she would make sure Mrs. Weatherford took shelter, even if she had to drag the older woman.

But the planes didn't come closer. Eventually, the residents of Britton Street joined her on their front steps, all watching in silence as the German planes continued their relentless assault through the burning sky.

Through it all, Grace could not stop thinking of the people. Had the residents there avoided the shelters as so many in the rest of London had? Would shelters even protect them in the face of such an onslaught?

How many would die?

She shuddered to even consider the casualties.

At long last, the rumble of falling bombs ceased and the all clear sounded. Grace turned to go into the townhouse once more and found Mrs. Nesbitt standing rigidly on the stairs next door. She lifted a brow at Grace. "Well, that's that, I suppose."

Grace said nothing and went into the townhouse to find Mrs. Weatherford in the Morris chair, exactly where she had left her.

That night, Grace wasn't scheduled to perform her ARP work, doing so only three times a week. But before she could even prepare for bed, the wail of the air raid siren came again.

A spike of adrenaline shot through Grace, and this time she didn't take no for an answer from Mrs. Weatherford. After opening the windows, cutting the mains and filling the tub, Grace forced Mrs. Weatherford down to the Andy. They stumbled in the near darkness, upsetting pots and gardening supplies on their way into the shelter.

The shelter smelled of wet metal, earth and disuse. More a shed than a place to remain for any length of time. The siren's call cut short, and silence filled the emptiness in its place. It was an expectant kind of quiet, one that promised more of what London had taken earlier that day. Every muscle in Grace's body remained tense, and her skin felt as though its fit was suddenly too tight.

She struck a match and lit the candle she'd brought along with their gas masks. The flame was small, but filled the cramped interior of the Andy like an electric light. In the distance came the familiar drone of planes, their ominous one-note tone amplified by the metal frame so it practically vibrated in Grace's chest.

Again came the thumps that meant more bombs. It was all Grace could do to keep from flinching with each distant whump.

"Do you think these are the last sounds Colin heard?" Mrs. Weatherford mused, her stare locked on the flickering candle flame. "Do you think he was frightened?"

"I think he was brave," Grace replied with confidence. "Knowing Colin, he was probably trying to save someone."

"I'm sure." Mrs. Weatherford nodded, and tears shone bright in her eyes. "It was me who killed him, as surely as it was the Germans." She sniffled. "I let him grow up to be too kind, too sweet. I never should have allowed him to be so…so sensitive."

Grace sat up from where she leaned against the rippled metal wall. "You would have been forcing him to be someone he wasn't."

"Yes," Mrs. Weatherford snapped. "But he would be alive."

"Not as the man we loved so dearly."

"I know." Mrs. Weatherford put her face into her hands and began to softly weep. "I know."

"You did right by him, Mrs. Weatherford." Grace shifted onto the other bench and gently rubbed the older woman's shoulders as she grieved the loss of a man far too good to die so young. "You let him be who he wanted to be, and you supported and loved him. He would not have had it any other way."

Grace paused, aware that her next words would sting, and that they needed to be said regardless. "And you know he would hate to see you like this."

Mrs. Weatherford ducked her head.

They didn't speak again for the rest of the night. Eventually Grace returned to her seat on the opposite side of the shelter. Somehow she managed to fall asleep despite the distant bombing, with her head cocked at an awkward angle and her bum tingling with numbness where it pressed to the hard surface. The all clear woke her early the following morning, nearly startling her from the narrow bench.

"They didn't get close." Mrs. Weatherford rose stiffly from where she sat with a hand pressed to her lower back. "I'll go put the kettle on."

She gathered up the candleholder with its pool of melted wax, the wick blackened and spent, and limped from the

shelter. Grace went inside as well, but didn't bother with
tea. Her body ached from the uncomfortable position, and
her eyes were heavy with exhaustion. Never had she been
so grateful to have a day off from the bookshop.

She woke later to a familiar tar-like scent. The carbolic
smell grew stronger when she opened the door to her bedroom and made her way down a gleaming stairwell. Mrs.
Weatherford greeted her at the bottom with a sad, apologetic smile. She wore a dark housedress and no jewelry or
lipstick, but her gray hair had been pulled back in a neat roll.

"Thank you for what you said last night." Mrs. Weatherford self-consciously touched a hand to her hair. "You were
right about Colin not wanting me to be like that. I can do
this." She swallowed hard. "For him."

Grace embraced Mrs. Weatherford, holding the other
woman tightly. "We both can."

Mrs. Weatherford nodded against her shoulder. They spent
the remainder of the day cleaning the house and working
in the garden, now filled with beans, cucumbers, tomatoes
and peppers.

Through it all, a hazy cloud settled over the East End, a
shroud to the many who had died.

Midway through the day came yet another air raid, lasting
nearly three hours. Only this time, the noise of the planes
was accompanied by the boom of the anti-aircraft guns.

Gossip hummed in the neighborhood louder than the
bombers' far-off engines. It was said hundreds died in the
attack on the East End. Many had been left homeless, and
the fires from the night before still blazed out of control.

Grace listened attentively to each piece of news, stitch-
ing them together in her mind like a macabre quilt in an
attempt to create a whole story. No matter how much she

heard or even how many times it was repeated, she craved more. She was not alone in this desperation for information. Every wireless set in London was tuned to the broadcasts, and newspaper shelves were soon stripped bare.

That evening, Grace was on the ARP schedule to work the night shift with Mr. Stokes, starting at 7:30 and ending at 8:00 the next morning. Though it was only three days a week and Mr. Evans allowed her to come in later the following days, it often left Grace tired.

That night, however, she was beyond exhausted, her mind as gritty as her eyelids. Regardless, she would ensure she was sharp for her post. Of all nights to watch for visible lights, this would be one of the most important after what had happened to the East End.

"It's still burning," Mr. Stokes said under his breath, squinting in the distance where a subtle red glow flickered. "I've a mate who works for the AFS near there; he said the scene was like something out of hell."

Grace did not envy the Auxiliary Fire Service, who had the extraordinary task of putting out such a blaze.

She followed his stare. "I can't imagine how awful it must be."

"Terrible," Mr. Stokes answered. "Harry said hundreds of people died, some blasted so hard by the bombs, their clothes were ripped clean off."

Grace stopped walking, unable to even fathom something so awful.

"Pieces of bodies were all over the street." Mr. Stokes spread his hand through the air. "They had to keep stopping to clear away bloody bits from the road so they could drive on."

Mr. Stokes had always been one to amplify the gory details. Only in this particular case, she didn't think he was exaggerating. And while she'd never offered much complaint before, his gratuitous attention to the gruesomeness raked over her nerves.

Not noticing her silence, he continued. "A shelter was bombed too. On Columbia Road. A bomb fell straight down the ventilation shaft and…" He spread his hands slowly apart and imitated the rumble of an explosion. "Whole families killed off all at once."

"Mr. Stokes," she said sharply. "How can a veteran such as yourself speak so cavalierly about the dead after the things you've no doubt seen?"

He frowned and shook his head. "I'm no veteran. They wouldn't take me in the Great War." He shrugged his narrow shoulders, his mustache twitching. "Said I had a weak heart."

A weak heart.

If they'd bothered to look deeper, Grace was certain they'd discover he had none at all.

A sharp wail cut through the air suddenly, the cry announcing yet another slew of bombers. Her blood ran cold with pure terror.

In the bombing the previous night, she'd been safely tucked inside the Andy. But wardens didn't lock themselves inside when there were people to protect.

No, they patrolled their designated sector, on the lookout for bombs and damage that might have been done so they could administer first aid to those who were injured. And help locate the ones who didn't survive.

She would be exposed there in the street, not even covered by the thin sheet of the Anderson shelter's crimped aluminum.

Vulnerable.

"Come now, don't tell me you're frightened." Mr. Stokes clapped a hand on Grace's shoulder.

She shot him a hard look, but it did little to chasten him. Instead, he laughed and shook his head. "This is why women shouldn't be allowed to volunteer for a job clearly meant for men."

She stiffened at the offense, a sharp retort on her tongue, but he'd already wandered off toward the stream of residents exiting their homes. He waved his arm as though directing traffic, shepherding the frightened masses from the Borough of Islington toward their designated shelter.

She gritted her teeth and recalled her training. She knew what to say. What to do. She need not allow the Nazis to get the best of her.

The siren cut short and voices filled the air, asking any number of questions all at once. Where were they to go? How long would the raid last? Would it be quite as long as the previous night?

Would they be bombed?

All questions neither Grace nor Mr. Stokes could answer.

But there was something about their worried faces and the way their voices trembled with panic. It reminded her of why she was there, to help the masses in their time of need. To be the example of calm when they were frightened.

Soon, her even-toned instructions joined those of Mr. Stokes, leading with well-trained guidance and offering support. She led them to the shelter, their numbers far greater than during any of the air raids before.

As people entered the brick shelter lined with sandbags, Grace recorded their names, recognizing all of them from Mr. Stokes's nightly roster of house numbers. It made sense to her then, as she put the addresses to faces, how knowing who lived where and who was safely sheltered held such importance. The drone of planes caught at her awareness, tickling the insides of her ears and running a chill down her spine.

They were louder than before.

And growing closer still.

Mr. Stokes glanced sharply behind them and slammed the door to the shelter shut. Grace looked in the same direction, searching the darkness for something, anything, with which to gauge the location of nearby planes.

Spears of light stabbed up through the night sky as the anti-aircraft guns sought out their targets, the beam rolling over the dense underbellies of clouds. When Grace had seen the planes in the park, they had been flecks in the distance. Now, they looked much larger. Closer. Like an enormous black bird pinned in the center of the shaft of light.

A German plane.

Not above them, but near enough to make the hair on the back of her neck stand on end.

Without a moment's hesitation, an anti-aircraft gun boomed into action, its baritone shots rumbling in Grace's bones.

A dark, oblong object slipped from the bottom of the plane and sailed downward. A bomb.

She and Mr. Stokes stood transfixed as it glided toward its target, a whistle of air building around it as it went, followed by a fraction of a second of silence, so quick one could scarce blink. Then a flash of light. A soul-shuddering boom that rattled the ground where they stood. A cloud of smoke belched upward, flickering with flames.

And just like that, someone's house might be lost. A family might have been killed.

The reality of it happening in Grace's borough, to people she might know, was like a dagger in her chest. But she couldn't stand in awe of something so terrible. Not when she had a job to do.

It was difficult to tell from where they stood if the bomb hit within their sector. Adrenaline fired through her body. She charged through the empty street, lit by the nearby glow of a fire as well as the rekindled flames of the East End, which had clearly been struck again.

As she twisted her way through the blocks they were charged with monitoring, the sounds of war grew louder. Only this time, the rattle of the flying planes was muted by the whistling of falling bombs and the shuddering booms of their impact. All this combined with the constantly firing anti-aircraft guns as well as the RAF overhead in aerial battle with Germany. When a lull presented itself, the ringing bells of an AFS vehicle could be heard on its way to one of the many fires raging throughout London.

Grace's breath rasped in her lungs as she ran, her legs moving with such force, they felt as though they might separate from her body and go on without her. Her feet crunched over the street where millions of shards of glass littered the road, sparkling like rubies in the glowing red light of London's inferno. Every window of the houses on the left side of the street had been blown out, their shredded curtains hanging out like ragged black hair and their doors all knocked from their hinges.

The scrim tape, so carefully applied in each of those homes, had clearly done nothing.

"Miss Bennett, slow down." Mr. Stokes puffed at her side. "Do remember my heart."

But Grace did not slow. People who might be dying

wouldn't give a fig about his heart, she thought. She rounded the corner and skidded to a halt.

There in front of her was a massive gap in the neat row of townhouses, backlit by the flames. In its place was a smoldering pile of rubble where someone's house had been.

Their sector had been bombed, and now Grace's job as an ARP warden truly began.

THIRTEEN

GRACE DREW TO A STOP BEFORE THE BOMBED-OUT house on Clerkenwell Road, the muscles in her legs jumping from her exertion. The address was no longer visible in the rubble that had once been a home, but she could make out the two on either side well enough to identify the missing house number. For that number was tied to names in her mind, repeated by Mr. Stokes three times a week at several intervals on every watch.

Mr. and Mrs. Hews, an elderly couple, had lived in that house since they wed nearly fifty years prior. Mr. Stokes often mentioned Mrs. Hews's fondness for chocolate and how she'd always carried one just for him when he'd been a boy.

Mr. Stokes's footsteps slowed as he appeared beside Grace. "Mrs. Hews," he whispered, his expression stark as he observed the ruins.

"They were in the shelter." Grace recalled the names from

the list she'd assembled as people entered the door. "Mr. Stokes, they're safe."

"Good." He nodded. "Good. That's good."

They set to work, dousing the small flames that flickered in the rubble with their stirrup pumps and continued their watch on the rest of the sector. More bombs fell as the night went on, though no more were in their area of patrol. The better part of their night was spent sweeping up the fallen glass on the surrounding streets where all the windows had been blown out, and at one point chasing away looters from the Hewses' property.

Mr. Stokes waited for Mr. and Mrs. Hews when the all clear sounded, thinking it best that he be the one to share the dismal news. Their pain was difficult to witness. After all, a woman's pride was her home, and Mrs. Hews had put a lifetime of work into the grand little townhouse where purple cabbages grew in flower boxes that once held geraniums.

But in the end, it wasn't only Grace and Mr. Stokes who stayed on after the all clear to help them sort through the dusty rubble for anything salvageable. The inhabitants of the entire row of townhouses helped as well as neighbors from other streets. They ignored their own broken windows and blown-out doors to offer aid to those whose suffering was far greater than their own. A community brought together by loss.

Their close friends took the meager pile of possessions to hold for them while Grace directed the stunned couple to the local rest center to be sheltered until a new home could be found. After Grace's shift ended, she made her way back to Britton Street in such a fatigued state that her feet could scarcely function and clumsily stumbled over one another.

She fell into bed with her dirty clothes on and slept where she landed until she could rouse herself for her shift at the bookshop.

A bath worked miracles for her and by the time she entered Primrose Hill Books, she didn't feel nearly as exhausted as when she'd come home. Mr. Evans, however, frowned at her as she entered the store.

"Have you had enough sleep?" He set his pencil in his ledger so it lay neatly along the seam.

"Have any of us?" She offered a smile.

He folded his arms over his brown pullover, which had become baggy as the ration whittled away at his once rather stout frame. "I heard the Hewses' house was bombed on Clerkenwell Street. Were you there?"

"Only afterward." There was something in the seriousness of his tone as he asked that made her feel like a child about to be reprimanded.

"You could have been there when it happened." The white tufts of his brows inched together. "What would you have done if you'd been near the bomb when it fell?"

Grace hesitated. She hadn't thought of it, truly. After all, it was the East End that the Germans seemed to target. And the odds of her being hit by a bomb seemed far too slim to genuinely consider.

"I don't like it, Miss Bennett." Color blossomed in his face. "I think you ought to resign from your post with the ARP."

A customer entered the store, setting the bell ringing. Grace glanced over her shoulder and recognized the woman as one of their regulars, one who seldom required assistance.

"The ARP needs me now more than ever," Grace replied in a low voice.

"So does the store." Mr. Evans snatched up his ledger, sending the pencil flying from its spine, and strode toward the rear of the shop without another word.

Hopelessness welled in Grace, exacerbated by the tired fog clouding her mind. Mr. Evans was evidently worried she would be sacrificing her focus on the store for her efforts with the ARP.

She was determined to prove him wrong.

By the time the shop was set to close that night, she'd designed several new slogans with a couple already neatly printed on pasteboard. *Liven up your shelter with a new book* and *Let a book keep you company during the air raids.* They weren't ideal, but they were a start.

Regardless, Mr. Evans had scarcely said more than two words to her and merely offered a grunt at the new adverts.

She had little time to worry over his demeanor, however, for when she went home, she fell into a deep slumber. One that was rudely interrupted around eight that evening by the wail of yet another air raid. She dragged herself to the shelter along with Mrs. Weatherford where the sleep she so desperately needed eluded her.

The attack continued through the night, the same as the prior evening when she'd been outside helping the people in her sector. Only this time, she was locked in the darkened cocoon of the Anderson shelter, unable to see what was happening. But she could hear it.

The blasts of the ack-ack guns rattled the steel frame and bombs detonated so close, the whole structure shuddered as though it was going to cave in. Once it even seemed to lift off the ground before crashing back into place.

The whistles were sharp and loud just before going silent, followed by a boom so ferocious that the ground trembled. The all clear didn't come again until the following morning, and the women resolved to layer the hard benches with bedding to at least make them more comfortable for sleep. Already they'd cleared away the gardening tools to restore it to a proper shelter.

After all, it was beginning to look like the Germans were intent on bombing London every night.

When Grace woke later that morning, she learned on the news that St. Thomas's hospital had been hit, having received a direct blow along one major section. Nearby, a school had also sustained terrible damage. The Nazis were a foul lot, but it was truly low to target the infirm and children.

Anger burned through Grace, arming her with the need to continue her role with the ARP—to do her part to fight Hitler.

She was ready to declare as much to Mr. Evans when she went to the bookshop, but found the door closed and locked tight upon her arrival. He'd presented her a key some months before, and she dug it out of her handbag, unlocking the shop. Once inside, she flipped the sign to Open and pulled back the blackout curtains to let in a stream of cloudy sunlight as she called out for Mr. Evans. He did not reply.

Apprehension tightened along her back.

It was the only time in her employment he wasn't standing at the counter like a sentry, awaiting her arrival before disappearing into the back to resume his daily work. His work, she'd surmised in the last year, was mainly reading the day away.

And now, he wasn't there.

The building didn't appear damaged, meaning his flat

above would have remained intact. Images flooded her mind, colored with Mr. Stokes's terrible stories. What if Mr. Evans had been out the previous evening and was caught unawares?

She called his name again as she strode to the rear of the shop and pushed into the small backroom.

It was the smell of alcohol that hit her first.

Scotch.

Her uncle had drunk the stuff. It stank like paraffin oil and tasted far worse. Not that she was one for sampling paraffin oil.

Mr. Evans was slumped in his chair, half sagging over the tabletop. A bottle of amber liquid sat before his folded elbow, and his hand limply curled around a nearly empty crystal glass.

Were it not for that bottle at his side, she might have been truly worried. Though the image of him in such a state was still rather disconcerting.

"Mr. Evans?" Grace stepped into the quiet room and set aside her handbag.

He lifted his head, though his glasses rested askew across his face, and gave her a bleary look from the crooked lenses. His normally immaculately combed hair was mussed and his brown pullover atop his collared shirt, the same he'd worn the day before, was rumpled. "Go home, Miss Bennett." His words were thick with sleep and drink, and he lay his head on the table once more.

"I can't go home. It's morning and we've a store to run." She gently reached for the glass and pulled it from his hand.

He didn't stop her. Instead, he squinted up at her from under his bushy brows. "Did I ever tell you I had a daughter?"

"I wasn't aware, no." Grace cradled the glass in her palm,

its smooth surface still warm from his grip. He had clearly been there for quite some time. "Is she in London?"

He sat up slowly, swaying. "She's dead."

Grace winced at her egregious misstep. "Forgive me. I didn't—"

"It happened several years ago, same car accident as my wife." He adjusted his glasses with clumsy hands, setting them almost correctly at the bridge of his nose. "She would have been about your age now, my Alice."

A ghost of a smile flickered at the corners of his mouth. "You look like her. I suspect it's why Mrs. Weatherford sent you my way, the meddlesome woman. Her boy Colin had been friends with my daughter for the whole of their lives. No doubt she thought it might help ease the pain of Alice's loss or some such rot. Nonsense, all of it." His furrowed expression softened. "Though I suppose now Mrs. Weatherford understands the futility more so than before."

There was a sadness in his eyes that Grace felt in her core, the hollow emptiness of grief. One that had resonated since her mother's death and never went silent.

She carefully set the glass on a stack of boxes, away from his reach. "Does it bother you that I look like Alice?"

His gaze slid to Grace and paused as though considering her appearance in earnest. Tears filled his eyes, and his chin began to tremble. Quickly, he looked away and a hearty sniff filled the room.

"In the beginning." There was a quaver to his voice, but he cleared his throat. "Every time I'd see you, I'd see my Alice. She had blond hair, like me. Before this." His fingers danced over his white, rumpled hair.

Grace said nothing, letting him speak.

"I thought I'd buried her here." He slapped his open hand

on his chest and gave an exhale that seemed to cause him great pain. "Now I know, such things are too great to be contained. It also makes me realize I wasn't only trying to push aside my grief, but also my guilt."

There was a thickness to his words, not from alcohol, but from emotion, and it made Grace ache for him.

Mr. Evans tilted the bottle to study the inch or so of liquid sloshing at the bottom. "I hope she knew how much I loved her. How much she meant to me." He set the bottle firmly into place and looked up at Grace.

"I'm sorry I was cross with you for staying on with the ARP." His jaw worked beneath a sprinkling of fine, white whiskers. "You're not Alice. I know that. *I know that.*" He looked away. "But I can't lose you too."

A stubborn lump worked its way into Grace's throat. One she couldn't swallow away. She'd never had anything close to a father in her life. Not when her own had been killed before she met him. And certainly not with her uncle, who saw her more as a workhorse than a niece.

"I'll be careful," she said. "But I have to continue with the ARP. Mr. Evans, this is me never stopping—just as you said."

The corner of his lip lifted in a half smile. "I give terrible advice sometimes."

"You give excellent advice."

He pushed up from the table and paused a moment, teetering a bit where he stood. "I haven't ever told you this before, Grace, but I'm proud of you."

A warmth blossomed in her chest at his praise. No one had ever said those words to her before, not like that.

Mr. Evans framed his fingertips on the table. "I think I should retire to bed now."

"I can handle the store," she offered quickly.

"I know you can." He reached out and took hold of her shoulder, giving it an affectionate squeeze. "Mind you look after yourself as well, eh?"

"I will," she promised.

With that, he nodded and wandered toward the door leading to his flat above the shop, his glasses still askew.

Grace managed the shop that day, using her ARP skills that afternoon to usher the customers to local shelters when an inevitable air raid called out the arrival of more German planes. Those same sirens wailed again that night and the following night, as well as in the afternoons.

People did not ignore the sirens now. Not like before. Not when the damage was so considerable, the worst of which being when South Hallsville School in Canning Town was struck, killing many of the survivors of the East End who were sheltering within.

It was a hard blow for all of London.

Aside from the destruction of the Hewses' home, Grace's sector remained untouched during the air raids. Regardless, she and Mr. Stokes were asked to increase their night watches from three times a week to five. Mr. Evans, who never again brought up their discussion about his daughter, allowed her to start a bit later each day to account for the extra ARP shifts.

It was past noon several days later when she entered the bookshop and discovered a small tabby cat sleeping in a sliver of sunshine just inside the door. This discovery was followed almost immediately by the excited trill of Mr. Pritchard's voice as he offered his ever-present opinion on the state of Britain.

"Did you hear the king and queen were bombed in Buckingham?" he said as she set her things in the back room.

"The bloody king and queen, Evans. They're just like us, they are. We're all in this together."

Grace could practically see Mr. Evans wince at the other man's language when customers were present in the store. She hung her handbag and threaded through the shop, ensuring their patrons were tended to.

"You said a bomb was lodged in the ground before St. Paul's?" Mr. Evans pressed, clearly trying to rush the other man along.

"Yes," Mr. Pritchard exclaimed. "Right before the clock tower. The whole cathedral would have been blown to pieces had the thing gone off. The bomb disposal unit had to come see to it. Fascinating stuff, that."

No sooner had he spoken than the air raid siren started its afternoon wail. Tabby immediately leapt to his feet and trotted over to Mr. Pritchard, who scowled at the interruption by "Moaning Minnie," his beady eyes bright with irritation. "Blast these nuisance raids. I think Germany wants to win by driving us all mad."

Regardless of his grousing, he followed Grace out of the shop, along with the other customers and Mr. Evans. The tube stations had opened up for shelter despite the government's initial decision to keep them closed. The repeated bombings made their use necessary, especially with so many now seeking safety.

It was to Farringdon Station that Grace led them all, utilizing her experience as an ARP warden, despite not being on duty. For those who preferred not to pay the one and a half pence to enter the station, she guided them first to the brick shelter at the corner. Before the siren had quieted, she was settled against the tiled wall beside Mr. Evans and lifting the front jacket of her book.

She'd only just started *Middlemarch* the night before and was several chapters in, her mind locked on Dorothea and the young woman's plight with her new, much older husband. The siren overhead cut off and the shuffle and muttered conversation of dozens of people inside the tube echoed against the rounded walls. Wind billowed in from the gaping tunnels on either side of the platform, issuing a low, haunting note and tickling Grace's hair across her cheek.

She blocked all sound out, propped her open book on her knees and began to read. Outside came the now familiar sounds of war, the booming ack-ack guns firing at enemy aircraft as the RAF dove and shot at the Germans in an effort to fend them off. Amid it all, and far less often than at night, came the distant thud of falling bombs.

"What are you reading, miss?" a woman asked from beside her.

Grace looked up to find the young mother she'd comforted weeks before. "*Middlemarch* by George Eliot."

Guns pounded overhead. The woman glanced up anxiously. "What's it about?"

"A woman named Dorothea," Grace replied. "She has a handsome suitor intent on marrying her, but he's not the man who draws her eye."

"Why is that?"

"She quite prefers an older man, a reverend."

The young mother gave a nervous chuckle. "Does she?"

"She does." Grace pinched her finger between the pages of the book to ensure she wouldn't lose her spot and sat up a little straighter. "She even marries him."

"What was so appealing about him?" a middle-aged woman in a blue housedress asked.

A low whistle sounded outside, followed by an explosion

that made the ground vibrate and the lights flicker. Mr. Evans nodded encouragingly at Grace, a small smile playing on his lips.

"She's pious," Grace answered. "And he is a scholar in addition to being a reverend, with intellectual pursuits she finds fascinating."

"What about the handsome man?" a voice asked.

Grace grinned. "He pursues her sister."

Someone laughed. "Brilliant!"

"Does it work out then?" a burly man in a yellow pullover asked. He hardly looked the type to care with his tousled dark hair and rumpled clothes more likely suited for a pub.

"With the sister and the handsome suitor?" Grace asked. "Or Dorothea and the reverend?"

The man shrugged. "Both, I suppose."

The crack of the anti-aircraft guns rang out overhead as a plane swooped low enough for the hum of its engine to echo through the cavernous tube station.

"I don't know." Grace glanced at the book, still pinched at her location. "I haven't read that far yet."

"Well," the housewife said. "Go on."

Grace hesitated. "You want me...to read it?" Everyone on the platform of Farringdon Station watched her expectantly. "Out loud?"

The lot of them all nodded, and quite a few smiled.

Suddenly, she was the painfully shy girl of her youth again in scuffed shoes that pinched at her toes, standing before the class with a bit of chalk in her hand and every set of eyes on her. Her stomach coiled itself into a knot.

"Please," the young mother said. Another barrage of gunfire came, and she cowered down into herself.

Mr. Evans's expressive brows crept upward in silent question.

Despite every brutally shy bit of Grace's makeup screaming at her to refuse, she opened the book, licked her suddenly dry lips and began to read. Her tongue tripped over the first couple of sentences, and she was awkwardly aware of how many people were witnessing her missteps. And when a bomb exploded somewhere far off, its thunder distracted her so thoroughly, she forgot what line she'd been on.

But as she continued to read, the crowd around her faded away and her mind focused only on the story. Her world curled around Dorothea's, experiencing that miserable honeymoon in Rome with a man who hoarded his scholarly aspirations to himself. As the pages turned, they met Fred, the wastrel who had his sights set on marrying a woman in his uncle's care while Dorothea's previous beau set his intent toward her younger sister.

When the anti-aircraft guns fired, Grace raised her voice to be heard. When the lights winked in and out, she continued on as best she could, recalling from her peripheral vision what words were to come next. And when a new character spoke, she invented a voice for each and every one of them.

A howling screech came overhead, followed by a boom that plunged the tube station into darkness.

"Here." There was a rustling as someone dug in a handbag, followed a moment later by the weight of a torch being nudged into Grace's hand. She flicked on the beam and continued to read, bringing the entire group with her through the story. The all clear sounded and broke through her reading, making her blink at the abrupt transition between the fictional world and reality.

She returned the borrowed torch with thanks and discovered she was already several chapters into the book.

"Will you be here tomorrow afternoon?" the housewife asked.

"If we have an air raid." Grace tucked a scrap of paper between the pages to mark her place and cradled its weigh in her palm.

"Then she will," the burly man said.

The young mother, who Grace learned was called Mrs. Kittering, nodded at the book in Grace's hand with a hopeful smile. "Perhaps you can bring *Middlemarch* with you?"

After promising to resume where they'd left off, Grace and Mr. Evans returned to the bookshop.

"You mentioned once feeling helpless amid this war." He flipped the sign to Open in the window. "But down there, reading to all those frightened people, you had power."

"I confess, I felt rather foolish reading aloud like that." Grace stacked the discarded books left on the counter during the air raid and set them aside in case the customers returned for them.

He shook his head. "Not foolish at all, Miss Bennett. You'll change this war yet." He tapped his blunt fingers on the cover of *Middlemarch*. "One book at a time."

FOURTEEN

THE DAMAGE FROM THE ATTACK THAT AFTERNOON
was considerable, leaving a massive crater carved into the
street in the middle of the Strand. Over six hundred German planes had crossed into Britain, their bellies heavy with
bombs. But while they had come with the intention to destroy more of London, the RAF was prepared to defend.

The Luftwaffe came back that night, of course. They always did.

Grace was on duty, grateful that her sector, once more,
remained blessedly untouched. It would not remain thus forever. Not when the rest of London had been chipped away
to reveal ribs of support beams and blown-out windows
reminiscent of the empty sockets of a skull.

The following day, when the air raids blared their warning, Grace put *Middlemarch* in her large handbag and escorted
Primrose Hill Books patrons to Farringdon Station. The

people she'd read to the day before were waiting for her in a small cluster. Their faces lit up when they saw her, especially after taking note of the book she pulled from her handbag.

They showed up the following day and the one after that as well, each time the number growing slightly larger.

However, mid September, the weather was quite dismal. Bad enough even to discourage German bombers from attempting their daily afternoon raids. It was a rare, uninterrupted day, absent of a single air raid siren.

Grace did not squander it and instead combed through a list of recently released books to see how many she might order from Simpkin Marshalls. The door chimed to announce a customer as she was nearly done, a disruption she did not mind.

When she lifted her gaze, she found the burly man who attended every one of her readings at Farringdon Station. He had his cap in his large hands, wringing the gray wool.

"Afternoon, Miss Bennett." He ducked his head respectfully. She'd never seen him without the cap settled over his head. His hair beneath was a mix of gray and brown, slightly fuzzed with a bit of his scalp showing at the top.

"M'name's Jack," he said. "I wanted to thank you, not only for reading to us from your book, but also for saving my life."

"Saving your life?" Grace repeated in surprise.

He nodded. "I was in the area the day you started reading, rather by accident. Usually, I'm near Hyde Park in the afternoons, repairing some of the buildings there." He tilted his head in a humble gesture. "Much as I can. But lately I've been finding jobs around here to make sure I'm in the tube to hear you read during air raids. Had I not, I'd have been in Marble Arch Station where I sheltered before."

Grace put her hand to her mouth to cover her shock.

Two days before during a particularly brutal attack that destroyed nearly all of Oxford Street, a bomb had come through the ceiling of the Marble Arch Station where people were waiting out the attack. The carnage had been considerable, as detailed by Mr. Stokes until Grace had begged him to stop. Those who had not been killed by the bomb had been shredded by the exploding tiles. The injuries had been horrific.

"I'm so…" Grace stammered, unsure what to say. "I'm so pleased you weren't there. That you've remained safe."

Jack sniffed and wiped at his nose with the back of his hand, cap still clutched between his thick fingers. "That's not the only reason I'm here."

"Oh?" She smiled. "Can I help you find a book?"

He twisted at his cap again. "You hadn't finished *Middlemarch*. A couple of us queued at Farringdon Station anticipating an air raid. When it didn't happen, well… We were wondering what's next in the story."

"We?" She followed his side gaze to the large plate-glass windows of Primrose Hill Books and found a crowd gathered outside the store. Mrs. Kittering was there, as well as many others Grace recognized, and waved with a hopeful smile.

Grace turned her attention back to Jack, who gave her a hesitant grin. "Would you be so kind as to read to us still, even though we aren't in the tube?"

She glanced to Mr. Evans who looked at her with a paternal pride that crinkled the corners of his blue eyes as he offered her a nod of silent consent to their request.

Biting her lip, Grace considered the size of the store. Last year, such a request would have been impossible. But now…

"Yes," she replied. "I absolutely can."

And so it was she settled on the second step of the circular metal stairs while everyone else sat about on the floor or propped themselves against the wall to listen to her read from *Middlemarch*.

Mr. Evans's white hair was visible along the top of a bookshelf one row over and remained there for the duration of her reading, as though he too was listening.

After that, she read every day, either in the tube, or at Primrose Hill Books when there was no air raid. But while the days were filled with stories and the many people who came to listen to her, the nights were filled with bombs.

It was, in a single encompassing word, wretched.

The evenings when Grace didn't work alongside Mr. Stokes, she was getting only a few moments of miserable sleep in the cramped Anderson shelter buried in the backyard.

One such evening, she and Mrs. Weatherford had prepared to go into the Andy with their bedding and a small box containing necessities: a candle, their gas masks, though Germany no longer seemed interested in poison, Grace's latest book, *The Waves* by Virginia Woolf, and a vacuum flask of tea.

Rain was pouring down when the air raid siren went off, sending the women racing out into the deluge and through the muddy garden. The Andy rose in the dark like a sleeping beast, its hump wild with bristles of hair where sprigs of tomato plants sprouted from the dirt layering it. But when Grace stepped into the shelter, her foot sank up to the ankle in a pool of icy water.

She cried out in surprise and leapt back out.

"Is it mice?" Mrs. Weatherford asked, jerking away in horror.

"It's flooded." Grace shook her damp shoe to little effect. "We'll have to go to Farringdon Station until the Andy has dried out." She made her way back to the house, one foot weighty and sodden from the soaking, issuing a derisive squish with every step.

Mrs. Weatherford rushed behind her, but didn't set about to prepare to go to the tube station.

"If we hurry, we might still manage a decent spot," Grace said by way of politely trying to rush Mrs. Weatherford.

Already it was past eight, which was usually when the Germans began their nightly raids. Most likely they had been put off by the inclement weather. But that also meant the tube station would be packed with people like sardines in a tin by now. Grace had seen it on her nights as warden. People lay side by side wherever they might find the space to do so, strangers nestled as closely as families. Not only on the floor of the platform, but up the stairs and escalators and even some brave souls who slept beside the tracks.

Mrs. Weatherford sat at the kitchen table and poured herself a cup of tea from the Thermos.

"There isn't time for all that." Grace's nerves scrabbled with an anxiety she could no longer temper. "We must be going."

Mrs. Weatherford offered a little sigh and set aside her cup. "I'm not going, Grace. I only go in the Andy to soothe your mind, but I confess, I never seek shelter during the day when you aren't here." She blinked, slow and tired. "I'll not go to the tube station."

The ire deflated from Grace, replaced instead with a heavy ache. "But it won't be safe." Her protest was weak. She already knew there was scarcely any point in arguing.

Mrs. Weatherford didn't bother replying and merely stared

dejectedly at the floor. Her face was lined with anguish where she sat in the white-and-yellow kitchen, a place that had once felt so cheerful and now seemed dull and stark. While she had once again begun to have a care with her appearance, she wore only dark clothes in place of her floral housedresses, each one belted tighter and tighter on her frame as she lost more and more weight.

There were no more WVS meetings or elaborate meals or anything to show she was doing more than simply surviving, as if life was a book full of blank pages to be turned. Uneventful. Holding no purpose but to get to the back cover and be done.

Grace remained in the townhouse with Mrs. Weatherford that night, resolved to find some way to encourage the older woman to join her at the tube station going forward. Each attempt afterward, however, was met with the same refusal and once, a sobbing confession for a wish to join Colin. Grace could not argue against something as powerful as grief.

The rest of September passed with nightly bomb raids and more afternoon attacks than not. Somehow, London adjusted.

After all, no one in the world had the spirit of the British. They were fighters. They could take it.

Shops began to close at four every afternoon to allow employees the opportunity for sleep before their night shifts began. Nearly every person had two jobs now. The ones they operated by day and the ones they volunteered for by night, whether putting out fires, watching for bombs, searching through the rubble for survivors or offering medical aid in the many various places it was needed—London came to life at night to help.

Grace found she now could sleep rather effectively in small moments, falling immediately into a deep, dreamless slumber in short snatches of time.

Queues at tube stations and shelters began before eight when the first sirens would inevitably begin to sound, people arriving early on to ensure they received a prime location on the floor. Or in a bunk if they were truly fortunate.

As a result, people grew used to sleeping fully clothed. Some even confessed to bathing in their knickers, far too frightened to be caught unawares and be found dead in the buff.

Yet even with the upheaval and uncertainty, letters continued to pour into the postal service despite the bombings and damaged buildings, operated by way of candlelight with signs declaring they were still open. It was a sad sight to behold, however, when a postman stood before a home reduced to a pile of rubble with a letter held in his hand.

Whatever had stifled the Royal Mail service in the beginning of the war had begun to ease somewhat and Grace received letters from Viv and George with more regularity. It was ironic that their correspondence expressed as much concern for Grace's safety now as hers did for them.

George had suggested a new book, *South Riding* by Winifred Holtby, after she'd told him she'd begun reading in the tube station. A copy had been delivered to her at the store just that morning from Simpkin Marshalls, its dust jacket crisp and glossy with newness.

The day held a chill from the previously sodden weather, but a beam of light streamed in through the window. No customers had entered the shop yet and Mr. Evans was busy with his "work" in the history section, so she found herself sitting in a little nook by the window.

A sliver of sunlight broke through the clouds and shone on her with a gentle warmth. Grace paused for a moment and ran her fingers over the book cover, savoring the quiet peace. Relishing the joy of reading.

The jacket was smooth, the print black against a yellow background dotted with small red houses. She slid her fingertip under the lip and drew it open. The spine, not yet stretched, creaked open, like an ancient door preparing to unveil a secret world.

She turned the pages to the first chapter, the sound a quiet whispered shush in the empty shop. There was a special scent to paper and ink, indescribable and unknown to anyone but a true reader. She brought the book to her face, closed her eyes and breathed in that wonderful smell.

It was startling to think a year prior to this, she hadn't been able to appreciate such small moments. But in a world as damaged and gray as theirs was now, she would take every speck of pleasure where it could be found. And much pleasure was to be had in reading.

Grace cherished the adventures she went on through those pages, an escape from exhaustion and bombs and rationing. Deeper still was the profound understanding for mankind as she lived in the minds of the characters. Over time, she had found such perspectives made her a more patient person, more accepting of others. If everyone had such an appreciation for their fellow man, perhaps things such as war would not exist.

Such considerations were easy to muse over there in a rare beam of sunlight, but far more difficult to hold tight to in the blacked-out streets of London with Mr. Stokes.

The improved weather brought with it an influx of bombers who sailed easily through the clear skies to unload their destruction. It was on one such night that Grace found herself on duty when the familiar droning of planes announced their unwanted arrival.

They flew like a murder of crows in the blackened sky, their presence evident in the scrolling beam of a searchlight. In previous raids, they would have opened their bellies by now.

And yet still they came, growing larger, louder until the small hairs in Grace's ears trembled at the noise. The ack-ack guns cracked in the thin night air; the hint of their smoke in the distance acrid. She craned her head back to stare up at the formation above her head. A searchlight passed over a plane just in time to see as its bottom split open and a large, pipe-like shape slid free into the sky.

A bomb.

Above her.

She watched, transfixed. Her mind screamed run, run, run, but her legs wouldn't listen. The bomb whistled a note that pitched higher as it gained speed. As it came closer.

That shrill note called her to her senses and she turned from it, grabbing Mr. Stokes's arm as she did so, pulling them back behind a wall framed with sandbags. The whistle became a shriek and her entire body went cold with fear.

The sound stopped abruptly and her heart with it.

That was the worst moment, when it fell, in the split second before it detonated. When you didn't know where it had gone.

The explosion was an immediate burst of brilliant light and a powerful bang that made the world go eerily silent. A flash blew hot as an open oven at her back. The force of it shoved Grace and sent her sprawling forward several feet.

Her body smacked hard into the ground, knocking the

wind from her lungs. She blinked, stunned, as a pitched whine rang one lofty note in her ears, tuning out any other sound.

Her cheek ached where it had struck the pavement, her chin tender where the leather strap of her hat had kept it on her head as she landed. She huffed out a breath and a cloud of dust billowed up in front of her face.

Slowly, the world came back to her, starting with the booming anti-aircraft guns, odd and distant like an underwater echo. She lay a moment more, taking in the broken bits of rubble around them, waiting for a rush of pain to announce a missing limb or a fatal wound.

Her chest throbbed where she'd landed. But nothing more.

She pushed herself to sitting with arms that almost seemed too weak to lift her. With shaking hands, she patted her jacket, pressing over the thick, gritty layer of dust for any indication of injury.

There was none.

She looked to her left and found Mr. Stokes sitting beside her in a similarly dazed fashion.

They had survived.

But others might not have.

All at once, sound rushed back at her. Not just the ack-ack guns, but the whistles of bombs and the explosions. So many explosions.

She and Mr. Stokes appeared to recover their senses simultaneously. They looked to one another and immediately jumped to their feet. The wall they'd been standing behind had a hole at its center, the sandbags ripped to shreds.

Had they not been behind it, those shreds of fabric might have instead been their bodies.

It was a realization Grace couldn't allow herself to process at that moment. She tucked it into a neat box, locked tight in her thoughts, and set it to a dark, dark corner of her mind.

Several homes had been obliterated to rubble before them, and the glow of fire pulsed like wounded hearts within. Quickly Grace assessed the numbers on the homes and deduced that three of the ruined dwellings had inhabitants she'd seen to the shelter herself. However, the one to the left, which was still standing, belonged to Mrs. Driscoll, the middle-aged widow who had stopped coming to the shelters a fortnight ago.

Grace pointed to the home. "Mrs. Driscoll."

She needn't have said more. Mr. Stokes broke into a run toward the standing townhouse and continued through the gaping entryway, its door having been blown off. Grace followed and waited for him to go in and return, as he'd always instructed her to do.

Except he did not reemerge.

Grace cautiously entered behind him to find Mr. Stokes standing in the parlor, staring at something. "Mr. Stokes?"

He said nothing.

She came to his side and followed his stony gaze. It took a moment to realize that what she was looking at had once been a person. Had once been Mrs. Driscoll.

Grace's stomach roiled, but she gripped her hand into a fist to hold herself together as she added this sight into the neat little box in her mind, along with her fears of what could happen to Mrs. Weatherford in such a circumstance.

"Mr. Stokes," Grace said.

He didn't look at her.

"Mr. Stokes," she said sharply.

He turned his head to her slowly, his gaze wide and distant, in a dreamlike state. A single, silent tear spilled over his lower lash line and crawled down his cheek. He blinked, as though startled to see her standing there.

"We can't do anything for her now," Grace said in a matter-of-fact tone she didn't know she could possess in such circumstances. "We need to see if there are survivors we can help. I'll go next door to Mr. Sanford's." She nodded to the wall to indicate the townhouse standing on the other side of Mrs. Driscoll's and hoped the elderly man hadn't suffered the same fate. He had stopped going to the shelter as well. There were too many who had.

They wanted a night of sleep in their own beds. They wanted normalcy.

But one couldn't wish the world into its previous state. Not when it was rife with dangers.

"Will you go around to the townhouse beside Mr. Sanford's?" Grace asked of her partner.

Mr. Stokes nodded and shuffled outside. She followed behind him, pausing only to ensure the mains had all been cut off, to prevent an explosion.

She did not turn to look back at Mrs. Driscoll again as she left.

The rest of the night was a blur, a forceful redirection of thoughts into that box in her mind. She focused on calling up her training, binding the bloodied limbs of survivors, helping put out meager fires with her stirrup pump, or sand if the oiled ground and odor indicated a recently dropped incendiary. It was one task after another until the sun rose and the night watch came to a blessed end.

On her way home that morning, despite Grace's resolution, that locked box in the back of her mind began to rattle.

As if it too were a bomb whistling toward her. She threw

open the door to the townhouse and raced upstairs as its shriek in her mind went silent.

And the box erupted.

The horrors she'd seen peppered her thoughts like shrapnel.

Sorrow for Mrs. Driscoll. Fear that Mrs. Weatherford could end up like her. Shock at how close Grace had come to being blown to pieces herself. The destruction. The gruesome injuries. The blood still smeared on her jacket. The death.

Mrs. Driscoll's was not the only body they had found that night.

Grace threw open her bedside drawer and dug frantically at the contents until she found the identity wristlet with Viv's neat script detailing Grace's name and their address at Britton Street on the smooth oval surface. Grace's hands shook so hard, it took several tries to secure it on her wrist. Once there, she slid to the floor and let herself be pulled under by the powerful wave of so much horror.

She had to deal with it now, to face its overwhelming and extraordinary force. So she could return to her shift tomorrow and do it all again.

FIFTEEN

BY SOME MIRACLE, GRACE FOUND SLEEP THAT morning, but as soon as she woke, the memories of the bombing were there. It was as if they'd been lying in wait, hiding in the shadows of her mind for her awareness to return.

They followed her as she made her way to the bookshop, each bombed-out building a nudge at her wounded thoughts. Buildings she saw every day on her quick walk to Primrose Hill Books had been reduced to heaps of brick with broken beams jutting from the destruction. The grocer who always reserved a few raisins for Mrs. Weatherford when he had them, the apothecary who helped them through the cutworms, the café on the corner where she was supposed to go on a date with George. And so many more. They were not the only losses. Many homes were shells of themselves, their missing walls revealing the rooms inside like a child's macabre dollhouse.

People she passed on the street observed the damage with dull curiosity. A couple strode by, powdered with dust and clutching filthy bundles in their hands, the man's face hard set and the woman's eyes red-rimmed from crying. No doubt they had lost their home that night.

They were lucky to have not lost their lives.

Grace entered the bookshop and anxiously swept a loose wave of her hair over her right cheek. She'd taken to wearing her hair in pinned rolls to keep her face clear as she worked. Except that the bruised scrape on her cheek had stubbornly refused to be covered with makeup, and Mr. Evans would no doubt worry.

He looked up and narrowed his eyes, immediately suspicious. Grace patted her hair once more, self-conscious, and his attention drifted to the wristlet.

His jaw set. "I heard Clerkenwell was hit last night."

Grace couldn't look at him. Not with the tears welling in her eyes. She would be strong. She was better than this.

His steps thumped softly over the carpet as he came around the counter. "Grace," he said softly. "Are you all right?"

Brushing him off with a simple yes would have been easier, but the tenderness in his tone and her aching need for comfort was too great. Even as she shook her head, his arms went around her, like a father's, pulling her into an embrace of comfort such as she hadn't known since her mother's.

Tears fell, and the details from that night spilled from her lips while he held her. Her burden eased as she shared what she'd seen, leaning on his strength, not realizing how much she had needed it.

"I was in the Great War," he said as she wiped at her eyes

with a handkerchief. "You never forget, but it becomes part of you. Like a scar no one can see."

Grace nodded at the logic of his statement, the roil of her emotions finally calm for the first time since she'd allowed herself to break apart.

Perhaps his comfort and advice were what gave her courage later that afternoon when a particularly bad raid echoed over the tube station. The cacophony of war overhead came nonstop and with such intensity, it was impossible to differentiate one sound from the other. Without her wits about her, she might have surrendered to the flicker of panic racing in her mind with every whistle, every thundering boom that reverberated in her chest. They only made her read all the louder.

Afterward, she learned just a mile away, during the height of rush hour, Charing Cross had been heavily bombed.

That evening, Grace was far more successful in hiding her bruised face from Mrs. Weatherford as they ate a supper of fatty beef and a blend of beans and carrots from their garden. She did not, however, succeed in convincing Mrs. Weatherford to seek shelter.

It was a discussion they had almost daily. At this point, Grace presumed Mrs. Weatherford had stopped listening to her carefully detailed reasons. Except now, Grace knew full well what could happen if a bomb struck Britton Street.

Preparing for her ARP work that night took a considerable amount of fortitude. Even as she attached the pin to her lapel, her hands trembled. After all, she never knew what the night would bring.

Mr. Stokes did not seem to act his usual self either. He didn't bother to lord his knowledge over her, nor did he make any mention of the bombing of Charing Cross, which no doubt would have had gory details to regurgitate.

For once, he was quiet.

And as much as Grace thought such a thing would be a blessing, she discovered his silence dug at an uncomfortable place inside her until she recognized it as worry.

For Mr. Stokes, of all people.

After several hours of listening to the rest of London be bombed, a sound so commonplace, it faded to the background like static, and their own sector remaining quiet, Grace could stand it no longer. "I presume you heard about Charing Cross," she said finally.

He pressed his lips against one another in the moonlight. She marveled for a moment in his thoughtful pause at how adept she had become at seeing in the blacked-out London streets. She could even make out a slight nick on the side of his jaw that he'd sustained in the blast the night before.

"I heard," he said, his voice gravelly and hoarse. He swallowed. "Those poor people."

And that was it. No terrible details of dismemberment or smoke-belching destruction. No destroyed homes and victims blasted to gruesome states.

They didn't speak again for a long time. Not until they strode past Mrs. Driscoll's townhouse. The widow's remains had already been seen to by one of the rescue services and removed. Mr. Stokes stopped in front of the still-standing townhouse and looked at it for rather a long while, his hands thrust in his pockets.

"I didn't thank you, Miss Bennett." He lowered his head. "For last night. I... I nearly forgot myself, and you reminded me what we were there for."

His humility struck Grace even more fully than had his silence earlier. "We're partners."

"You kept a level head and people are alive because of you." His gaze shifted toward Grace. "I admire your ability to stay so focused."

"I suspect," she said slowly, unable to help herself, "it's because I'm a woman."

A slow smile crept over his mouth. He gave a mirthless laugh. "I am a lout, aren't I?"

She tilted her head, declining to speak when he already knew the answer.

From that night on, they got on quite well with one another, finding something of a friendship amid the shared danger and tragedy they encountered together.

And they had need of it, for just a week later, on a night heavy with fog and anticipation, more bombs fell in their sector. The damage was great, the casualties high. On and on the Germans dropped their explosives into the early morning hours.

As slivers of sunlight jabbed through the smoky air, the all clear sounded. Grace paced before a fallen home, knowing the occupants had sought shelter in a basement beneath. There was a chance, however small, that they might still be alive.

The men of heavy rescue pulled up in a battered lorry, though most vehicles were battered these days, and approached her with grim faces. Those men saw the worst the bombing had to offer. They were large, all of them, their bodies bulky from the weeks of shifting rubble, their eyes as hollow and empty as the gaping windows of blasted homes.

She directed them where to dig and helped where she

might, calling out the names of people she hoped to one day see again.

"Miss Bennett." A shrill voice cried out to her.

She straightened from a pile of bricks to find a young man running down the path to her.

"I'm glad I found you," he said, gasping for breath from his haste. "There's been a bomb. At Mrs. Weatherford's—"

Grace's blood chilled.

Mrs. Weatherford.

She turned from the boy and the men and the rubble, sprinting down the streets toward the townhouse with an impossible speed. When she arrived, she found its face intact. But she knew better than to trust such things. One need only open a door sometimes to discover nothing there.

She raced up the steps and wasted not a moment as she threw open the door and froze with shock.

Everything was exactly as she had left it, the wooden floors gleaming beneath the fading carpet, the door to the kitchen propped open, revealing the cheerful yellow and white room.

She shouted for Mrs. Weatherford as she stumbled into the parlor, finding it empty.

She darted to the kitchen with another ready breath sucked in to call out once more and nearly ran headlong into none other than Mrs. Weatherford.

"I was told there was a bomb," Grace cried out.

Mrs. Weatherford gave a tired smile. "There is, love. But it's not gone off, you see?"

She pointed from the kitchen window where a massive bomb had landed directly on their Anderson shelter, crunching in its center. It was an ugly thing, nearly as long as Grace was tall with a fin jutting from its back and a layer of grit over its dull metal body. Within that body, however, were enough explosives to reduce homes to ruin and chew through tender skin.

Another shiver rattled down Grace's spine.

Had it gone off, Mrs. Weatherford would have been killed. Ripped to pieces. And Grace would have been the one to come upon her.

"I've already notified the ARP post so a bomb disposal unit could be sent round." Mrs. Weatherford spoke in a flat tone, as if she hadn't a care. As if she didn't acknowledge the danger.

Grace shook her head. "You could have been killed. If it had gone off, if it does go off, the explosion would have leveled the house and you would be…"

"But that didn't happen, dear." Mrs. Weatherford motioned Grace to the table and poured her a cup of tea. The small chain bracelet Grace had given her recently hung from her limp wrist, the flat oval at its center printed neatly with her name and address.

But even if she was wearing the wristlet, Grace wouldn't be put off so easily. She pulled at Mrs. Weatherford, drawing her from the kitchen. "You could have been…" Grace's voice faltered. "You cold have been hurt…like…"

Like Mrs. Driscoll.

"But I'm not." Mrs. Weatherford sighed, almost appearing saddened by it. Regardless, she offered no protest as Grace nudged her out the front door.

"You could have been." Grace blew her whistle to the ARP wardens just coming onto their shift and directed them to clear out the area before the bomb removal unit arrived.

When at last they were several streets away, with a cup of lukewarm tea from a WVS sponsored canteen, Grace managed to quell her panic and leveled a gaze at Mrs. Weatherford. "I know life has been difficult."

Mrs. Weatherford closed her eyes in a slow, painful blink.

"Please," Grace pleaded, her voice thick. "I have seen some terrible sights. I've witnessed what these bombs can do to people."

Mrs. Weatherford's stare drifted to Grace's coat, now exposed in the daylight to reveal the grit and blood.

Things Mrs. Weatherford had never noticed before.

Several other people lingering near the mobile canteen unit appeared in a similar state, volunteers as well as bomb victims.

"Do you know what it would do to me to find you in such a state?" Grace's voice was hoarse with the strain of her whisper. "I can't—" Tears stung her eyes.

Mrs. Weatherford touched a hand to her mouth. "Oh, Grace. Dear, I'm so sorry."

They said nothing else in the hours that dragged on before the disposal unit could come to take the unexploded bomb safely away.

That night, however, when Grace had a night off from her ARP shift and was readying herself to join the queue at Farringdon Station's entrance, Mrs. Weatherford wordlessly joined her with a small bundle of belongings packed at her side.

From that night on, Mrs. Weatherford slept in the tube station without argument.

As the month of October went on, the bombings continued, peaking midmonth when the moon was full and bright. A bomber's moon, they called it. And aptly so.

By the brilliant lunar aura, the Thames was lit like a silver ribbon curling through London's blackout, and the Germans could clearly make out their targets.

Hundreds were killed, far more injured, thousands were left homeless and so many fires raged within London that the ARP wardens were deployed to assist the firemen in their seemingly endless fight.

Despite London's flesh being peeled back night after night to reveal more of her skeleton beneath, Churchill still sought to keep as much information from Germany as possible. This meant the casualty numbers listed on the broadcasts in the evening weren't given a location. It meant stores that had been bombed could reopen in a new area, but not state where their previous location had been. Worse still, it meant the dead could not receive a proper obituary in a timely manner, but were listed at a delay and with simply the month of their death.

Through it all, life in the battered city went on, its people taking whatever pleasure wherever they could and trying to savor the final vestiges of fine weather before the ice and snow swept in. Especially if the upcoming months were to be as frigid as the winter before.

So it was that sometime past the middle of October on a particularly lovely day with almost no clouds or rain, Grace found herself longing to forego an extra wink of sleep for a chance to walk in the vestiges of a sunny day. An order from Simpkin Marshalls failed to arrive that afternoon, and she found her opportunity.

When she'd suggested to Mr. Evans that she go by and check, he'd smiled with understanding and told her to take her time. And take her time she did. Grace strolled to Paternoster Row, making the short walk last a few extra minutes more than necessary. There was a nip in the air, yes, but nothing the sunshine couldn't warm away.

Grace had been back to Paternoster Row many times after that fateful first visit. The bustle of foot traffic hadn't diminished since the start of the war; if anything, it was busier with more people seeking books to entertain them through the long nights in their shelters.

The glossy red buses once so prevalent had suffered heavy losses due to the frequent bombings. She'd witnessed far too many on the sides of bombed roads, crumpled like discarded children's toys. One was still visible from time to time, amid the green, blue, brown and white coaches sent to replace the ruined public transportation.

The vendors along the pavement still sold their fare made with recipes altered to accommodate the ration. And though patrons complained the food was never quite up to snuff, they still queued to buy.

She knew all the vendors by now, as well as the shop owners and publishers. She entered the shops at a leisurely pace, greeting the owners by name and perusing their new arrivals, not as a competitor, but as a reader. It was a glorious thing to walk down a street devoted to books, where lovers of literature could congregate and indulge in their passion with like-minded souls.

And though she now understood everyone's insistence that Mr. Evans relocate his shop to Paternoster Row, she could not imagine Primrose Hill Books anywhere else than in its present location, tucked amid a row of townhouses on Hosier Lane.

Her mood was so fine that day, she even chanced a visit to Pritchard & Potts where she found Mr. Pritchard dangling a string before Tabby. The cat raked a paw through the air with fanatical determination, so set on his prize, he didn't even turn at the sound of the bell. Mr. Pritchard, however, startled and dropped the string, which was immediately pounced upon by Tabby.

"Miss Basset." Mr. Pritchard cleared his throat and gestured toward the cat now tangled in the length of string. "I was…ehm…trying to hone his reflexes to help him learn to catch mice."

Grace smiled despite his perpetual inability to recall her name and seeing through his poorly crafted ruse. "I'm sure it's quite helpful."

Mr. Pritchard's shiny gaze darted about his shop, and she realized he was no doubt seeing the chaos through her eyes. He tucked his head deeper into the bulk of his dark jacket and tutted. "I am impressed with what you've done with Mr. Evans's shop." He shoved his hands into his pockets, his thin lips pressing thinner still. "If you've any suggestions…"

Primrose Hill Books was well established now and far enough away that Pritchard & Potts would never be considered legitimate competition. And so it was that Grace offered the older man several tips on advertising and how far a bit of organization could go. While he scowled at the latter suggestion, he nodded intently to her advice on adverts.

She spent far longer at Pritchard & Potts than she'd intended. Indeed, far longer than she'd ever thought she could endure. On her way rushing home afterward, however, she was not in too great a hurry to miss the large pasteboard in the window of Nesbitt's Fine Reads touting "Live Readings Every Afternoon."

Just like the ones Grace had continued to do.

She bit back a laugh at such a blatant copy from her austere neighbor. Truly, she wasn't even cross about it. After all, if it offered more people books to bring joy in such dark times, who was she to be offended?

Certainly, Mrs. Nesbitt's afternoon reading did nothing to decrease the crowds in Primrose Hill Books. During bomb raids, Farringdon Station's platform was nearly spilling over with people. Those whose jobs didn't allow them the ability to come to the shop during afternoons without air raids quickly asked others what they'd missed as everyone pressed in close to hear her over the sounds of war.

They had finished *Middlemarch*, of course, then had moved onto several other classics, including *A Tale of Two Cities* and *Emma*. The latter had been at Mrs. Kittering's insistence.

The afternoons when sheltering wasn't necessary were Grace's favorite. Mr. Evans had procured a thick pillow for her to use as she sat upon the second step of the winding stairs, and she never once had to compete with a whistling bomb. It was on one such quiet, rainy afternoon she first saw the boy in the back as she read *South Riding*. The book had resonated with her after she'd read it on George's recommendation.

It is through books that we can find the greatest hope, he had written in his tight, neat script. Words the censor had no cause to cut away. *You remain ever in my thoughts.*

The letter, as all the ones he'd sent before, were precious to her. But those two lines specifically scored themselves on her mind, repeated multiple times a day.

And truly, *South Riding* was a book of great inspiration. Set after the Great War as communities came together and a headmistress inspired hope in a place where there was little to be had. It was an empowering tale about people who could overcome whatever life threw at them.

The same as the British did now.

The boy who attended the reading was tall and slim with a cap shoved low over his mussed dark hair. He wore a men's jacket that hung on his skinny adolescent shoulders and pants that swung about his ankles. All of which were filthy.

He slipped into the reading after it had started, sitting in the shadows of a towering bookshelf. His attempts to not be seen, however, only made him more noticeable. Grace was keenly aware of him, how he'd tucked those long legs beneath him and raised his cap to reveal his dirty, gaunt face while listening intently. He remained where he was all the way up to the last word of the story, then departed as quickly and quietly as he'd arrived, once more tugging his cap low.

It was not the only time Grace had seen him. He showed up every day after, wearing the same ill-fitting attire, just as grimy, just as determined to remain unseen.

But how could one not see a child in such sore need?

She left small gifts of food where he sat, an apple or a bit of bread, but he never so much as looked at it, clearly assuming it belonged to someone else. He required help. And she knew just the one to give it.

She waited until she and Mrs. Weatherford sat down at the kitchen table that evening for a bit of Woolton pie, a vegetable concoction with a potato pastry crust. Mrs. Weatherford had made the meal several times since she'd heard the recipe on *The Kitchen Front*, which she listened to religiously every morning after the eight o'clock news on the BBC.

Grace poured a bit more gravy on the tasteless crust and decided then was as good a time as any to broach the topic. "I wonder if you've thought about doing more work with the WVS?"

Mrs. Weatherford touched the napkin to her lips. "I

haven't." There was a crispness to her tone Grace had expected. "I cannot say I could do anyone a bit of good in my state."

"You do a considerable amount for me." Grace took an appreciative bite of the pie.

Mrs. Weatherford gave a purse of her lips that almost resembled a smile. "Well, you do enough for the two of us. You must keep your strength up."

"What if someone needed you?"

"Nobody needs me."

"I do," Grace protested. "And there's a boy who could use some help."

"A boy?" Mrs. Weatherford regarded Grace with tired, barely tethered patience.

Grace explained how he'd come to listen to her read and the state he was in. "I don't believe he has parents to care for him, and he's too old to go to an orphanage."

Mrs. Weatherford sat back in her chair. "The poor dear."

Sadly, many children were in such a state. Although orphanages were filling up with those who actually went, it wasn't uncommon for the older kids to take their chances on the streets instead. They didn't need anyone, or so they thought. The state of them suggested otherwise with their tattered clothing and hollowed cheeks.

Mrs. Weatherford shook her head. "But what can I possibly do?"

Grace lifted a shoulder. "I hoped you'd know. I haven't a thought how I can help, but I feel like someone must do something before he wastes away. There are too many other people in need for anyone to care for the likes of him."

Mrs. Weatherford went silent at that. But Grace saw her eyes narrow, flickering with a hint of the spark that once gleamed there. Though the older woman carried on with disinterest, her mind was clearly winding through possible solutions.

The ARP shift that night was difficult. There were so many bombs, one Grace and Mr. Stokes had narrowly avoided, and far too much death. The Germans had begun implementing the use of landmine bombs, which floated down on parachutes and whose explosions caused damage that could spread as far as two miles.

No matter how many victims Grace saw to, she still found herself affected by every one. Each name scored on her heart, each memory burned into her brain. She was not alone in how death had affected her. The heavy rescue service, the men who dug through rubble for bodies, or whatever was left, passed a flask around as they worked, unable to perform their grisly tasks without the aid of spirits. They too never would grow used to what they witnessed.

So, when Grace, weary and soul-worn, came home that morning to the scent of baking bread, it did much to lift her downtrodden disposition. Especially when it had been half an age since Mrs. Weatherford had baked, putting to use the secret bags of flour. It was a good thing she had so frugally tucked them away. The months had shown them that just because something was not rationed did not mean it was any easier to come by.

And Grace thought she knew who would receive that coveted loaf.

In the afternoon, Mrs. Weatherford arrived just before Grace's reading, her gaze sharp as she scanned the surrounding faces. The boy arrived just before Grace began and settled in to listen. As she finished the last passage, the boy rose and so too did Mrs. Weatherford.

Grace gave part of her attention to the paragraph in front of her as she watched Mrs. Weatherford out of the corner of her eye.

The older woman approached the boy in his secluded corner. He stiffened and regarded her quietly with his large eyes as she offered the bread. He stared at it for so long that Grace thought he might decline.

Mrs. Weatherford nodded, saying something Grace couldn't hear. Then, quick as a bullet, he grabbed the loaf, tucked it under his jacket and skittered out of the shop.

Mrs. Weatherford met Grace's gaze and offered a proud nod. She had done it. If nothing else, the boy would have food for one day.

Except Grace knew Mrs. Weatherford better than that. There would be many more days after this one. At the town-house that afternoon, the mail wasn't on the floor where it usually remained after being pushed through the slot by the postman. It had been added to the stack near the door, which appeared noticeably smaller as though it had finally been sorted.

At the top was a letter addressed to Grace from Viv. And beneath that one, another from George. Such a double blessing was indeed good fortune, for when Grace opened them, she found they both contained a similar message that sent her squealing with girlish delight.

Both Viv and George would be returning to London for Christmas.

SIXTEEN

IT HAD BEEN THE END OF OCTOBER WHEN GRACE received the letters from Viv and George stating they'd be visiting in time for the festivities. A week later, London experienced its first night without a single bombing.

The weather had been terrible. Rain lashed sideways, thunder growled like a beast and lightning streaked the cloudy sky. Grace had been on duty with Mr. Stokes, both anticipating the air raid that blessedly never came. The hours of that shift had stretched on for an eternity, boredom after so much excitement and an unending assault of blistering rain.

The next morning, those who had sheltered in the tube station emerged with bright eyes and well-rested smiles. It had been hard not to envy their night of solid rest and dry clothing. But the following evening when Grace was off from her ARP work, she had her turn.

It was a beautiful thing to sleep the night through, without the all-too-present cry of the air raid siren.

It wasn't to last, of course, but the bombings did become more sporadic.

If nothing else, the rare nights offered a chance to rest and a welcome relief after weeks of onslaught. Farringdon Station had no doubt saved the lives of the many people who slept safely tucked underground beneath its fortified ceiling, but it was not ideal lodging. The floor was hard, the tea sold below was twice the cost of what a café would charge outside and the sounds of so many people shifting, talking, coughing and snoring echoed around at all hours. Not to mention the smells, which were best left without elaboration.

While it wasn't the luxury of sinking into the softness of one's own bed, sleeping a night without the interruption of a wailing siren, even on the floor of a tube station, was better than nothing.

As the season changed, the weather in England turned abysmal and never had Londoners been gladder for it. Fog, rain and high winds kept the Germans grounded often. Unfortunately, that only made the nights of attacks all the more brutal.

Newspapers were filled with information on bombed areas that offered censored details, citing a blanket statement of tragedy when they could not. And all the while they reminded Londoners their children could still be relocated to the country free of charge.

Grace could not imagine what it must be like for a child to experience the constant bombings. Like the boy who came to her readings.

The adolescent slowly became less skittish around Mrs. Weatherford. Her patient kindness reminded Grace of Colin, handling the frightened child with the care he'd shown with wounded animals. It was recollections such as those that struck the tender place inside Grace she knew would never heal.

Nothing could replace Colin.

But it was good to see Mrs. Weatherford slowly coming back to life.

It wasn't until midway through December that her perseverance finally paid off as the boy lingered after the reading to speak with her. Grace approached the two cautiously, worried she might run him off.

"He knows you're with me." Mrs. Weatherford waved her over. "Come meet Jimmy."

The boy doffed his cap and lowered his head, revealing the sorry state of his greasy hair, dark with dirt. His eyes lifted and met hers, brilliant, clear blue and large in his skinny face. "Thank you for all the readings you do. And for the food."

Behind the boy, Mr. Evans lifted his furry brows, as if to ask if his assistance was needed, but Grace gave a discreet shake of her head.

"It's our pleasure to help," Mrs. Weatherford replied. "Might I inquire as to where your parents are?"

Jimmy shifted from one foot to the other. "Dead."

Though Grace had been expecting the answer, she couldn't help the squeeze of sorrow. He was too young to be on his own.

"What happened to them?" Mrs. Weatherford prodded.

The boy lifted a shoulder. "They went out one night, just before an air raid, and never came back. Bombs, I suppose," he replied in a soft, almost childish voice. He rubbed his jaw where a sprinkling of soft, dark hair had begun to show.

"They told us—" His eyes bulged at his slip. "Me. They told *me* they'd be back soon and never returned."

But Mrs. Weatherford never was one for part of a story. "Us?" she pressed. "Come now, Jimmy. You know we mean you no harm."

He toed the floor with his scuffed shoe. "My sister, Sarah, and me." He flicked a bashful glance at Grace. "She likes your stories too. I worry bringing her out, with her being so young. But I share what you read when I go home."

"Come to our home for Christmas," Mrs. Weatherford said. "Bring your sister. I have some clothes you can have."

The latter part of her statement was said flippantly, but Grace knew it to be poignant. Those weren't simply "some clothes"; they had been Colin's.

The boy glanced about with obvious unease. "I'll think on it."

"Please do," Mrs. Weatherford said, and gave the address. "We'll have a lovely Christmas pudding and maybe some treacle tart."

Jimmy swallowed, as though he could already taste the sweetness. He nodded, murmured his thanks and quickly dashed from the store.

"You must join us too, Mr. Evans," Mrs. Weatherford called. "Better to be with us on Christmas than to be alone."

Mr. Evans stuck his head out from a shelf he'd sequestered himself behind. "Are you being meddlesome, woman?"

"Are you being a curmudgeon?" She pursed her lips and studied him expectantly.

He scoffed in reply.

"Arrive at two then?" she asked in a light tone, her eyes sparkling in a way Grace loved to see.

Mr. Evans disappeared behind a shelf. "Fine. Two."

Several days later, Grace was off from the bookshop and curled up on the sofa as she read *A Christmas Carol* by Charles Dickens. She'd read several of his works, but had specifically saved that one for Christmas.

The townhouse parlor had been decorated, but not in the usual fashion. The ornaments on the tree had lost their sparkle since the lights were required to be off during blackouts, and rather than boughs of fresh evergreen, they had to make do with painted newspaper garland. The festive cards had also been affected by the paper ration and wilted on the mantel, smaller than before and too thin to be properly propped upright.

It wasn't the kind of Christmas she'd had as a girl with her mother, but then no one had that kind of celebration anymore. Most people weren't even in London for the holiday. Not with the war on.

Anyone with relatives in the country found excuses to go see them. Well, anyone but her.

She was interrupted in the beginning pages of her book when a rattle sounded at the door before it swung open.

Mrs. Weatherford was already home, in the kitchen, preparing supper, working miracles with the things that passed as sausage these days. Which meant it could only be the one other person who had a key to the townhouse.

Viv.

Grace squealed with delight and bolted from the chair. Viv dropped her kit and responded in kind, bright vermillion lips parted in a wide smile.

Still lovely as ever with her red hair in rolled curls under her service cap, she managed to look far more chic in the khaki uniform than others did in their most stylish outfits.

"Grace." Viv threw her arms around her. The embrace

was still scented with a sweet perfume, though no longer as strong as it'd once been, and now harboring traces of damp wool and the nip from the air outside.

Grace squeezed her arms around her dearest friend. "It is so good to see you."

"It's been far, far too long." Viv put her icy hands to Grace's cheeks. "How I've missed you, Duckie."

"Viv?" Mrs. Weatherford pushed through the kitchen door and stared for a moment with tears gathering in her eyes. "Oh, it's so good to see you, love."

Viv grinned. "It's good to see you too." She went to Mrs. Weatherford and enfolded her arms around the older woman for a long moment. It reiterated her shared pain at Colin's death in a way that couldn't be conveyed in letters alone.

The agonized expression on Mrs. Weatherford's face against Viv's shoulder said she understood exactly. The older woman pushed back and dabbed at the corners of her eyes with a handkerchief. "You go get settled now and I'll put the kettle on. You can stay…" She swallowed. "You can stay in whatever room you like."

She rushed out before explaining what she meant. But then, no explanation was truly necessary.

Colin's room.

"I'd still like to share our room." Viv pulled off her service cap and set it on the hat shelf by the door. "After all, I've been sharing a room with three other ladies in the ATS all this time. That is, if you haven't become too used to having all that space to yourself."

"It's been far too lonely." Grace picked up Viv's kit before her friend could grab it, and carried it up the stairs.

Once in their shared room, Grace set her bag on the metal

rail bed Viv slept before, still immaculately made since its first washing after her departure.

While Viv unpacked, the two picked up right where they had left off, as if the gap of time between them had never passed.

Grace told her about gardening and their experience with cutworms, which made Viv laugh. She told Viv about Mrs. Weatherford and Colin and Jimmy, which made Viv cry, and she told her about the ARP warden position and working with Mr. Stokes. Grace omitted, however, the dangers of the job and the horrible sights she'd witnessed.

Not that it mattered when Viv knew her so well. After she'd finished sharing how things had gone on in London, Viv approached and gently touched the wristlet on Grace's arm. "It's worse here than I thought," she said softly. "You can try to mask it, but I know what the ARP wardens do. I know your job has great dangers."

"We all do our bit," Grace said, not wishing to delve into such matters on so happy an occasion as finally seeing her friend safely returned. "What of you? Everything you try to say gets blotted out by censors, so I'm left to supply my own details."

Viv's smile returned. "Oh? Then pray tell what it is I do in the war."

"You're a spy," Grace said. "You went to France and rescued several boats full of men during Dunkirk, then flew over to Germany in a mink stole to personally pry the secrets from Hitler himself. You did such a fine job of it, we have all the intelligence we need and the war will soon be over."

Viv laughed. "Oh, if only that were the case. I've actually been working as a radar operator, if you'd believe it."

She folded a pink cardigan and tucked it into a drawer. "As it turns out, I'm better at maths than I realized."

"I'm not surprised," Grace said earnestly. Her friend had always underestimated her own intelligence. "How is it working with radars?"

Viv sat back on her heels in front of the chest of drawers. "It's exciting, but it's also sad. We see the men off as they go to Germany to bomb. Some of the women are married to the men who fly out." Her mouth twisted as she appeared to bite the inside of her lip.

A lot went unspoken in this war. Far too much was easily assumed in the silence.

Grace had seen enough German planes shot down to know that whatever Britain gave to the Nazi bombers, they received right back. Not all of those men came home.

"The dance halls have been divine though." Viv got to her feet and pulled a bottle of red nail lacquer from her bedside table drawer where she'd left it before departing for the ATS. "The men there practically line up to dance the night away and dawn arrives before you know it."

She unscrewed the top, and a familiar sharp odor filled the room. It smelled like late nights at the farmhouse in Drayton, summer afternoons in a field, picking flecks of floating seed from the glossy polish surface and talks of someday going to London.

Grace smiled softly at the memories. Never would they have thought they'd be here, her working as an ARP warden as well as at a bookshop and Viv performing the task of radar operation with the ATS.

"Men have always lined up to dance with you," Grace teased.

"Not like this." Viv ran the brush over her thumbnail,

leaving a cherry red streak down its center. "Do you ever go to the West End?"

The West End of London, where hotels opened their basements as dance halls through the duration of the long nights. It was easy to get there, but not to return home since the tube stations closed at night for shelters and so many taxis refused to run amid the bombs. As a result, most people going to the dance halls would bring a fresh change of clothes and paid a fee that covered their entrance to the hall, a night in a room and a quick breakfast the following morning.

"I think you know me better than that." Grace settled onto her bed with her legs tucked underneath her.

Viv inspected a freshly painted nail then slid her gaze to Grace and laughed. "We must go. Everyone talks about what a lark the West End in London is at night. Trust me, you'll love it."

On her own, Grace would have hated it, she knew without a doubt. Not that she'd had the nights to spare anyway. But with Viv, she could see the possibility for a jolly good time.

Grace nodded. "Let's do it then."

Viv beamed. "You'll have the best time. I promise."

She wasn't wrong. The next night, Grace found herself at The Grosvenor House Hotel for one of their two-shilling cocktail dances. They'd donned their best swing dresses, Viv in a bright red confection with a crimped skirt that matched her nails and lips while Grace borrowed one of Viv's in ice blue with folded sleeves. They bundled up in warm coats against the bitter December freeze and took a hack to Park Street. The Grosvenor greeted them with a mound of sandbags piled high around its perimeter and its windows blacked out against the darkening sky.

They left their overnight bags at the front desk and were shown to the Great Room where the pulse of jazz reverberated off the glossy floors and high ceilings. People toward the front of the room whirled about on the dance floor, stockinged legs kicking out with the jitterbug and ladies swishing their hips with such enthusiasm their knickers peeked from beneath their swirling skirts.

Excitement pulsed through Grace, penetrating that ever-present fog of exhaustion that had encased itself around her in the past months.

Viv ordered two French 75s and met Grace's questioning look with a grin. "It's my favorite," Viv shouted over the blast of lively music. "They say it has more punch than a French 75mm. Meaning it will even get you out on the dance floor, Duckie."

The beverages arrived in tall glasses with bubbles dancing up their sides. The drink was tart and sweet with a fizz that tickled Grace's tongue and set a warmth glowing through her. It took only one to melt away her inhibitions and pull her toward the beat of the live band playing their souls out on the stage.

Grace and Viv danced on and on through the night, with soldiers, with men who had jobs that kept them from conscription, and even with each other. By the end of the night, Grace's cheeks hurt from laughing and her veins were still buzzing with the electricity of the night, the drinks and the joy of dancing.

It was the first time since the start of the Blitz, as the papers termed the interminable onslaught by Germany, that she'd been able to set it all aside. She didn't once think about the bombs, or the destruction they caused, or how no matter how hard she worked, she could never make the world right.

She was alive.

She was young.

And she was having fun.

This was what life in London was supposed to be for her and Viv—a celebration of youth and happiness and everything she'd set aside for far too long.

The effervescence of it all kept the smile hovering on her lips through the following morning after they freshened up and stepped out of the Grosvenor into a world of snow flurries and smoke.

In the daylight, the familiar odor of war hit Grace like a punch, and all the exhilaration crushed out of her. Rubble and fragments of broken glass littered the street just beyond the immaculately swept entryway to the hotel. Several fires still burned in the surrounding buildings, the oily scent on the air indicative of incendiaries.

It was then she realized the flecks whirling in the air weren't snow at all, but ash.

"Would you like me to ring you a taxi?" one of the hotel's attendants asked.

"How could this have happened while we were inside?" Grace asked through numb lips. "I never heard any of it."

"The sand bags." The attendant puffed his chest proudly. "We've so many, it blots out the bombings completely."

A chill threaded through Grace's veins that had nothing to do with the bite of icy wind. They were never informed of an air raid being sounded. It was all too easy to imagine what a bomb would have done to such a large roomful of people. Everyone dancing, carousing, oblivious. A shudder rippled down her back.

The realization was immediately replaced by the heavy press of guilt.

While residents were outside being bombed, losing their homes and their lives as volunteers worked all night to save who and what they could, Grace had been dancing.

A pain lashed through her. She could have been out here, helping. She could have been able to offer first aid, comfort, advice to the rescue crews on who might be where and in need. She could have manned a stirrup pump to help with dousing the flames. She could have—

Viv tucked Grace's arm in the crook of hers. "Come, let's go to the station."

"I could have helped." Grace let herself be led away, barely acknowledging the attendant's warning to mind their step.

"You could have been killed," Viv said, sharper than Grace had ever heard her speak.

In truth, they all could have been killed. Thick walls and sandbags didn't do much. Even underground. She'd heard of too many shelters whose occupants thought themselves safe, only to be bombed or buried in rubble.

And the hotel had never even told them of the air raid.

Their feet crunched over broken glass, and heat wafted toward them from a pile of shattered bricks with flames still burning somewhere within.

"You walk outside while this is going on?" Viv asked quietly.

"Of course," Grace frowned. "I should have been out here last night."

"No." Viv stopped in front of Grace and met her eyes. "You are working yourself ragged. You needed the distraction, at least for one evening, and I'm glad you took it." She looked around in horrified awe before turning her attention back to Grace. "Good God, the things you must see."

Then she threw her arms around Grace and squeezed her in a hug that smelled like the old Viv, all sweet floral perfume that overwhelmed the acrid odor in the air. "You're so brave," Viv whispered. "So very brave."

Brave.

The word took Grace aback. She wasn't brave. She was simply doing what any ARP warden would, what she'd been trained to do. Of all the words Grace might describe herself with, the last would be brave.

When Viv straightened, she wiped the underside of her eyes and looked up, fluttering her lashes with a self-deprecating laugh. "I'll ruin my makeup going on like this. Come, let's get home so you can have a proper rest before this afternoon."

Warmth flushed over Grace's cheeks at the reminder. George would be by to pick her up later that afternoon for a date. It had been over a year since she'd seen him last.

Several men she'd danced with the night before had asked her to dinner or for her to write. A few had even boldly asked her to kiss them, declaring hers might be the last lips they'd ever taste. She'd turned every one of them down, though as gently as possible, and took care not to dance with anyone more than once, lest they mistake her interest in them.

That afternoon, after a bit of a nap and a lot of fuss from Viv over exactly what dress to wear, they'd agreed on a cherry-red shirred dress in a silk Grace thought far too fancy and Viv insisted was exactly perfect. This was paired with matching pumps and a black purse with red piping. Her hair was styled in the latest fashion, courtesy of Viv, with reverse rolls curled back from her face.

Viv even managed to talk Grace into a bit of red lipstick, which admittedly did look becoming with the dress. It was the boldest outfit Grace had ever worn, and it made her feel as smooth as the silk of her last pair of new stockings.

"I think he may fall over when he sees you," Viv said with a rise of her perfectly plucked brows.

Grace's cheeks flushed at her reflection.

"Especially if you blush like that." Viv clapped her hands with delight and they made their way downstairs.

Mrs. Weatherford, who was waiting in the entryway for them, put a palm to her chest. "Oh, Grace."

Grace went hot all over, nervous that Mrs. Weatherford might declare it all too much. Certainly it was far more than Grace had ever done with so much red and in silk, no less.

"You're so very beautiful, my dear." Mrs. Weatherford shook her head and breathed out a long exhale. "If only your mum could see you now."

Before Grace could reply, the doorbell chimed and she nearly stumbled off the last step.

She and George had agreed on an early dinner to ensure they couldn't be interrupted by air raids and so she could still resume her shift that night as warden. A glance at her watch confirmed he was a minute early.

Mrs. Weatherford's mouth formed an O of anticipation, and she scooted back from the door so Grace could draw it open. It was all Grace could do not to yank the handle, and instead pulled it far slower than she truly wanted.

On the other side was George. The man to whom she'd written letters for months detailing every bit of her life, with whom she had shared her innermost thoughts. The man who had introduced her to the world of reading.

And now, for the first time in over a year, she was finally seeing him again.

SEVENTEEN

GRACE'S PULSE TRIPPED OVER ITSELF AS HER GAZE found the striking green eyes of George Anderson.

After so many months, there he was—in person, with his dark hair neatly combed to the side and wearing a crisp blue RAF uniform, his arms tucked patiently behind his back like a soldier at ease. His mouth opened as he took her in, but he didn't utter a single word.

He swallowed and cleared his throat then said, "Miss Bennett—Grace—you look…" He shook his head as though trying to find the right word.

Never had she seen him at a loss for what to say. In their previous interactions, he'd always been so smooth and confident. That she had rattled him gave her an undeniable thrill.

"Stunning," he said finally with a lopsided grin. "You look stunning."

He brought his arms from around his back and extended a

book toward her. The royal purple cover was embossed with
a gold image of a man standing on a barrel amid a group of
people with the looping title in gilt at its top. *Vanity Fair.*

"I would have arrived with flowers, but it appears they've
all been replaced with cabbages." He tilted the book as
though reconsidering it. "So I brought the next best thing.
I thought you might enjoy it, and you hadn't mentioned
reading this one yet in your letters."

"I haven't." Grace took the book, feeling suddenly shy
in front of this man whom she'd shared so much of herself
with. "And this is far better than flowers."

Grace turned inside the townhouse to set the book on
the small table by the door and found Mrs. Weatherford and
Viv watching with raised brows and wide, expectant smiles
stretched on their faces. Grace laughed. "Let me introduce
you to my dearest friends, Mrs. Weatherford and Viv."

George stepped into the townhouse and was introduced
first to Viv, who politely greeted him, then, once he'd turned
to Mrs. Weatherford, she fanned herself with openmouthed
appreciation.

For her part, Mrs. Weatherford tittered on with flushed
eagerness as she chatted with him about his return to London and asked after his family who lived in Kent.

Once introductions had been made, George returned to
Grace and offered her his arm. He led her outside and together they walked to a waiting taxi.

Her jittering nerves prior to his arrival melted into a bliss-
ful, electric happiness. There was something about knowing
one another's intimate musings and considerations. After all,
it was so much easier to share oneself by pen than voice, and
it had established between them an undeniable connection.

While it might be only their first proper date, they knew one another. What's more, they understood one another.

He opened the door for her to let her in before joining her in the close quarters of the cab. The scent of his shaving soap filled the small space, a familiar smell she recalled from their earlier interactions in the bookshop so long ago.

"I want to hear all about how your book readings are going," he prompted.

Grace told him of the people who came and the stories she read as he listened with a smile hovering on his lips. All the while, the taxi sailed through the streets, weaving through the occasional Diversion signs to avoid craters from bombs.

She'd expected they might dine at a small eatery, something like the Kardomah Café, whose layers of sandbags rendered it safe enough to double as an air raid shelter. So, when they stopped before the multiple arched entryway of the Ritz, her mouth went dry with shock.

Never had she been to a place so fine, exploring any possibility only in her imagination on late night chats with Viv while they were still locked in a doldrum life at Drayton.

"I thought…" Grace stammered. "I thought we were going to a café."

George grinned at her. "If I only have the opportunity to take you out once during my three-day pass home, I want to make it count." He exited the hack, then offered her his hand. "If that's all right."

She put her fingers to his warm palm and allowed him to help her from the taxi. "Quite."

He tucked her hand into the crook of his arm as attendants opened the doors to welcome them into the splendor of the Ritz. They were led into the dining area where many tables were set for two with fresh linens and plush chairs.

As grand as she had anticipated it might be, it was far, far grander.

There wasn't simply one chandelier, but several. They were all linked throughout the oval-shaped ceiling by garlands and seemed to drip down like jewels from a fine necklace. Every inch of the place was resplendent with opulence, from the scrollwork-patterned rug thick underfoot to the painted walls and ceilings.

It was as though they'd stepped into a pocket of London where the war didn't exist. Where people wore clothes that weren't sensible for running to a bomb shelter or stumbling over rubble-strewn streets. Where the scent of food in the air held luxuries like sugar and quality meat. Somewhere unseen, a pianist's fingers danced effortlessly over the keys, producing the most delicate tune that made her think of summer and laughter.

At the head of the room was a stately Christmas tree with not a scrap of painted newspaper to be seen among its glittering ornaments.

They were shown to a table set for two in the corner with a small bunch of what appeared to be dahlias in a vase on the table.

George grimaced at the flowers. "And all I could find were cabbages."

Grace laughed, giving way to the giddy rush racing through her. "You're not the Ritz."

The waiter arrived and presented them with the menu. At the top, in a fine looping script was Le Woolton Pie. Grace smiled, imaging Mrs. Weatherford's face when she found out the Ritz was serving Woolton pie with a fancy name.

Grace opted to forego Le Woolton Pie and chose a perfectly cooked roast beef instead, which emerged succulent and tender, a refreshing change from what they managed to purchase from the butcher, which often seemed more fat than meat.

George ordered the same with a carrot salad to start.

"Carrot salad?" Grace made a show of raising her brows. "Is it true that they help you see in the dark?"

"The government says they do." He winked.

Various posters had appeared recently encouraging carrot consumption and touting their ability to help people see in the dark. Especially pilots.

"And what do you say?" Though Grace asked the question playfully, she was indeed curious. After all, she'd been eating more carrots than usual and had noticed little different when on patrol in the blackout.

He grinned. "It works well enough for the Germans to start feeding them to the pilots too."

"Truly?"

He laughed and she realized he was intentionally edging around her question. It was something he did when it came to his efforts in the war. When she'd asked if he'd been in France, he'd replied with one word: Dunkirk. The guarded look on his face and the understanding of what he must have seen kept her from asking any more.

He was stationed at Acklington in Scotland with 13 Group as a fighter pilot who flew a Hawker Hurricane. And he'd been at Dunkirk. Outside of those few bits of information, she knew little else. With the sensitivity of sharing details about the war, especially regarding the RAF, Grace was well aware there was a lot that couldn't be said.

After all, loose lips sink ships. Be like dad and keep mum. And all those other slogans about staying silent.

"Now tell me, how did you know I would love *The Count of Monte Cristo*?" she asked.

This was a topic he could speak on freely, as was evidenced by the way his handsome green eyes lit up. "Everyone loves *The Count of Monte Cristo*."

"It seems you did especially." She trailed off her words and took a sip of wine, hoping he would fill her in on the story behind the old book.

"My grandfather gave it to me." Tenderness touched George's smile. "Every year when I was a boy, we would take the train to Dorset to stay in his cottage. It's on one of the cliffs, overlooking the sea. There's an extensive library." He widened his hands to reflect its enormity. "It takes up half the house and is filled with classics. But that one was always my favorite. Once I attended university, I couldn't go anymore, so he had the book mailed to me."

"Dorset." Grace leaned back in her seat and gave a wistful smile. "I've heard it's beautiful."

"It is." George curled his fingers around his wineglass, his head tilted in musing. "I miss it, the way the wind smells of the ocean, and how it tugs insistently at my hair and clothes when I stand near the edge of the cliff. On fine days, we would go down to the beach where the sand is hot and the water is cold."

Grace could imagine herself there in that moment, the pull of the fierce coastal breeze at her own hair and clothes. "It sounds lovely."

"Maybe someday you'll have to go." He lifted his glass to her in a silent toast and drank a sip of wine.

The waiter appeared then with the most decadent meal Grace had ever been served. While they ate, she recounted how life in London had changed and he told her about two other pilots he'd become friends with back in Scotland, sharing what bits and pieces of his life that he was allowed.

Graced glanced at the blacked-out window beside their table. "It doesn't even feel as though the war is on while we're here."

George gazed around the room. "We could pretend, if you're game?"

"Pretend?" Grace smiled even as she repeated the word. She hadn't pretended at anything since she'd been a child. It felt so silly and impractical that it immediately drew her appeal.

"Oh yes." He took a sip of wine, his head tilted in consideration. "As though the war never happened. You're working at a bookshop, a lovely store assistant with a sharp mind and a keenness for good books."

Grace couldn't help but chuckle. "And you're a charming engineer with an affinity for literature and a wonderful sense of humor who always knows how to say the right things."

He gave a laugh that made his smile look almost boyish. "I'll take it. Tomorrow, we'll have plans to walk through the streets as snow sifts around us like down feathers, listening to the carolers singing at Hyde Park. I'll have a handful of flowers for you." He lifted a brow and eyed the small vase of purple-red dahlias pointedly. "Roses, I think."

"And we will find a theater that's playing *A Christmas Carol*," she added.

"I love that book." George paused as a waiter approached to ensure they had all they needed. "It might be a bit childish, but I read it every year around this time. I'm actually in the middle of it now."

"I am too," Grace confessed. "I was saving it for just before Christmas."

"Charles Dickens always writes a thoroughly detailed and memorable tale."

Charles Dickens happened to be a particular favorite of Grace's as well, and the mere mention made her sit forward with excitement. "Have you read *The Pickwick Papers* yet?"

His eyes narrowed in thought. "I'm sure I have, only it's been ages. I can't say I remember it."

"Oh you must read it again." Grace leaned closer to him in her enthusiasm. "Mr. Pickwick and several of his companions, the 'Pickwickians,' go on a journey through the English countryside. It's quite the adventure with so many laughs, like—" She put her fingertips to her mouth to suppress the scene she'd been about to recall. "I don't want to spoil it. You'll have to read it and be surprised all over again."

His whole face smiled as her watched her, his eyes practically twinkling. "Consider it done. I'll be sure to let you know some of my favorite scenes in my next letter."

On and on their conversation went, lush with descriptions of books they'd read and recalling things they had shared with one another in their letters, expanding on details that were too lengthy to write.

It was so easy to put off the bombings in such company, in such a lovely room; to forget the ration's meager meals when dining on fresh beef in a hearty, aromatic sauce, to dream away the world outside when she was so focused on George.

All too soon, their date drew to a close as Grace needed to return for her ARP shift that evening and George had to catch one of the last tubes back to Kent to spend Christmas in Canterbury with his parents.

As Grace and George rode home in a hackney, the flow of conversation ebbed to a companionable silence as if they were both savoring the connection between them one last time until their next meeting. George saw her out of the vehicle and up to the doorway where the full effect of the blackout cloaked the stoop of the townhouse in a curtain of privacy.

Grace paused at the door, little more than half a step from him. It was the closest they'd been all night, save when they were side by side in the cab. She luxuriated in his clean scent and tried to sear every second of the magical night into her mind forever.

"Thank you for the most wonderful evening," she said, her voice breathier than usual. But then, how could she possibly speak normally when she could barely breathe.

"I confess, I've thought of this night for many months." George's hand found hers. It was a gentle touch in the dark, followed by the intentional curling of his warm fingers around hers.

Her skin tingled with anticipation like the moment of static in the air before a lightning storm. "As have I."

"I've enjoyed our letters," he said, his voice low, intimate. "However, I know war can be difficult. If you would prefer to leave yourself open for a man in London—"

"No," Grace replied too quickly.

They both laughed, shy, nervous chuckles.

"I look forward to every letter you write." She ran her thumb over the back of his hand, exploring the newfound closeness. "And whenever I encounter something quizzical or amusing, you and Viv are the first ones I think I must share it with in my next letter."

"I have no right to ask you to wait for me." He closed the half step between them, and the air became nearly too thin to breathe. "We don't know how long this war will go on."

"You're worth waiting for, George Anderson." Her pulse raced.

He lifted his free hand, gently touching the left side of her cheek and lowered his mouth to hers. It was a sweet, tender kiss that robbed her of all thought.

He wasn't as eager as Simon Jones had been back in Drayton, and she was glad for it.

George wasn't that kind of man. He was thoughtful and careful and put his soul into everything he did. Though the kiss was gentle and light, it touched her in a deep place she knew would forever belong to him.

"Good evening, my beautiful Grace." He swept his forefinger down her chin, lingering a second before regretfully falling away. "I look forward to your next letter. Promise me you'll be safe."

"Only if you do as well." She gazed into his eyes, already lost in them. "I'm eager for your return already."

He grinned at her, a flash of white teeth in the darkness. Grace pushed through the front door, startling Viv and Mrs. Weatherford, who had been curiously close in the entryway.

Mrs. Weatherford looked guiltily at the ceiling as Grace shut the door.

"Taking tea in the entryway?" Grace teased.

"Oh, do stop." Viv waved her hand. "You know full well we were trying to listen in on you. It was quite rude of you both to speak so softly that we couldn't hear a word."

The hack's engine outside rumbled, carrying George away. Who knew when they'd see one another again? Months, if they were lucky.

She touched her fingers to her mouth where the warmth of his lips still lingered. She would wait those months happily for him. Years even, if that's what it took.

There wasn't another man like George Anderson.

"Well." Mrs. Weatherford puffed with impatience. "Do tell us."

With the older woman being in better spirits than Grace had seen her since before Colin left for war, she couldn't help but share all the details. Well, nearly all. She left that kiss tucked closely against her heart. For her and her alone.

Christmas lacked many of the luxuries Grace had enjoyed in London the previous year. Carolers were absent from the streets due to the constant bombing. All the theaters that might have once been open were now few and far between, many having been rendered inoperable by damage.

But by some miracle, Grace and Viv managed to squeeze into a show for a pantomime on Christmas Eve, a festive play that recalled them back to their childhood, though the production was far better than what they'd had in Drayton. On Christmas Day, Mrs. Weatherford, as always, followed the rules to conserve fuel by cramming the oven full of crockery in an attempt to cook all their food at once, which was quite the accomplishment in light of the feast she'd prepared.

As everything Mrs. Weatherford did when it came to rationing in the kitchen, she made it work beautifully. The government had doubled their tea and sugar rations in preparation for Christmas, and Mrs. Weatherford put those to good use as well, in addition to her secreted stores.

There was treacle tart and figgy pudding and Christmas cake, though the latter was missing most of the dried fruit usually prevalent through the confection. All of it was adorned with frosted bits of holly, made by soaking the waxy green leaves in Epsom salts—a festive suggestion from the Ministry of Food.

Though Mrs. Weatherford remained seemingly in high spirits, Grace could see the cracks in her forced joviality. It came in the moments she thought no one was looking, when the smile wilted from her lips and a pained look pinched at her features in a sudden onset of agony.

Grace knew that hurt.

Loss.

For Colin.

His absence was felt like a missing limb. No—a missing heart.

His smile, his kindness, his light—no Christmas would ever be the same without him. And no amount of frosted holly leaves or painted newspaper garland could make that go away.

Though they'd agreed to no presents that year in light of conserving for the war efforts, they all had a little something for each other. Mrs. Weatherford had procured scented soaps for both Grace and Viv. Viv had knit them both thick mufflers, and Grace had managed to get Mrs. Weatherford and Viv a bit of chocolate. It was wrapped in wax paper as the foil was now needed for materials, and the chocolate was crumblier and less sweet than it was before. But seeing them beam with delight upon opening their gifts told Grace that chocolate would still always be chocolate, no matter how it came.

Dinner was as delicious as it was lovely, the addition of sugar a magical touch in such restrictive times. Mr. Evans came with a bottle of wine he'd been saving for just such an occasion, and he and Mrs. Weatherford spent a good part of the afternoon bickering with each other like siblings, each with a good-natured twinkle in their eye.

Jimmy and his sister, however, did not join them, and

their absence was very much felt. Most especially by Mrs. Weatherford. The package under the unlit tree with Colin's old clothes, altered to accommodate Jimmy's skinny frame, was left where it lay alongside another bundle of several girls' dresses and a coat Viv had tailored for his sister.

Viv had to return to Caister the following day. It was a sad realization that sifted like ash over the fleeting joy Christmas had brought and left the townhouse feeling darker and more alone than ever.

Mrs. Weatherford, especially, was affected by Viv's departure, as though she were losing Colin all over again. The only time she managed to rouse herself from the house was the day after Boxing Day when she went to Grace's afternoon reading at Primrose Hill Books with a great box of leftover Christmas cake, several rolls and the children's presents.

Jimmy arrived, albeit shamefaced when he saw Mrs. Weatherford, but didn't run from her and Grace after the reading.

"They were feeding us at the rest center." He took his cap off, his expression heavy with remorse. "I didn't want to take your rations."

The boy's consideration, in a devastated world when he had nothing and they had so much by comparison, needled into Grace's chest.

"You needn't ever worry about us," she said.

"We had far more than we could possibly eat." Mrs. Weatherford set the box before him and lifted the top.

She'd set the Christmas desserts in a large glass bowl nestled beside the wrapped presents for Jimmy and his sister.

He looked up in surprise. "You're sharing too much."

Mrs. Weatherford waved him off. "I made it for you both, and you weren't there to eat it."

"Open the larger package," Grace urged, knowing what it would mean to Mrs. Weatherford to see him unwrap the gift.

Jimmy hesitated only a moment before drawing the parcel from the box. He didn't rip into the package as children often do. Instead, he untied the string holding the parcel together, wound it around his hand into a neat bundle and set it inside the box. Only then did he gingerly fold back the paper so as not to cause a single tear.

It was the care of someone who had nothing, someone who knew they might have need of such materials later. It wasn't only the item inside that was the gift, but the wrapping as well.

He stared for a long while at the clothes. Three collared shirts, three pairs of trousers, two pullovers and a thick coat.

All at once, he sniffed hard and swiped at his nose with the sleeve of his dirty jacket.

"It's too much," he croaked in a thick voice. He lifted a watery gaze at them, his mouth pressed hard together.

Mrs. Weatherford shook her head. "It's not nearly enough."

That afternoon, Mrs. Weatherford cast off the weight of her sorrow and marched back to the WVS to resume her aid. This time she homed her focus in on seeing to the orphans of the Blitz. She went at the task with fire and purpose, which was as true a Christmas miracle as Grace had ever seen.

Two evenings later, Grace was preparing herself for another shift for the night period with Mr. Stokes when the air raid siren screamed through the peaceful quiet. The sound of it nearly startled Grace. The nights since Christmas Eve had been quiet in London, an unspoken ceasefire. Overhead, the thick clouds indicated the night was not ideal for bombing, especially not so early in the evening.

Though it was only a few minutes past six, Grace led Mrs. Weatherford to Farringdon Station to join the queue of people waiting to get in and rushed to the ARP post. After all, there was no sense in being in the shelter for less than an hour, especially when an opportunistic entrepreneur might claim her spot on the tube station floor and try to sell it to a tardy soul later for two shillings.

Mr. Stokes was already at the post when she arrived, clearly having had the same idea. He smirked when he saw her, his thin lips stretched beneath his mustache. "The German planes are early tonight."

"It would have been polite to at least wait until our night shift started." Grace buckled her tin hat under her chin with a leather strap.

Mr. Stokes grumbled his agreement.

Outside, the vibration of passing planes reverberated with such intensity, Grace could feel the engines humming through the soles of her shoes.

This night would be bad.

She left the safety of the sandbag-laden post and went out into the wet chill of a late December night. However, it was not blackness that met her eyes, but a glow of orange in the distance, where a nearby part of London was on fire. Close to the Thames. By St. Paul's Cathedral.

The planes rattled by overhead, emptying their bellies to strike an area several streets over. As objects fell, they spilled out small cylinders and a familiar sound met Grace's ears. A swish, followed by the tapping of dozens of these sticks crashing through roofs and striking the pavement, violently sputtering flames upon impact.

"Incendiaries," Grace called out to Mr. Stokes as she slung the coil of tubing for the stirrup pump over her shoulder.

She didn't have to look behind her to know he followed closely. They both knew there were mere minutes between them and the many new fires that could easily flare out of control.

Two streets over, they found the first incendiary, sparkling with white splinters of light as it furiously expelled its magnesium innards. Nearly all doorsteps now had either a bucket of water, sand or even sandbags set out in preparation. Grace grabbed a sandbag, hefting its weight before her face to protect herself, and dropped it atop the glare of light. As the bag burned, it would spill out the sand and douse the sparks before they could do any damage. There was no need to wait to see if it would be effective. Not when there were so many more.

"Miss Bennett," Mr. Stokes called. Already he had his foot set on the stirrup pump beside the bucket with the hose extended to Grace.

She grabbed it and ran toward the nearest house where several bushes were on fire, pressing the switch on the nozzle to go from jet to spray until the flames were extinguished.

As always, they had to have a care to avoid the magnesium, which would explode upon contact with water. This was only a concern in the beginning of the fire when the incendiary was casting out its brilliant green-white sparks, but one that was exceedingly dire.

On and on they repeated their actions down the length of the street, putting flames out with sandbags and spray, alternating at the stirrup pump lest one of them tire too quickly.

Finally, they managed to control all the fires. Panting, they sagged against the wall of a building they'd just extinguished, tired and hot despite the December night, but victorious.

Another barrage of planes buzzed overhead.

Swish.

Grace's stomach slithered to her toes.

Plop.

The first incendiary struck the pavement several yards from their feet and sputtered to life with a hiss of sparks.

Plop.

A second fell not even a breath later.

It was no longer possible to identify an individual incendiary falling, not when so many clattered around them, like kirby grips being dumped from a tin.

All at once, Grace and Mr. Strokes were fighting a fresh wave of magnesium flames that lit up the street like daylight. They turned the corner of the block as they battled the blaze, and Grace realized they were on Aldersgate Street, near the fire station. Except it too was on fire, its firefighters outside the burning walls with water jetting from a wheeled water tank.

In the distance, toward the mouth of the river, came another familiar drone. Another swish. And the raining of more incendiary bombs upon London.

The firemen battling for control of their own station would be of little help. There was nothing for it, but to fight.

No matter how long that battle may be.

Grace and Mr. Stokes managed to put out the fires in their sector while the blaze near the river grew brighter.

They'd passed Primrose Hill Books several times to ensure it remained secure, confirming it had indeed. Mr. Evans had taken to keeping Mrs. Weatherford company in Farringdon Station. At least Grace could be at ease knowing they were both safe.

While the sky glowed with orange and red intensity, the bookshop remained quietly tucked in the shadows of the blackout. It was on one such check-up that they came upon a fireman, his face streaked with soot and glossy with sweat.

"If your sector is clear, we need help." His gait increased to a run as he pointed in the distance. "Paternoster Square. Bring whatever you can."

EIGHTEEN

A CHILL PRICKLED DOWN GRACE'S SPINE DESPITE THE heat caused by her exertions. What of the booksellers' district on Paternoster Row, which connected to the square? What of Simpkin Marshalls who so readily provided all the books to the bookshop? What of the printers and publishers and all the many stores?

Grace and Mr. Stokes wasted no time. Armed with their stirrup pump and an empty bucket, they followed the fireman, running several blocks. The blaze became more visible with each step, glowing as if it were one solid inferno with firefighters on all sides, spraying the flames from their taxi-drawn wagons.

The thundering report of the ack-ack guns firing at the Germans was louder too, along with the whistling of dropping bombs and the inevitable explosions that followed.

The closer Grace and Mr. Stokes drew to Paternoster

Square, the hotter the air became, until it was like trying to breathe in an oven.

"Grace, we need to stop," Mr. Stokes panted at her side, bending over to catch his breath.

He said something else, but a bomb whistled nearby, went silent for a breath of a moment, then detonated with a deafening explosion that set the ground underfoot rumbling.

"We can't stop now." She picked up her pace, running at full tilt, rounding the corner of Paternoster Row and stopping.

Where holy men once blessed the streets, hell had descended.

Choking plumes belched up from the flames and singed pages scattered through the debris-ridden street like the feathers from wings that had been ripped apart.

The street glowed red with the consuming conflagration, yet several buildings remained untouched, most likely those whose owners employed fire watchers on their roofs. Though they were few and far between.

The stores full of dry books were like tinder waiting for a match. Most had fire crawling across their slate roofs, dancing wickedly over their costly wood interiors and stretching out from their shattered windows, the exterior paintwork blackening with soot.

Simpkin Marshalls, who often touted their stock of millions of books, burned like a funeral pyre.

The building to Grace's right blazed brighter as though it were igniting from within. Inside, shelves of books were being licked apart by flames as they raced with greedy delight over rows and rows of neatly organized spines.

The building seemed to pulse, as if it were a breathing beast, set on devouring everything in its path.

Someone called her name and the beast of a building roared, powerful and terrifying.

She couldn't move. Couldn't tear her gaze from the horrific scene before her. So many books. Millions. Gone.

Something solid collided with her, knocking her to the ground. She landed hard as a blast of blistering heat rushed at her. Bits of sand and dust stung her cheeks and the backs of her hands.

Dazed and momentarily bewildered, she blinked up to find Mr. Stokes covering her with his body. The heaving building was now rubble, its tumbled bricks glowing red.

"Are you hurt?" Mr. Stokes shouted over the cacophony of war.

Grace shook her head. "We need to find water."

He looked around sadly. "We need to find survivors."

He was right, of course. The fire was too great to contain. All around them firemen were emptying their tanks into the blaze to no effect.

Pritchard & Potts was only several shops away from Grace, one of the few that was absent flames, though a chunk appeared to be missing where a blast had caught its right side and demolished the shop beside it.

Fortunately, Paternoster Square wouldn't have many people in the buildings, with most having gone to the country, intent on returning in the new year. But some had nowhere to go.

Like Mr. Pritchard.

He would be in his flat above Pritchard & Potts without a doubt. Especially when he had so often decried public shelters, complaining about those who littered the floors of the tube stations and bricked-up buildings.

Grace rushed over to the shop and found the door missing, blown off by the bomb that had struck it. Inside, the bookstore was dark, lit only by the glowing flames coming in through the shattered windows. Books had been thrown from their shelves and littered the floor, splayed and broken like fallen birds.

A whistle sounded outside, followed by a crash that made the entire structure tremble. Plaster sprinkled down from the ceiling, and several more books tumbled from their shelves.

"Mr. Pritchard," she called out.

He did not reply.

This was no time for decorum. She found the door leading to his flat and didn't bother to knock as she rushed up the stairs. Even as she did so, the building seemed to sway slightly, unsteady on its foundation.

By the flickering orange light from outside, she searched the flat, its state in as much disrepair as the shop below. Her breath caught as she noticed what appeared to be a skinny leg jutting from beneath a tipped curio cabinet.

"Mr. Pritchard," she said again.

When she received no response, she knelt by the cabinet, confirming it was indeed the old man beneath. She shoved at the furniture to no avail. A bomb crashed somewhere nearby, and the building shuddered as if it wished to crumble in on itself.

It very well might.

But the cabinet did not matter, not after she tried to find a pulse in the limp, slender wrist. There would be no saving Mr. Pritchard.

He was already dead.

Another bomb crashed, this one with such force, Grace's balance faltered. That's when she heard it, a pathetic mewling cry.

She rushed to the sound, straining, and looked beneath the sofa to find a very frightened Tabby. She scooped him up with such haste, he did not bother trying to fight her. Instead, he clung to her as she raced from the building.

Outside, Mr. Stokes was standing in the middle of the street while fires raged on either side of him. Men with the AFS pointed their hoses into the flames, their uniforms soaked with runoff from the brass nozzles, but still they didn't move from their position.

Mr. Stokes glanced at Tabby and said nothing. "Any other survivors?"

The image of Mr. Pritchard pressed lifelessly beneath the cabinet flashed in her mind. She hugged Tabby a little tighter and shook her head.

Wind swept through the narrow alley, fanning the flames into wild excitement and sending flecks of sparks shooting every which way. The heat around them expanded, pressing in on Grace until she felt as though the marrow of her bones was melting like wax.

When she was a girl, she'd thought the glowing embers in the fireplace beautiful, like fire fairies. There was nothing beautiful or magical now. The flames were cruel in their greed and merciless in their destruction.

"We need to leave." Mr. Stokes's face glistened with sweat, and his eyes darted over the swelling fires. "They've no water to spare. There's nothing we can do here."

She took Tabby with them as there was nowhere to leave him, depositing him at St. Paul's Cathedral, which remained blessedly free of flames thus far. One of the parishioners who sought refuge there offered to mind the cat for Grace, enfolding the small frightened feline into her arms.

After that, Grace and Mr. Stokes returned to the blazing streets. The planes were overhead still, not visible in the haze of smoke, but audible with their droning engines and the repeated dropping of bombs and the maddening plop, plop, plop of incendiaries.

A firefighter stood in front of a burning building, the hose in his hand limp and empty. "They've bombed the mains," he said as they approached to help.

"What of the water relays from the Thames?" Mr. Stokes asked.

The water relays were there as a safety measure in the event the bombings cut the water mains that fed the hydrants. The Thames could then be tapped as a water source.

The man didn't turn from where he watched the fire devour the building, his gaze bright with helplessness. "The tide is too low."

Grace's skin prickled with the intense heat. "You mean…?"

The man lowered his head in defeat. "There's no water. We have no choice but to let these fires burn themselves out."

And burn themselves out they did. While Grace and Mr. Stokes went on to try to help any people who might have survived, the firemen could only watch as the flames consumed building after building with insatiable greed, jumping from one to another the way it'd done nearly three hundred years prior during the Great Fire of London. The inferno had rendered central London to char and ash then and appeared to be doing so again.

She shuddered to recall the scenes she'd read in *Old St. Paul's* by William Harrison Ainsworth when the great fire devoured London. Except she couldn't stop it as the main character had.

Grace and Mr. Stokes continued to rescue who they could

as the longest night of her life pressed onward. Through it
all, she drew from a stream of desperate energy she didn't
know she could possess when so thoroughly fatigued.

After what felt like a lifetime, the morning came, bringing
with it an end to the hours of bombing and perpetual dropping of incendiaries. Smoke still hovered in a thick blanket
over the ruined buildings that crackled with fires that could
not be extinguished.

Exhausted and defeated by so much destruction, Grace
made her way toward St. Paul's in the hopes of collecting
Tabby. Dread gripped her in its icy grasp as she strode toward the cathedral through smoke too thick to discern if
the old church still stood.

She held her breath, hoping it too hadn't fallen prey to
the attack as the rest of Paternoster Square had.

Suddenly a gust of wind blew, its chill startling against
the heat of smoldering brickwork and flames. The plumes
shifted and rolled as they cleared away to reveal a patch in
the sky and the miraculously unmarred dome of St. Paul's
Cathedral.

During the first Great Fire, the cathedral continued to
stand for three days before finally falling. It had been rebuilt
and still stood now. But it was so much more than simply a
building. It was a place of worship, of succor for lost souls.

It was a symbol that in the middle of hell, good had still
prevailed.

It was a mark of the British spirit, that even in the face
of such annihilation and loss, they too had kept standing.

"London can take it," Mr. Stokes said in a gravelly voice
from beside Grace. The ethereal sight had clearly moved him

with the same flood of patriotism as he echoed the slogan the government had encouraged since the start of the Blitz.

Even more astonishing, Tabby had remained put, now wrapped in a thin blanket and contentedly sleeping at the end of a pew. Grace lifted the pale blue bundle with her soot-blackened hands, and Tabby blinked awake with his amber eyes.

No sooner had she lifted the small cat against her than he nestled close, clinging with gentle claws. Cat properly in hand, Grace allowed Mr. Stokes to walk her back to the townhouse on Britton Street, too tired to argue that he needed to be home in bed as much as she. Regardless of their exhaustion, and though it was never discussed, they took the longer path to curl around the front of Primrose Hill Books, where it still sat as snug and safe as it had ever been.

She appreciated that the shop remained unharmed, especially when so many had experienced such loss.

Mr. Evans was no doubt back in his flat above the shop after the all clear had sounded early that morning.

Not all homes or people were as lucky. In their sector in Islington, many homes had roof damage from the incendiaries, and a number of properties had been bombed. However, the destruction was nowhere near the devastation of Paternoster Row.

Now, away from such a blazing inferno, the air was colder and a shiver ran down Grace's back.

Mr. Stokes simply nodded at her when they arrived at her townhouse before he turned to stagger slowly in the direction of his own home on Clerkenwell Street. Mrs. Weatherford pulled the door open before Grace had finished climbing the stairs.

"Grace." Mrs. Weatherford put her hand to her neck as if

she was struggling to breathe. "Oh, thank God you're safe, my girl. Come in, come in."

Grace was too tired to do much more than trudge up the remaining steps and into the townhouse. Her throat burned from hours of breathing in the hot air, and her chest felt as though it was clogged with soot.

"I heard it was awful." Mrs. Weatherford closed the door and fluttered anxiously around Grace. "Was it? No, don't answer that. I can see it on you that it was. My poor dear. Thank God you're safe, you're home. Do you want a spot of tea? Some food? Can I get you anything at all?" She paused in her worried onslaught and looked at the bundle Grace carried.

The weather was so cold outside that the heavy fog seemed laced with shards of ice. Once they were away from the inferno of London's center, Grace had covered Tabby with the blanket to ensure he'd remain warm. Now, she peeled the thin layer of cloth back, revealing a sleepy-eyed cat who had experienced just as terrible a night as them all.

Mrs. Weatherford put her fingers over her lips. "That isn't…is that…?"

"Tabby," Grace croaked through her raw throat.

Mrs. Weatherford touched a hand to Grace's cheek in silent emotion, then let it come to rest on Tabby's head. "You were the last—" Her voice caught. "You were the last wounded creature Colin saved." Suddenly remembering herself, she looked up sharply at Grace. "Mr. Pritchard."

Grace shook her head. She'd made sure the rescue crews knew his location so that his remains would be seen to properly. "I hoped you would keep Tabby," Grace said hoarsely. "He's very frightened, I believe, and could use someone to love."

Mrs. Weatherford gave a shuddering exhale. "I feel very much the same, little Tabby." She lifted the cat from Grace's arms, bundle of cloth and all.

Grace bathed after that, leaving smears of black soot in the small bathroom, but too exhausted to care. She'd meant to clean it when she woke, but found it already done later, practically gleaming with the telltale scent of a good carbolic cleanse.

Downstairs, she found Mrs. Weatherford, who waved off her thanks while cooing over Tabby. For the cat's part, he appeared to be just as besotted with Mrs. Weatherford as he stretched up to rub his face against hers. Much to her delight.

After the quick meal of vegetable and rabbit stew, Grace left the townhouse to make her way to the bookshop. After all, life went on and she still had a job to do.

There was a bite in the damp air that made her suck in her breath as soon as it hit her. The odor of burning hung acrid on the wind and recalled everything from the night before.

"It's you," a curt voice came from the other stoop next door.

Grace blinked against the cold to find Mrs. Nesbitt standing stiffly at the railing of her townhouse. Soot was smeared over her otherwise neat macintosh and her eyes were red-rimmed.

She elevated her head to tilt her glare over her sharp nose. "I've just been to my shop. Or what's left of it."

Such a sight surely must have been devastating. Grace turned fully to Mrs. Nesbitt, genuine in her empathy. "I'm terribly sorry."

"You should be," the other woman hissed.

Grace ought to be used to Mrs. Nesbitt's stinging rebukes, but those barbs never failed to strike their mark. "I beg your pardon?"

"You were out there last night." Mrs. Nesbitt pinched at her gloves, angrily removing them, one finger at a time. "You could have done more. Were it not for the stock I keep here at the townhouse, I would have nothing left. Nothing." She jerked the gloves from her hands and slapped them into one bare palm. "There is no excuse for so many businesses to have burned like that. None."

It was on the tip of Grace's tongue to defend her actions and those of the many volunteers who had fought last night. There had been too many incendiaries dropped. The mains had been hit, and the Thames had its lowest tide of the year at that exact time. But she owed no justification to this woman. Not when she and everyone else had given it their all.

Anger singed away the chill in the air.

The report on the wireless that morning had stated over a dozen firefighters had been killed, and over two hundred were injured. Brave men whose families would never welcome them home again, tell them they loved them again.

"How fortunate for you that several people lost their lives fighting the fires last night," Grace said in a hard tone. "There are now openings for you to fill, as the rest of us are clearly so inept."

Mrs. Nesbitt's cheeks went red. "You impudent—"

But Grace was already jogging down the remainder of the stairs, not bothering to listen anymore. Not when it was too tempting to march up to the other woman and slap her bony face.

Steam huffed from Grace's lips in white puffs, and she walked so fast that the muscles in her legs burned with the effort. Primrose Hill Books appeared before her without her realizing how quickly she'd gone.

She shoved in the door harder than she meant to.

Mr. Evans snapped his head up. "Miss Bennett?"

"That woman," Grace declared with all the vehemence she'd been swallowing. "That horrid woman."

"There's no one in the store at the moment." He came around the counter, folded his hands and rested them where the swell of his belly had once jutted. "Tell me what's happened."

Grace told him what Mrs. Nesbitt had said and relayed what had happened the night before, faltering when she shared Mr. Pritchard's passing.

Mr. Evans exhaled thickly through his nose, his gaze distant. "He never did see the point in going to a shelter. It's a pity how many share that opinion." He shook his head slowly. "The poor bloke. Thank you for caring for Tabby."

"I think Mrs. Weatherford is glad to have him."

Mr. Evans gave a ghost of a smile. "He'll do her good, I think. And as for Mrs. Nesbitt..."

The mere mention of the woman's name caused Grace to simmer anew with rage.

"I think," he said slowly, "Mrs. Nesbitt is so wounded by what's happened to her shop that she's lashing out at the first person she can." Mr. Evans tilted his head in apology. "And that happened to be you."

"She didn't have to be so cruel." Grace was being petulant, she knew, but the woman was truly odious.

Mr. Evans adjusted his thick glasses. "You recently read *A Christmas Carol* as I recall."

Grace nodded.

"You saw how Ebenezer's unhappy childhood made him

who he was. Imagine how he might feel if his business burned to the ground."

It was an apt comparison between Ebenezer Scrooge and Mrs. Nesbitt to be sure. One Grace had never thought to put together before that moment. But it was true how anger could be used to mask hurt, especially when hurt was such a very vulnerable emotion.

Even Mr. Evans had used his gruffness to mask his memories of his daughter when Grace had first started to work at the bookshop.

Who knew what Mrs. Nesbitt had experienced in her life to make her so hard and bitter?

It was a fresh understanding Grace had never stopped to examine before.

"Thank you," she said. "I never thought to consider it in that fashion."

Mr. Evans patted her cheek affectionately, the way a father might do. "You've a good soul, Grace Bennett."

"And you're an excellent teacher."

She thought about that conversation through the day as she worked. It made her reevaluate even her own uncle. Ugliness in a person was not born, but created. Perhaps he had endured a hardship that had made him so cruel.

Suddenly she regarded him in a different light. Not with anger, but compassion. And with the knowledge that his mistreatment had nothing to do with her, and everything to do with him.

She mulled over all of this as she stared at the empty shelf in front of her, which had been cleared out the day before to make way for a new order expected to come in from Simpkin Marshalls. An order that would now no longer be fulfilled.

An idea struck.

"I wonder…" Grace said aloud. "If we might set up a small area of the shop for the booksellers of the Paternoster Row bombing."

Mr. Evans, who was engrossed in a book some paces away, looked up at her over the rim of his glasses. "How so?"

"We can offer space to any of the shops who have books that weren't burned and can keep track of whose stock they belong to when sold." After all, she and Mr. Evans had tailored their recordkeeping into an immaculate art. "Then the owners can still generate a profit from at least some of their stock."

"It might be a difficult task to take on," Mr. Evans hedged.

"Do you doubt me?"

"Never." Mr. Evans's face broke out in a grin. "Take all the shelves you need."

He allowed Grace to leave early that afternoon, to set off on her mission to see how best to get in touch with the owners from the bookshops on Paternoster Row. It would be Grace's first time seeing the booksellers' hub since the fires the night before, and her trepidation grew with every demolished building she passed. The odor of smoke preceded her arrival, and her stomach sank at what would meet her eyes.

NINETEEN

THERE WAS HARDLY ANYTHING LEFT OF PATERNOSTER
Row. Its remains lay beneath a shroud of smoke where fires
still smoldered deep within the wreckage. The once busy
street was nearly leveled. Buildings that had risen high on
either side were now little more than bricks and dust while
several single walls stood uselessly with empty squares where
windows had once been.

Grace approached a man in a suit pacing before a flattened
plot of land that had once been an elegant shop with glossy
green paint lettering on its sign and small newspaper birds
hanging from the interior of his display windows. "Are you
the owner of Smith's?"

He looked at her, dazed with a numb expression she saw
far too often in her ARP work. His nod was almost imper-
ceptible.

"Smith's was such a lovely shop. I'm so sorry." She ap-

proached him carefully. "I'm with Primrose Hill Books on
Hosier Lane." She regarded the devastation that had most
likely been the man's livelihood. "We are setting aside shelf
space to aid the bookshops impacted by the bombing. You
can…" A band of emotion tightened at her throat. "You can
bring any of your stock to us, and we'll ensure you receive
the profits when they're sold."

She handed him a small card where she'd written the information for the bookshop.

He accepted it wordlessly and stared.

"I'm so sorry," Grace said again, feeling helpless once more
and hating it. "I wish there was more I could do."

"Thank you." He spoke softly and turned his sad gaze
from her to the rubble of his establishment.

She saw only one other person, to whom she made the
same offer and received the same bewildered response.

Not that any of it mattered. Surely no books had survived.

Dejected, she turned from the remains of London's book
district and made her way home to give in to the fatigue
grinding at her eyes like grit. On the way to Britton Street,
however, it occurred to her that she knew of exactly one
bookshop owner who did have a supply of books that were
unmarred by the night's conflagration.

Mrs. Nesbitt.

A war played out in Grace's mind, with one side arguing that it would be the right thing to do, fighting with
the spiteful side that had been hurt by Mrs. Nesbitt's sharp
words and wanted to retaliate with more spite. Exactly as
Mrs. Nesbitt had done.

It was that final thought that made up Grace's mind. For
she would never allow herself to become so bitter. Even to
the likes of Mrs. Nesbitt.

Grace was halfway up the short steps to Mrs. Nesbitt's townhouse when a familiar voice called out to her. "Grace, are you confused?" Mrs. Weatherford asked. "It isn't even blackout and you're going to the wrong home. You need more sleep, dear."

Mrs. Weatherford wore the gray-green uniform of the WVS, indicating she'd likely just returned from a meeting. Her cheeks were flushed, and her eyes were bright with the spark of life.

Grace stepped down and quickly explained what she intended to speak with Mrs. Nesbitt about. Mrs. Weatherford's back stretched a little taller, her shoulders squared. "Then I shall go with you." Before Grace could decline, Mrs. Weatherford shushed her. "I'll not let you tackle that beast alone, especially not when you're going to her with such goodness in you."

And so it was that Grace and Mrs. Weatherford rapped upon the brass knocker of Mrs. Nesbitt's door.

The woman greeted them with a look about as warm as the frosty day. "Your home is next door." She lifted one sharply arched brow. "Or have you forgotten?"

"We're here to see you," Grace said.

"And could use a bit of tea." Mrs. Weatherford rubbed her cold hands together, not so subtly reminding Mrs. Nesbitt of her manners to guests. "We're likely to get chilblains out here."

Mrs. Nesbitt sighed and opened her door. "Do come in. I'll put the kettle on."

She showed them to the parlor where the plushness of the blue velvet sofa felt as though it had just been purchased. There was an austere beauty to the room, like a museum full of fragile items you weren't allowed to touch. Everything was neat and orderly from the freshly polished end table to the many various figurines and scattered pictures of what appeared to be Mrs. Nesbitt as a young woman.

Grace and Mrs. Weatherford both perched awkwardly at the edge of the cushioned sofa, afraid to lean back and leave an imprint in the brushed velvet. Mrs. Nesbitt arrived several minutes later with a tea tray and presented teacups made of a fine bone china so thin, Grace could see the light of the back window through it.

"What can I do for you?" Mrs. Nesbitt asked. "Aside from deplete my tea and sugar rations in a bid to be hospitable."

Grace detoured the path of her hand from the sugar bowl to her cup, opting to drink her tea plain. "We'd like to offer a space for you at Primrose Hill Books to sell your books. You'll receive your profit from them, of course, and we'll ensure people know they are books from your store."

Mrs. Nesbitt's brow crinkled upward. "Are you in earnest?"

"Yes." Grace sipped her tea. It was weak, of course. Most likely the leaves had already been steeped a time or two. Nothing but the best for her unwanted visitors.

To her great surprise, Mrs. Nesbitt's eyes filled with tears and she looked away. "This is what I deserve for never loving Mr. Nesbitt." She dabbed her eyes with a lace handkerchief meant more for decoration than actual purpose. "I only ever married him for the bookshop, to have my father finally take notice of me. To—" She caught herself and regarded Mrs. Weatherford and Grace as if they were interlopers. "Do you not see? God is punishing me."

"Are you truly so arrogant to assume that God would have London bombed just to take a jab at you for a selfish act?" Mrs. Weatherford heaved a sigh. "Mrs. Nesbitt, I suggest you put some sense into your head and take advantage of a good offer when it's sent your way."

Grace nearly choked on her tea.

For Mrs. Nesbitt's part, she sputtered with indignation. "How dare you come into my house and say such things."

"Because someone needed to." Mrs. Weatherford plopped half a spoonful of sugar into her tea. "You need to apologize to Grace and tell her you'll accept the generous opportunity. Then you'll prepare yourself to come to the orphanage with me to read."

"The orphanage?" Mrs. Nesbitt blinked in stunned disbelief. "To read?"

"You did daily readings at your shop, did you not?"

Mrs. Nesbitt slid a glance toward Grace, then lifted her head and sniffed. "Yes."

"Your schedule appears to be clear, and there are children in sore need of books." Mrs. Weatherford stirred her tea.

"Well." Mrs. Nesbitt tossed her head.

Grace and Mrs. Weatherford looked at her expectantly.

Mrs. Nesbitt made a show of slowly adding a bit of sugar to her tea before taking a sip with one pinky elegantly elevated from the slender handle. She set the cup onto its matching saucer with a plink and took a breath.

"I shall take you up on your offer, Miss Bennett." She stared at the luxurious thick pile carpet underfoot as she spoke. "Thank you."

"And the orphanage?" Mrs. Weatherford prompted.

Mrs. Nesbitt lifted her gaze. "I'll prepare to leave once we finish our tea."

Mrs. Weatherford gave a triumphant smile. "Smashing."

1940 passed into 1941 without much fanfare on Mrs. Weatherford and Grace's parts. There was far too much to do otherwise. Over the next month, Mrs. Weatherford had to persuade Mrs. Nesbitt to join her at the orphanage less and less, as she began to go of her own choosing. The shelf designated for Nesbitt's Fine Reads received much attention, which pleased Mrs. Nesbitt greatly.

She was not the only shopkeeper to have taken Primrose Hill Books up on their beneficence. With so few open buildings available in the bombed-out city, word spread among the booksellers of Paternoster Row, and five additional sellers had a shelf devoted to their store, including Smith's. Grace fashioned small newspaper birds to adorn their designated space and rotated books from each seller along with Primrose Hill Books' own stock for her afternoon readings. Soon the customers in the shop were not only those they knew from their own store, but from the other booksellers as well.

Jimmy attended her readings still, the orphan well-fed now and with properly fitting, clean clothes, with little Sarah in tow, which made Mrs. Weatherford enormously happy. The people who listened to Grace read at the tube station also continued to come, along with several of their friends and the owners of other bookshops along with their patrons.

The offer to give space to the other stores had helped not only the booksellers, but inadvertently benefited Primrose Hill Books by keeping their stock from being depleted too quickly. Not only was Simpkin Marshalls no longer able to provide books, but finding a new supplier had been difficult with the paper ration on. What's more, customers who came in to support other sellers often purchased an item from their shop as well.

Grace wrote to George about Paternoster Row and how Primrose Hill Books had become such a popular place for readers to linger in discussion of literature. Hearing their conversations made her miss him terribly, to long for the ease with which he so eloquently described books and enticed her with new story plots. He expressed an eagerness to attend the shop upon his next visit to London, which he hoped would be in the next several months.

I long to be among the familiarity of Primrose Hill Books again, he'd confessed. *Where the literary conversations are ubiquitous and a particularly beautiful assistant brings stories to life with her lovely voice.*

It had warmed her heart to read those words. And yet the idea of reading in front of him made her anxious as well, the same as the first time she read aloud in the tube station.

Viv's letters had also been brimming with anticipation, especially since her duty station would be shifting to London in several months as she was being considered for a new assignment she couldn't elaborate on. Her exuberance lit the entirety of the letter and had Grace eager to see her friend once more.

One rare, quiet morning at the bookshop, Mr. Evans was at the counter tallying up a row of numbers in his ledger. "You told me once I was a good teacher." He set the pencil in the spine and glanced up at Grace. "Well, I want you to know I've learned a good bit from you as well."

Grace tossed him a skeptical look and replaced a book from Stephens Booksellers into a gap.

"Look what your compassion has done." He indicated the shelves of books designated for other stores. "You give every part of yourself to help others. Not just with what you do with the ARP. But here, with the other booksellers, with the people you read to. Out there, you save lives. In here, you save souls."

Heat spread across Grace's cheeks at such praise. "I think you might be exaggerating." She murmured her reply, but truly the pleasure of his words ran through her with a glow of warmth.

Judging from the tender smile on his face, he was well aware.

Mrs. Nesbitt pushed through the door with her usual air of self-importance. But this time, she didn't look herself. Gone was the dark macintosh belted at her thin waist and a pillbox hat stabbed through her hair with a wicked hat pin. In their place was a dull green WVS uniform and cap.

"Oh come now, don't look at me as though you've never seen a woman in a WVS uniform before, Miss Bennett." Mrs. Nesbitt strode toward her shelf of books, her sensible low-heeled shoes clicking over the floor.

Grace said nothing as she admired the change Mrs. Weatherford had wrought in Mrs. Nesbitt.

"I just finished the accounts if you'd like to see." Mr. Evans lifted the ledger in preparation to show Mrs. Nesbitt the neat row of numbers she typically asked for on her visits.

"No, thank you," she replied airily as she lifted a bright yellow children's book from the shelf. "I only came to collect a few things to bring for the orphanage. Their stock of books is abysmal, truly." She selected five more, then rattled off their titles to Mr. Evans. "Have these removed from my stock. They'll be staying with the children."

Mr. Evans lifted his bushy brows with incredulity at Grace. "Consider it done." He pulled the pencil from where it lay nestled in the spine and jotted the titles across the page.

"Thank you, Mr. Evans," she replied in a crisp tone.

"It isn't me you should be thanking." He nodded to Grace.

Mrs. Nesbitt paused before Grace and studied her thoughtfully. Her hard features softened, if only for a moment. "Thank you, Miss Bennett. For everything."

With that she lifted her head, haughty once more, and departed from the shop.

★ ★ ★

The next month flew by in a whirl of activity with Grace's daily readings growing in popularity along with the bookshop. Where Foyles continued to attract celebrities for their infamous teas, Primrose Hill Books had become distinguished for Grace's readings and the many discussions about the books afterward as people clustered together to rehash what they'd heard.

Mrs. Weatherford came every day in her WVS uniform, her sharp gaze picking out any orphans in need of care to tuck under her wing. She had once more resembled the woman she had been, albeit with more threads of silver in her neat hair. The only time Grace had seen Mrs. Weatherford truly upset was when March rolled in with a new item on the ration list: jam. To which she woefully replied, "What's next? Cheese?"

The bombings continued with such regularity that London no longer resembled her former glory. But even exhausted and war torn, she continued to shelter her people night after night, day after day. Lorries maneuvered around craters in the road, housewives queued for rationed food they made stretch into many meals and people brushed debris from their doorways in the morning when they collected their milk bottles. Life went on.

The weather had been horrendous with heavy fog, intermittent snow and ice, but little sun to be seen. The people of Britain had come to love that abhorrent weather and the reprieve it promised from bombers.

The Germans were so put out by the overcast skies, they'd come to do what was referred to as "tip and run," in which they'd pass over the city, loose a few bombs without aiming and depart quickly. The damage from such haphazard attacks was often minimal and the loss of life far less than it had been in previous attacks.

Grace continued to write to Viv and George, though finding posts that were still functional to mail them could prove difficult. Oftentimes, a postman stood with a sign stating simply "Post Office Here" with a counter lit by a candle thrust in a bottle. Telegram boys had it even harder, running about in their smart uniforms with pasteboard slung on a string about their necks declaring they were accepting telegrams. Those wishing to send one would then use the boy's back as a makeshift table to write out their messages.

Work with the ARP was no less taxing, but far less frightening. One could only see so many planes or be near so many bombs before the trigger of fear stopped firing. When air raids went off now, Grace and Mr. Stokes took their time, not bothering to rush until the drone of planes could be made out, or the cracking ack-ack gun informed them the Germans were near.

April offered a new month to begin planting. This time, Mrs. Weatherford expertly labeled the garden before she began planting. Tabby had certainly found a close companion in Mrs. Weatherford as the two were nearly inseparable. So it was no wonder that when the older woman went out to the garden to plant, along came Tabby trotting after her, batting about at bits of dirt. "Don't worry, Grace," Mrs. Weatherford said after the seeds had all been sown into the rich soil. "I didn't bother to plant any lettuce."

In the days that followed, as shoots began to push up from the earth and the weather turned mild despite the rain, the bookshop continued to thrive with new customers. However, it was around then that Grace noticed Mr. Evans had begun to seem rather unwell. It started with a small box he brought from the back room. He staggered under the scant weight, huffing and puffing for breath by the time he arrived at the front counter. Grace had asked after him, but he'd waved her off.

Several days later, she found him in the small back room with his hand to his chest, his face flushed a purple-red. She'd insisted he go to the doctor, which of course he did not, the stubborn man.

Just after the first week of April, on a chilly morning that left frost dusted over the slate roofs like sifted flour, Grace found Mr. Evans leaning heavily over the counter upon her arrival.

"Mr. Evans?"

He didn't look up. Instead, he issued a tight groan and flexed his left hand.

Grace pushed the door open to scream for help from passersby on the street, dropped her handbag and ran around the counter as she shrugged off her jacket. Her body went through the motions that had been trained into her as a warden, even as her mind reeled that this time she was helping Mr. Evans.

She eased him back to the floor, bracing herself against his weight. "Try to remain calm and breathe evenly." She spoke in the soothing voice she used when working with bombing victims. Only this time there was a tremble there, a break in her composure.

Mr. Evans flailed and gasped as though he could not find air, his face set in a hard grimace of pain. This man who had always been so strong, so unflappable. To see him in such a state, feeble and unable to breathe, it was too much. A tidal wave of emotion that threatened to drown her if she let her head go beneath the surface.

A sheen of sweat glistened on his brow and his face was unnaturally white, his lips a pale blue. Whatever was wrong with Mr. Evans was happening inside his body, something that required a physician. The aid she was used to offering was for a visible trauma she could address.

Powerlessness clawed at her with a frantic desperation. All the reassurances in the world wouldn't help him.

His hand caught hers, ice cold and damp with sweat. "Alice," he ground out.

"You'll be fine," Grace said firmly.

But he wouldn't be. She knew that and had no idea what to do to make it better.

He stiffened suddenly and his eyes went wide, practically bulging from his face as though he'd been given a great surprise.

"Someone will be here to help soon." Grace's voice broke on the words. "Someone will be here soon."

There was a light in everyone, one that dimmed when death took them, like a torch whose battery ran down. Grace had seen it once before in an old woman crushed by a collapsed building as she'd tried to cling to life.

That light in Mr. Evans's eyes, the one that shone with intelligence, kindness and dry humor—that light that had been so bright and so alive—went out.

"No." Grace shook her head as a knot lodged in her chest and ached in the back of her throat. She put her fingers to his wrist, but felt no pulse. "No."

Gingerly, she turned him onto his stomach and bent his arms so the backs of his hands braced his forehead on the carpet. She couldn't fix what was broken inside him, but she had been well trained on the procedure to restore someone when they were no longer breathing. She put her palms between his shoulder blades and slowly pushed her weight onto him for the length of an exhale. Next, she pulled his arms back by the elbows as she inhaled, willing him to do so as well. Over and over she did this in an effort to force him into breathing once more.

The doorbell chimed, a sharp, ugly sound in light of such unspeakable pain. "Is someone in need of help?" a man's voice called.

"Here," Grace cried out.

The man wore a suit and carried a black leather bag at his side. His salt-and-pepper hair was disheveled and exhaustion bruised the undersides of his dark eyes.

Grace explained what had happened with the efficiency of an ARP warden relaying her efforts to medical staff. Only now, she knew the person. She loved him like the father she'd never had. And this time, that person was dead.

The physician put a hand to her shoulder. "You did everything you could. There's nothing more that can be done." His brows pinched with genuine sincerity despite the many times he'd no doubt said those words. "I'm sorry."

Sorry.

It was such a paltry word for the enormity of such an event. A life snuffed out, one that had been so integral in Grace's world. He had been a mentor, a friend, a father figure.

And now he was gone. Forever.

Sorry.

Mr. Evans was taken away, leaving the shop unnaturally silent. For the first time since the start of the war, Grace closed Primrose Hill Books early and wandered home, her feet carrying her without thought.

She opened the door to the townhouse to Mrs. Weatherford's exclamation. "Dear me, where is your coat?" Mrs. Weatherford drew up short. "What is it, Grace? Is it Viv? Dear God, please tell me it isn't Viv."

Grace shook her head, though she scarce felt the action of doing so. "Mr. Evans."

Mrs. Weatherford's face crumpled, and the two women clung to each other through yet another devastating loss.

Yet even so, Grace opened the store the next day, and the day after that, and the one following as well. Customers asked after Mr. Evans and while their concern showed their love for the man who had meant so much to Grace, each question dug into the open wound of her sorrow.

Her mind felt rubbery and unwieldy in its grief. Every time she unlocked the door to the shop, she expected to see Mr. Evans there, marking meticulous notes in the ledger while offering a distracted greeting. And every time the emptiness of that space behind the counter hit her like a fresh knock to the heart.

No matter how much she failed to grasp the reality, no matter how much she didn't want to believe it, Mr. Evans was gone.

It took attending his funeral for her to finally accept his loss. That moment where his casket was lowered into the ground. It had rained that day and was as if the world was mourning the enormous loss of such a man as Percival Evans.

She still did the readings every afternoon. Getting through them might not have been possible if he wasn't in her head, encouraging her with that proud smile. Each night she closed, she put the money in a lockbox in the backroom the way she always did, not sure what would happen to it. She wasn't even sure what would happen to the shop. Perhaps a cousin in the country he had never mentioned?

It wasn't until nearly a week later that she had her answer. After her reading one bleak afternoon, an older gentleman approached her.

It wasn't uncommon. Many new listeners liked to speak with her about the book, or see what others she might suggest. Usually she would welcome such discussions. But not today. Not when her chest threatened to cave in.

"Miss Grace Bennett?" the man asked.

"May I help you?"

"I'm Henry Spencer, solicitor with Spencer & Clark." He smiled at her. "I'd like to have a word with you if I may."

Grace looked to Mrs. Weatherford, who was standing near enough to have overheard. The older woman made a shooing motion with her hands, indicating Grace should go with the man.

Grace waved him to follow her to the back room and apologized for the cramped space. Not being able to order from Simpkin Marshalls meant they were finally using their stockpile of books. Though many of the boxes had been cleared out, the tidy space was still rather small.

"I generally do not come to the establishment of my clients," Mr. Spencer said. "However, Mr. Evans was a friend. I wanted to ensure I had a chance to speak with you privately."

An ache clenched in Grace's throat.

"Mr. Evans had no family, as you know." Mr. Spencer reached into his pocket and withdrew several keys. "He has left it all to you. The shop, the flat above it, everything he owned is now yours."

Grace blinked in surprise. "Me?"

"Yes, Miss Bennett. From what I understand, you've made Primrose Hill Books what it is. I'm sure he knew no one would care for it like you." He handed her the keys and had her sign a document, which she did in a trembling script caused by hands that shook too hard.

She recognized the key to the shop, which was a mirror of her own. "What are these other two for?" she asked.

He indicated the larger one. "This is for the flat. I'm not sure about the other."

No sooner had he said it than Grace realized she knew exactly what it was for: Mr. Evans's safe.

She could recall the day he'd shown her those precious books that had been salvaged from Nazi flames. It had been months ago. It felt like it had been a lifetime. And yet, it also seemed like it had been only yesterday. With him imparting his wise words, sharing a greater piece of himself not only with her, but with the world.

The bookshop was now hers, and she found herself more determined than ever to make Primrose Hill Books shine— no longer for herself, but for Mr. Evans.

TWENTY

GRACE CLOSED THE COVER ON *THE ODYSSEY*, ONE OF the books she'd seen Mr. Evans thumb through often when he was alive. And one she now read aloud in the afternoons.

Were it not for the bookshop, the passing of the last month would have been much more difficult to endure.

She had lost herself in books. In the selling of them and the reading of them.

"Are you getting on well, dear?" An older housewife, who always wore a string of pearls at her throat and was called Mrs. Smithwick, put a hand on Grace's arm.

Grace nodded. The same as she always did when asked how she had been faring. "Reading through the books I know he loved really helps," she replied honestly. "Thank you."

"I never thought books that ancient could be so interesting." Mrs. Smithwick gave a conspiring wink.

"Nor did I." Grace smiled lightly to herself. "Mr. Evans had loved them all though. I'm glad we've given this one a go."

"Keep reading them all," Mrs. Smithwick said with encouragement. "And we'll be here to listen."

Grace nodded her thanks and set the book behind the counter to ensure it wouldn't become mixed up with the others. It was one she had taken from the massive bookshelf in Mr. Evans's flat above the shop.

The pages were worn soft at the edges from the countless times he'd read through them. One corner of the cover was dented and the ink inside had several smears as if he had rested his fingers over a certain passage. It was careworn and precious.

There had been little time to clean out his flat between her running of the shop and her long hours as an ARP Warden at night. The bombs fell with less frequency now, but her efforts were still needed. She'd been too exhausted to do much with Mr. Evans's effects, let alone prepare the small residence to move in to. Truthfully, she had been glad for the option to stay on with Mrs. Weatherford for a spell longer. Grace didn't feel strong enough to be on her own just yet.

There had been so much death.

Too much.

Her mother. Colin. Mr. Evans. Mr. Pritchard. All the bombing victims she'd seen in those harrowing months.

There had been so much loss in so little time. It built up inside her like a tidal wave battering at a weakening dam. The more it swelled, the harder Grace worked.

Mrs. Weatherford didn't like what she saw and commented often on Grace's worn-down appearance, always shoving food toward her to get her to eat more. But Grace didn't have an appetite for anything. Not Woolton pie, which they'd taken to calling Le Woolton Pie ever since her date at the Ritz, not even poultry when it could be found.

How could she with so much destruction and loss around her? Every day homes were destroyed and people were killed. The nights were blanketed in darkness, their food was bland and marbled with gristle. Through it all was the ever-present wail of the air raid siren, reminding them that this state of things would continue on and on and on with no end.

The war had been interminable and felt as though it would last forever.

After announcing Mr. Evans's death, Grace had been slow in her replies to Viv and George. The only words that she could summon were far too heavy for war letters. It wouldn't do to weigh them down with her burdens.

She went through the motions of reorganizing the display in the front window, letting her focus drift to the aesthetic where she didn't have to consider the numbness inside her.

A familiar face appeared at her side.

Mrs. Nesbitt's gaze skimmed the neatly arranged books amid paper flowers made from painted newspapers. They were meant to represent the incoming spring despite the dull, drizzling weather.

"Are you putting up another display?" She sniffed. "Is that not your second this week?"

Grace lifted a shoulder. "It may bring in more customers, which will benefit us all."

Mrs. Nesbitt hummed with an argument she was too disinterested to share and picked at a stray bit of string on her WVS jacket. "Having you drop dead from exhaustion will benefit none of us."

Grace offered a mirthless chuckle.

"I don't speak in jest," Mrs. Nesbitt said dryly. "But with sincerity. Miss Bennett, no amount of work you do will bring him back."

Of all the hurtful things Mrs. Nesbitt had thrown at Grace, this bite had the sharpest teeth.

Tears burned in Grace's eyes. "Please leave."

"You've told me things I needed to hear in the past, and I'm now returning the favor." Mrs. Nesbitt's demeanor softened. "Though it does pain me to do so, whether you believe it or not."

As much as her barb had stung, the sudden compassion of the irascible woman only made the ache in Grace's chest grow worse.

"I can assist you if need be, by working a day or two until you hire an assistant." Mrs. Nesbitt sighed at the great sacrifice she was suggesting. "But you can't keep going on like this."

It was the same thing Mrs. Weatherford had said to Grace. It struck her suddenly where Mrs. Nesbitt's true motivation must have originated—Mrs. Weatherford herself.

"Did Mrs. Weatherford put you up to this?" Grace asked.

Mrs. Nesbitt scoffed. "I have eyes, my dear. And you are a stiff wind shy of collapsing."

Grace diverted her attention from the woman, not wanting to acknowledge what had been said. Mrs. Nesbitt offered nothing further and instead turned on her heel to leave.

That evening, Grace was fit to be tied with frustration over Mrs. Weatherford sending Mrs. Nesbitt—of all people—to chastise her for working too much. She pushed open the door, ready to confront the woman she'd always known to be a friend.

"Grace," Mrs. Weatherford called out in a morose tone.

"Grace, is that you?" Her footsteps sounded in the kitchen, followed by a cooing change to her voice that indicated Tabby was close at her heels.

Mrs. Weatherford pushed through the kitchen door. "Oh, Grace," she lamented. "They've added cheese to the ration list now. Cheese!" Her eyes shifted heavenward.

"Did you send Mrs. Nesbitt to speak with me?" Grace asked, trying her best to keep the sharpness from her voice.

Mrs. Weatherford snorted. "I'd never send that woman to see to my personal business."

"So you didn't tell her to approach me about working too hard?" Grace put a hand to her hip, skeptical.

At least until Mrs. Weatherford gave a bark of laughter. "As though you'd listen. But I'll keep saying it, and you'll keep ignoring me up until the day you understand why I'd been warning you." Mrs. Weatherford lifted Tabby into her arms. The cat nuzzled her chin, and she spoke around his head-butting affection. "I assure you, I'd never send someone on my behalf when I'm more than capable of haranguing you on my own." She hesitated. "Though I did wish to speak to you on another matter."

Grace braced herself for something awful. As it seemed most news was these days.

"I've considered going through the necessary channels to adopt Jimmy and Sarah." Mrs. Weatherford set Tabby down amid a puff of dispelled cat hair. "I wanted to see where your thoughts might lie on the matter of them living with us."

The children had been doing so well, their progress noticeable with each week that passed. Not only did they both attend the readings now, but they were often at Mrs. Weatherford's townhouse, either for supper or to help out in the garden. They brought laughter back into a house that had gone far too silent, and the idea of having them there permanently left a smile tugging at the corners of Grace's mouth.

"That's how I thought you might feel," Mrs. Weatherford said with a grin. "I'll speak with them tomorrow to see if the idea would be amenable to them as well."

Grace nodded in reply and went up the stairs to her room. Fatigue had her in a tight grip, exactly the way she liked it. There would be no painful memories shuffling about her mind when she tried to find sleep, leaving her restless and tossing back and forth. It would be a sweet surrender to darkness later that night.

She opened her wardrobe to hang her coat and caught sight of her ARP uniform. They'd recently been given the new blue serge attire, with men in battledress and women in tunics with skirts. She wouldn't have need of it this night when she was off duty.

Grace forced herself to stay awake and take supper with Mrs. Weatherford, who used the ration and guilt to encourage Grace to eat. Any meal made with bacon, butter, a sprinkle of cheese or a decent cut of meat was too precious to waste.

Once their meal was done and the dishes washed and put up, they prepared for a night at Farringdon Station. Though the air raids were less frequent, it was still preferable to spend the night in the tube station as a precaution.

Waiting for an air raid siren to go down to the tube would mean no available space on the crowded station floor, so they went out into the dusk with their bundles of blankets in preparation to queue when Grace noticed the overcast sky had begun to clear. A shiver prickled over her skin, leaving the small hairs along her arms standing on end.

There would be a bomber's moon that night. They would need all the cloud cover they could get.

Especially with the Thames at low tide.

Apprehension tingled in the back of her mind. Exacerbated, no doubt, by her weariness.

They made their way into the underground, stepping over people who had already set up their place to rest for the night and locating a spot where they might settle down together. But no matter how tired Grace was, peace would not find her.

Usually she could sleep through the talking and snoring around her, so weary she'd be in a dreamless state within minutes. That evening, however, her slumber was repeatedly broken with haunting memories clattering about her mind like a pocketful of pebbles.

The air raid cried its wailing tune sometime after eleven that night, muffled by the layers of earth and pavement overhead. The subsequent bombing, however, was not so easily muted.

The screeching bombs. The pounding fire of the ack-ack guns. The thundering boom of explosives obliterating everything in its path wherever they descended. Plaster sifted from the ceiling in chunks and chalky dust. The lights flickered, going out completely for spells at a time.

They were used to these sounds, yes, but whatever went on overhead was far worse than ordinary bombing nights.

The apprehension lodged in Grace's chest amplified.

Mrs. Weatherford clutched her large green bag to her, part of one hand thrust inside where Grace knew she was stroking Tabby. They weren't supposed to bring pets down with them, but Mrs. Weatherford refused to leave the small cat, and he had the good sense to stay quiet in his sack until they could return home in the morning.

As the night crept on, the sounds continued with one hour banging into another until dawn when the onslaught finally came to an end. The foreboding rattling inside Grace crystalized into something cold and sharp. Insistent.

Something was not right.

She could *feel* it.

Like an ant tickling over one's skin, or the pregnant moisture in the air before a deluge. Something was not right.

The all clear finally issued its one-note call and those who'd sought shelter in Farringdon Station queued for departure. It was an agonizing wait that clawed at Grace's patchwork patience. She could scarce stand in place, shifting from one foot to the other.

People slowed as they exited, and Grace saw why when she emerged from the station. The sky was alight with fire, clouded by great billows of black smoke. Homes were cracked and sagging, some gone entirely, knocked from the rows of townhouses like a missing tooth in a jagged grin.

Grace's pulse raced at an unnatural pace. Sweat prickled at her palms.

"Oh, Grace," Mrs. Weatherford gasped. "It's awful."

Grace quickened her pace toward the townhouse. She was nearly out of breath when she rounded the corner, anxious over what she might find.

Mrs. Weatherford huffed behind her. "I can't run with Tabby."

But Grace wasn't listening as she studied the tidy line of townhouses on their street. Their home was intact, just the same as it'd ever been, save for the tomatoes sprouting from the window boxes rather than the former purple and white petunias.

The sense of dread inside her yawned wider.

Ice chilled the blood in her veins.

The bookshop.

"Go on without me," Grace said to Mrs. Weatherford.

Before the older woman could ask what she meant, Grace was sprinting toward Hosier Lane with her bed bundle clutched to her chest. The acrid, smoke-filled air burned her throat and stung her eyes, but she didn't slow as she darted around people returning home from a night hunkered in the tube station.

She had to reassure herself that it was safe, that it had survived the brutal onslaught. After all, Mr. Evans had entrusted her with the shop.

But with each step closer, the band of unease tightened.

When she rounded Hosier Lane, she stopped short, discovering why.

The street smoldered with extinguished fires. The building to the right of the bookshop had been struck in a blast, demolished to piles of broken brick. Primrose Hill Books still stood. But was not intact.

Glass had been blown out of every window, and shredded pages limped in an unseen breeze among the detritus on the pavement. The door was missing, and the contents inside were a scattered mess. Overhead, part of the roof had detached and the stucco near it scorched with flames that luckily had not consumed the structure.

Grace's heart seemed to shrink inside her chest, sucked into a realm of pure dread. She stood, numb, unable to shake herself from the sight. A gust of wind rustled her skirt and carried with it a flurry of ashes and heat from a nearby fire.

The shop was inoperable.

The source of her strength had been torn inside out.

Grace dragged herself into action, stepping toward the damaged building as the bedroll slipped from her hands. The world around her crackled from nearby fires, and the crunching of glass underfoot mingled with the ragged draw of her breath.

Any hope that Primrose Hill Books might look better up close was dashed as she stopped before the place she had poured her soul into, the culmination of a lifetime of Mr. Evans's hard work and the community she had built around the world of reading.

Grace struggled to find her breath, gasping around the pain that shattered open inside her, white hot and visceral. A small painted newspaper flower she'd designed for the window display rolled over bits of broken glass and dust, stopping at the toe of her shoe. She bent to pick it up. Its twisted paper stem was cool and hard where she pinched it between her fingers, its pink petals as immaculate and clean as the day she made it.

She had to go inside. To see for herself.

If nothing else, to ensure the precious books within the safe had survived.

She entered the gaping doorway and walked slowly through the mess, careful to not tread upon the fallen books. They would need to be salvaged. If they could be.

In her bewildered state, she wondered how she might sort her books from those belonging to the other bookshops, remembering belatedly she'd stamped their names inside with blue ink. Thank goodness for the organized detail with which she'd handled everything before.

Not that it would help the other shop owners, as the

bookshop was now almost as useless as theirs. None of them would have a place to go.

Tears prickled in her eyes at that realization, at her inability to help those who had come to rely on her.

The back room door was missing, and the small table had been mangled into a ball of metal in one corner. The safe was fortunately still lodged within the wall. She wrestled with a cabinet drawer and withdrew a torch. With shaking hands, she unlocked the safe and held her breath.

Mr. Evans's legacy was in those precious books he saved and collected.

The door groaned open and an exhale whooshed from Grace's lungs. The books that had once been rescued from the flames of Hitler's hatred had again survived a near demise. They were safely tucked inside the wall safe, framed on all sides within a shell of thick metal.

She had a mind to draw them out and bring them home with her to Britton Street. But thought better of it, knowing they were best left in their iron box. She was beginning to close the door when a slip of paper caught her eye.

An envelope.

A corner of it jutted from between two books whose German titles she couldn't read. She plucked it from its location and read her name on its back in Mr. Evans's slanted writing.

Her breath caught.

She slid her finger beneath the flap and drew out the neatly typed letter within.

Dear Sir or Madam,

I'm writing you to recommend Miss Grace Bennett's services to you. She has been employed at my shop, Primrose Hill Books, for the last six months. In that time, she has taken my cluttered shop and turned it into something quite elegant, thereby increasing its popularity, and sales, tremendously.

Miss Bennett is a polite young woman with immeasurable compassion and a keen intelligence. She's rather brilliant, actually.

If you don't hire her, you're a fool. And I'm a greater fool for letting her go.

My bookshop has never been in better hands, my own included.

Sincerely,

Mr. Percival Evans

Grace could hear his voice in her head, his tone growing more vehement toward the end.

My bookshop has never been in better hands.

The wreckage around her said otherwise. Carefully, she folded the letter back into the envelope and locked it back in the safe.

She would be letting everyone down without the shop. The people who relied on her to sell their wares, her customers who came seeking the distraction of books, not to mention herself. Mr. Evans.

She had lost everything.

TWENTY-ONE

THERE WAS NOTHING FOR IT BUT TO GO THROUGH the debris and see what could be salvaged. Grace clicked off her torch to save the battery and left the small back room, careful to avoid tripping on any fallen items. Of which there were many.

Books, glass, bits of shelves that had splintered apart. All beneath a fine sifting of dust and ash.

The slim figure of a man filled the doorway of the main entrance. She slipped back into the shadows, regretting not having at least had her ARP whistle on her.

It was far too common for looters to slink into ruined shops and homes, especially after heavy raids like the one they'd just experienced. It was a sad thing when a family returned to a ruined home to find their remaining belongings had already been picked over. Most of the pilfering fiends scared away easily after being called out. But some were bold and remained where they stood.

"What are you doing here?" Grace said sharply, hoping the man might retreat.

The figure didn't move.

She wrapped her hands tighter around the torch. If nothing else, she could hit him about the head if he came too close.

"Miss Bennett?" Mr. Stokes replied. "Is that you?"

Grace exhaled a sigh of relief and stepped into the open where he could see her.

The electric mains had been turned off prior to her departure the night before, as always. And good thing too, else the shop might have gone up in flames when it caught fire. She would have to assess the damage to the lights before turning them back on.

Mr. Stokes walked into the shop, wearing a jacket and trousers, tiptoeing about to avoid stepping on books as he made his way toward her. "They told me the bookshop had been struck." He looked around and frowned. "I'm so sorry."

"Is your home safe?" Grace asked.

He nodded. "Many didn't fare as well. It was one of the worst nights we've had. They estimate the attack on London last night left over a thousand dead, God save their souls. Double that are injured, and blazes still being put out." He glanced up, squinting with assessment as his eyes adjusted to the darkness. "It's a good thing this place is standing at all. Some of it might still be saved."

There was a hopefulness to his tone Grace didn't share.

"Thank you for coming by to check on the shop, Mr. Stokes." She looked gratefully at him, realizing that he had unexpectedly become something of a friend in the last few months. They'd been through bombings together, seen death together, saved lives together.

She bent to retrieve a book at her feet, its cover splayed open and its pages bent. Before straightening, she collected three more books, pausing to shake a tinkling of shattered glass from them first.

When she stood, he arched a brow. "You don't truly intend to handle this all on your own, do you?"

Grace regarded the mess in front of her. Books were torn and battered, shelves were in pieces, the history section pasteboard dangled by only one corner and was covered in a smattering of dirt.

When she turned back to Mr. Stokes, she found him standing in a salute. "Mr. Stokes, light recovery crew, reporting for duty." He lowered his stiffened hand from his brow. "After all, these matters are best not done alone."

"How could I possibly say no to that?"

"You can't," he answered, grinning.

The two of them worked through the morning and well into the afternoon. The damage to most of the books was not as bad as expected, and though the roof was not fully intact, the flat was, which provided shelter enough for the bookshop. For now.

It was a fortunate thing indeed she had been so slow to clear out Mr. Evans's flat and was still living with Mrs. Weatherford.

Grace and Mr. Stokes swept up the glass and gathered the unsalvageable shelves to set outside for collection, pausing only to have a spot of tea and some fish and chips Mr. Stokes had procured.

The snatches of sleep Grace managed the previous night, however brief they might have been, provided enough energy to get her through the task. Her shirtdress was covered in a layer of dust and soot, and her hands were gritty with filth.

As they cleared the last of the wreckage from the shop floor, Grace looked to the pile of books. It was a haphazard stack, with some spines facing outward and some turned in or on their side. It wasn't sorted by bookseller, let alone category, and would be a hefty undertaking to put to rights once more. But then, so too would the shop.

It would be like starting from her first day at Mr. Evans's shop. Except he wasn't there and the whole world had so drastically changed.

Emotion bubbled up in Grace, confusing and overwhelming, leaving her uncertain if she wanted to laugh or cry. In truth, she was nearly compelled to do both at once.

"We've been able to save a good bit," Mr. Stokes said encouragingly.

"What's happened?"

Grace turned at the familiar voice to find Mrs. Kittering. A glance at Grace's watch confirmed that it was nearly time for the afternoon reading. Which meant Mrs. Kittering would not be the only customer to show. In the next several minutes, doubtless there would be dozens more.

She rushed forward to Grace, her large, soft brown eyes going wide as she took in everything. "I'm so sorry to see this. After everything you've done, after everything you've made of this shop."

The woman's sympathy lodged deep in Grace's chest, echoing the hurt already radiating inside.

"I'll sort it out," Grace replied with as much courage as she could muster. Admittedly, it wasn't much.

But she was British. What's more, she was a Londoner,

baptized as such by the firestorm of war, by bombings and incendiaries.

Behind Mrs. Kittering, several more people had begun to enter the shop, gazing in awestruck bewilderment as they beheld the damage.

Mr. Stokes squeezed Grace's shoulder.

"Thank you for your help, Mr. Stokes." She smiled gratefully at him.

"I can stay longer if you like." Despite the generosity of his offer, exhaustion darkened the undersides of his eyes. Still he hesitated to leave.

"Go on home, Mr. Stokes, I'll take it from here." Mrs. Weatherford's soft voice chimed into the conversation.

He gave her a resigned smile. Even he knew better than to argue with her. With a final salute, he left the shop, no doubt to fall into a deep, dreamless sleep.

"Grace, dearest." Mrs. Weatherford took her arm.

The support she offered was kind, but it was too much when Grace was so fragile. It would be too easy to fall into the comfort of Mrs. Weatherford's maternal embrace and shatter.

Instead she offered a grateful smile and shook her head.

Every now and again, Mrs. Weatherford backed down when she knew it was best to do so. Fortunately, this was one of those moments. She lowered her head in acknowledgment and returned to the step where Jimmy and Sarah waited for her with wide, questioning eyes.

Grace went through her large handbag with the gas mask tucked inside, and withdrew the book she'd been reading aloud, *Jane Eyre*.

"Miss Bennett, you don't need to do that," Mrs. Kittering said. "Not today."

But her protest only steeled Grace's spine more, as her mother had always encouraged. "Of all days, I think we need this now more than ever."

Or at least Grace certainly did. As a reminder of what she might hopefully rebuild again.

Someday.

Somehow.

She made her way to the second step of the stairs, which hadn't yet been brushed off, and swiped at it to clear the debris. A handkerchief appeared in front of her from Mrs. Smithwick. Grace smiled her thanks.

The stair was near enough to the window that she could make out the type on the page well enough to read without the aid of her torch. She sat down and looked at the faces of those gathering around her with uncertainty. It was then she realized she ought to say something.

But what? That she didn't know how long it would take to repair such damage? Especially when another raid might crumble what little was left. Or the first downpour might leak through the flat above and destroy the entire shop.

As if the cruelest of fates heard her thoughts, a low rumble issued forth from the broken windows, indicating the likelihood of a storm.

Despair pulled at her like an undertow, threatening to suck her down in a dark abyss.

"Thank you all for coming," she said in an uncertain voice. *Jane Eyre* sat on her knees, an emblem of what had brought them all together, of what had unified them in the face of war and danger. Jane had courage, a considerable amount for all she'd faced, and Grace tried to draw as much from the book's protagonist in that moment.

"As you can see, Primrose Hill Books has been struck by

last night's bombing, as were many, many Londoners." Grace folded her hand around the cover of the book. "I cannot tell you when we will be back in proper form again. I do not know—" Her voice caught and she cleared her throat. "I do not know if it will even be possible to continue."

She looked out at the sea of faces she'd grown to know so well. The professors who loved to gather in their philosophical debates, the housewives, like Mrs. Kittering, who found refuge from their empty homes between the covers of books, men from the heavy rescue who sometimes needed more than what could be found in a flask to make them forget what they'd seen. And even Jimmy, who sat with Sarah tucked protectively against him, both under the watchful gaze of Mrs. Weatherford. The older woman's worried expression told Grace exactly how bad the shop truly looked.

She nodded at Grace with the same kind of silent encouragement Mr. Evans once offered.

"I appreciate what all of you have helped Primrose Hill Books become," Grace continued. "Books are what have brought us together. A love of the stories within, the adventures they take us on, their glorious distraction in a time of strife. And a reminder that we always have hope."

Thunder grumbled once more in the distance. Louder this time.

Several people glanced up with concern showing on their faces. With part of the roof missing, the upper floor would only block out the water for so long.

Jack, the rough looking man who had been there from her first reading, turned his head and spoke to two others beside him. They glanced up at the ceiling with a frown, clearly of a similar mind.

"Even if we don't have Primrose Hill Books…" Grace

cradled *Jane Eyre* to her chest. "Remember that we will always have books, and therefore we will always have courage and optimism."

The faces looking back at her were solemn as mourners at a funeral. A woman nearby pulled a handkerchief from her handbag and dabbed at her eyes.

No doubt they suspected the shop could not continue.

And they were probably right.

Jack and the two men with him quietly left the shop as another crash of thunder echoed overhead.

"I'll continue our readings until *Jane Eyre* is finished." She indicated the book where the scrap of paper she'd tucked between the pages, a place marker, closer to the back cover than the front. "And after that—"

"Please don't stop your readings," someone called from the back.

"You're the last bookshop in London," another youthful voice cried out.

Jimmy.

Mrs. Weatherford put a hand on his shoulder and pressed her lips together, appearing very near tears.

Grace shook her head. "I'm certainly not the last." After all, she imagined Foyles would undoubtedly be around forever. Its owner was rumored to have lined his roof with copies of *Mein Kampf* in an effort to keep all six stories of discounted books safe from the Germans. It worked, although Foyles did have a near miss at one point that left a massive crater in front of the bookshop that they continued to operate around.

They all made do in such times.

"Though certainly there will never be another bookshop like ours." The sentiment clogged in her throat and she opened the book to remove the scrap of paper. If she didn't start reading soon, she might lose her courage. "And we still have a few more chapters yet."

Before she knew it, she lost herself to Jane's story, feeling the character's suffering, but reveling in her strength and bravery. All at once, the two chapters Grace had meant to read became three and she knew she must stop.

But she didn't want to. She wanted to continue reading. Jane's mettle in the face of homelessness and starvation after leaving Thornfield in *Jane Eyre* was far easier for Grace to lose herself in than facing her own hardships.

But people had to return to their obligations and so must she.

It was with much regret that she lowered the book to find it had begun to rain outside. Surely it would not take much before water would seep into the walls and the damage became irreparable.

Then Primrose Hill Books would be no more, and everything she'd worked for would truly be gone.

Several men had arrived outside the broken shop windows with Jack in the lead. He entered the store, his cap clutched in his large hands. "I'm sorry I missed your reading."

The other men came in behind him, shining torches along the walls and ceiling as they spoke together in low murmurs.

They couldn't be there to—

"I had to get my crew," Jack said. "So we can fix the shop for you."

"I beg your pardon?" she whispered, unable to believe her ears. Surely she hadn't heard him properly. Surely he didn't mean—

"We're here to fix up your shop." He called out several orders to his men.

One of the men layered a sheet of waxed linen on the inside of a blown-out display window and nailed it to the frame. The room darkened somewhat at the blocked light.

"We'll fix up the shop, then you can keep reading." He winked. "These blokes haven't heard your readings yet. Now they're interested."

Grace gave a little laugh that was somewhere nearer to a sob than she cared to admit. "I'll read them any book they'd like."

"They were hoping you'd say that." He turned to his men and issued a series of instructions before turning back to her. "Please get some rest, Miss Bennett. Your shop will be in safe hands. We've worked out a system to keep watch so looters can't come in, even through the night."

"Jack." Words stuck in her throat then, all the gratitude and genuine awe at such kindness. "Thank you." It was all she could manage of the welling praise and appreciation she wished to say instead.

Mrs. Weatherford approached and put an arm around Grace's shoulders, gently guiding her home where she gave Grace a warm meal and saw her safely tucked into bed.

Mind reeling at the twists and turns of that day, Grace gave in fully to the weariness that felt as though it was leaching her bones.

She woke to the gray glow of a rainy day limning the blackout curtains. Her mouth was dry as wartime cake, and her brain was fogged over with blurred memories. The severity of her fatigue had left her more addled than the French 75s she'd had with Viv at Grosvenor House Hotel months ago.

Suddenly she remembered everything. The bombed

bookshop, Mr. Stokes helping her clean and salvage, reading amid the ruination. And Jack bringing his crew to help.

She leapt from the bed then, rushing to dress and go see what they'd managed to accomplish in the afternoon. If nothing else, hopefully they would have the tarpaulin on the roof to prevent any more leaking into Mr. Evans's flat.

She freshened up and went downstairs where Mrs. Weatherford was sitting in the parlor with Tabby nestled comfortably in her lap.

"I wondered when you might finally wake." She chuckled and scratched the little cat behind his ears. He leaned into her ministrations as his eyes lazily closed. "I'm glad we were able to make it through the night without a single air raid."

"The night?" Grace asked, startled.

"Yes, dear. You've been asleep since we came home yesterday afternoon." Mrs. Weatherford looked up. "And good thing too; you've been in dire need of rest. Jack said it was for the best. He's a lovely man, isn't he? He said to assure you that the shop—"

"The bookshop." Grace hastened to the front door.

"Do eat something before you go," Mrs. Weatherford called.

But Grace was already rushing out the front door, practically running to Primrose Hill Books. Once more, her feet skidded to a halt before the shop in shock. She'd hoped for a tarp on the roof and saw now there was none.

There was slate.

Mismatched and oddly shaped bits that came together to form a solid roof. The windows were covered in waxed linen, stretched taut in their frames like drum skins.

Even the soot streaking the stucco from the fires had been painted over.

It was all as if it had never happened. Grace strode toward the door—the door!

Its trim suggested it might have been cut down from a larger size, but a fresh coating of black paint gave it a fine look. She put her hand to the dented brass knob and entered the shop.

A familiar ding cheerfully welcomed her.

Along with an extraordinary sight.

Shelves of various heights and colors, pieced from odds and ends of repurposed wood, once more offered an array of books lining the walls, and the shelves stacked at the shop's center had been dusted and filled as well. Pasteboard signs in a neat script hung once more where they ought to, and even several advertising displays had been replaced.

It was too much in the most wonderful way. An absolute miracle.

And many of the faces she recognized from her book readings were there, watching her with tired, bright smiles.

"I…" Grace's words caught. "You did all of this?"

"We worked through the night and most of the day," Mrs. Kittering said. "Lucky for us there wasn't a single air raid."

"It isn't all organized yet," Mrs. Smithwick said apologetically, fingering the pearls at her neck. "But we're working on it."

"You've done a fine job, Mrs. Smithwick," Jack said to her with a nod.

She beamed broadly, the wrinkles at the corners of her eyes crinkling.

"This is incredible," Grace breathed. If she looked for hours on end, she still might not believe that her shop was back in working condition.

"We had to use scraps to put it all together." Jack glanced

about, his eyes squinted in assessment. "But it's a sound shop, so long as the Germans don't try bombing it again."

"I don't know how I can ever repay you." Grace put her hand to her chest. Her heart felt too large to fit within its confines.

"Everyone wanted to do their bit to help," Jack said with a nod to the group.

He moved back and little Sarah took a step forward. Grace recognized the blue-and-white polka-dot dress as one Mrs. Weatherford had sewn from some of Viv's spare fabric.

Sarah sucked in a deep breath and announced in a very loud voice, much like an actress, "Every day you read to a crowd. But they're not just stories, for many of us, they're a sanctuary." She said the last word slowly and Jimmy gave her a thumbs-up. She twisted with apparent pride as children are wont to do and took a deep breath again, meeting Grace's eye. "And you're not just someone who reads to us. You're a hero."

Such words rendered Grace speechless. She wavered on her feet, light-headed with gratitude.

Jack approached her. "You saved my life, Miss Bennett. Were it not for your readings, I'd have been blown to bits at Marble Arch. Thank you."

He didn't wait for a reply and stepped back, lowering his head with gratitude. Mrs. Kittering replaced his position at Grace's side. "I was in a dark place when you found me sobbing in your store. You gave me the light to keep going. Thank you."

She departed and Jimmy stepped forward. "I couldn't have cared for Sarah the way you've done along with Mrs. Weatherford. You gave us food and clothes when we had none."

"And now a home," Sarah said as she peered shyly from his side. "Thank you."

"That makes me so happy," Grace said, realizing the children had agreed to come live with her and Mrs. Weatherford.

They left together, hand in hand, and Mrs. Smithwick stepped forward. "My Tommy was killed in the war and so was my Donald." She looked down and discreetly glanced over her shoulder. "You don't know it, but you saved my life as well," she said so softly Grace nearly didn't hear. "By my own hands. You showed me that when all seems lost to the enemy, one can always find a friend."

On and on they all came forward. A man whose leg Grace had bound after a blast with whom she'd shared by memory the details from *The Count of Monte Cristo*, distracting him from the pain. A professor who had been seeking a welcome place to find fellow readers, having discovered them at Primrose Hill Books. A shop owner who had lost everything with the Paternoster Row bombing. And even Mrs. Nesbitt, who apologized for her past transgressions and offered her thanks for everything Grace had done.

Last came Mrs. Weatherford who stepped forward with a watery smile. "You saved me, Grace Bennett. When I lost Colin and thought I had nothing left, you reminded me there was a purpose to my life. What's more, you pointed me in the direction I should go." She glanced at Jimmy and Sarah, the latter of whom waved with vigorous affection. "I knew your mother better than anyone on this green Earth and I tell you right now—she would have been so proud. Of your sacrifice and your courage and your strength."

She caught Grace in an embrace. "And I'm proud of you too, my dear," she whispered.

When they broke apart, Jack was standing at Grace's side with his hands jammed in the pockets of his overalls. "Begging your pardon, but we need your approval on something."

Grace shook her head, overcome with affection and appreciation for the effort so many had gone through, not only with her shop, but for making her feel so valued. She followed him outside where two men in working overalls waited, weary and paint-smeared. They held a large beam of wood lengthwise between them.

"We know the bookshop is Primrose Hill Books," Jack said. "But we all thought this seemed more appropriate for the time being, given the circumstances."

He nodded and the men flipped over the board, revealing a painted sign, reading The Last Bookshop in London.

Grace laughed, giddy with love and friendship and joy. It was indeed a perfect name, and she knew Mr. Evans would agree if he was still alive.

"It's brilliant," she said. "With one small modification. If I may?"

Jack lifted his brows in amusement, and Mrs. Kittering brought over a pot of paint and a brush. Grace wrote in a small, cursive script beneath the beautiful title, "All welcome."

"Well done, Grace." Mrs. Weatherford clapped her hands.

"Wait—one more thing." Before anyone could stop him, Jimmy ran forward and plucked the brush from the pot. He turned around, blocking what he'd written and stepped aside with a cheeky grin.

Below Grace's welcome to all was a roughly scrawled statement, defiantly proclaiming, "Except Hitler."

They all had a fine laugh at that while the men put the new sign above the door to the shop.

Sarah tugged at Grace's skirt.

"What is it, dearest?" she asked of the child.

Sarah gazed up at her, bright blue eyes imploring. "Will you read to us now?"

But it wasn't only Sarah who looked at Grace with expectation, so did everyone else, tired but eager.

"Nothing would make me happier." Grace led them all to the glossy black door. "Ladies and gentlemen, it gives me great pleasure to welcome you to The Last Bookshop in London."

Amid the cheer that rose up, she led them into the store where she took her place on the second step up. She hesitated a moment there, scanning all the faces who had made not only the bookshop whole, but also her heart. Her gaze flicked to the history section where Mr. Evans had often sequestered himself, and for a fleeting moment she felt him then as surely as if he truly was there.

She smiled through her tears, opened her book and began to read, bringing them all along with her to a world where there were no bombs. There might be loss, and sometimes there may be fear, but there was also courage to face such challenges.

For in a world such as theirs, with people of spirit and love, and with so many different tales of strength and victory to inspire, there would always be hope.

EPILOGUE

JUNE 1945

FARRINGDON STATION WAS FILLED WITH SOLDIERS and civilians, the latter of whom had arrived in their best clothes, which wasn't saying much with the ration of clothing that had been going on for several years. Grace was no different as she waited in a blue dress with a dusting of small white flowers along a hem that had begun to fade.

She didn't often leave the bookshop, especially not when it had become so busy. While "The Last Bookshop in London" had great sentiment behind it, she had officially renamed the shop to Evans & Bennett, now painted on a robin's egg blue sign which hung over the doorway. The store had maintained a strong following through the war, with most she considered more friend than patron. Today, however, was worth having Jimmy mind the shop in her absence.

He'd become a talented assistant, eager to help and almost as voracious a reader as Grace. It wasn't uncommon for him to slip off between the shelves to lose himself into a story. The act reminded her so much of Mr. Evans that she couldn't bring herself to reprimand him.

Grace checked her watch, the luminescent paint flecks on the small ticking hands, once so integral to her former position as an ARP warden, were a greenish white in the daylight. At night, however, it had served her well through many air raids.

Five minutes until three.

That fateful night when Primrose Hill Books had fallen and Evans & Bennett rose from her ashes was the last of the Blitz on London. Bombings still had happened from time to time through the next four years until finally just last month on May 8, 1945, when the war came to an end.

The celebration had been tremendous. Couples danced in the streets, people pushed up their trousers and held up skirts to splash through fountains, grocers spilled open their reserves of sugar and bacon, neighbors came together to enjoy a feast they hadn't seen in years and the anti-aircraft spotlights, which once hunted their enemy in the skies, now swirled over the clouds in victory.

Grace and Mrs. Weatherford took Jimmy and Sarah to Whitehall amid a press of eager crowds to witness Churchill's speech touting their success in defeating Germany. The king and queen appeared on the balcony, resplendent and regal to show their appreciation for the people and their pride for such triumph. The princess wore her ATS uniform, which had made Grace cheer all the louder, if such a thing were possible.

Britain had taken it and come out a hero.

At the tube station, Grace checked her watch again. As three o'clock ticked closer, the group on the station platform increased in number until the air practically hummed with anticipation.

Soldiers were coming home now with frequency, those who had been conscripted among the first to arrive, nearly all of whom were women. Without the war on, their efforts, which had been required to win, were no longer required. This was not met with enthusiasm by all, especially those like Viv, who had poured everything they had into their jobs.

She had been part of the first mixed battery of men and women manning the anti-aircraft guns, stationed in London these last four years in the East End where she was billeted with several other women in her unit.

At least until she'd been given notice that her service was unnecessary. The telegraph from Viv had been brief, stating only the time of her arrival at Farringdon Station and asking Grace to meet her.

Viv would be coming home.

The telegraph was all Grace needed to know Viv was not happy with her abrupt departure from the ATS. They had seen one another on many occasions with Viv's day passes, but never once had she asked Grace to meet her.

Finally, the train pulled to the platform and the doors hissed open, spilling forth a good many soldiers into the waiting arms of their loved ones. Viv was easy to spot in the mass of uniforms. But then, she'd always stood out with her red hair and bright smile. Some things never changed, not even after six years of war.

Grace called to her friend who rushed toward her, embracing as if they hadn't seen each other in years.

"Are you all right?" Grace asked.

Viv took a deep breath and nodded, her red lips drawing tight against one another. Despite her attempt to remain optimistic, disappointment lined the corners of her mouth.

All around them, people jostled, lost in the bliss of their reunion or rushing to get home.

"I really did a great job out there," Viv said.

Grace squeezed her with one last hug. "You really did."

"We both did." Viv slung her kit bag over her shoulder and took Grace's hand in hers. "Do you miss your work with the ARP?"

"I miss the excitement of it," Grace replied. And she did. Of course, it was preferable to be in a time of peace. But there had been a thrill that hung in the air in the past years, an appreciation every morning you woke up alive. The kind that came from a perpetual press of danger. She hadn't been aware of it then, but now she felt of its absence.

"Mr. Stokes comes to the shop so often, I haven't had the chance to miss him," Grace said with an endearing smile. "However, I am grateful for extra nights of sleep."

"We'll have new adventures anyway," Viv said, falling back on her old habit of looking for new horizons when she was downtrodden. And right now her attention was fixed on a soldier striding past them with broad shoulders and an array of pins sparkling on his chest. "With handsome husbands, perhaps?"

"And shops to run." Grace squeezed her hand, earning a laugh from her friend.

"How is your wonderful bookshop?"

Grace's thoughts turned to the store, polished and clean, organized by subject, its shelves still mismatched wood from when they'd been rebuilt with scraps, the readings she'd continued as the war raged on and all the people she considered close friends. The booksellers she'd helped after the Blitz destroyed their establishments had found their own shops in time, each with a shelf designated for The Last Bookshop in London out of appreciation.

She loved every bit of Evans & Bennett.

"Like that then?" Viv asked with a smile. "Enough to transform your entire face with happiness?"

Grace nudged her toward the escalators. "Like that."

As they rode up the metal stairs, it was all too easy to recall another time when she and Viv were at Farringdon Station together. When they'd left their home in Drayton, before the war had begun and they'd never dreamed they'd be surrounded by bombs or manning an anti-aircraft gun. Before Grace had ever found a love for books.

It was surreal to think such a bland, colorless life had been lived by either of them.

Grace had reached out to her uncle Horace in the days following the war's end, to confirm their safety and offer her love. Once upon a time, she might have felt doing so was turning the other cheek. Now she knew it to be compassion.

And he had replied, his manner still gruff, as he assured her that they were well and offering an invitation for her to visit should she fancy a jaunt in the country. In truth, it was more than she'd ever expected from him.

She owed the fragile repair of that relationship to Mr. Evans. Well, that and so, so much more.

Grace and Viv chatted on their way toward Mrs. Weatherford's townhouse, where Viv was staying in the room she and Grace had once shared. Grace now lived in the flat above Evans and Bennett, which was far too small to accommodate two beds comfortably. As they neared Britton Street, Viv clasped Grace's hand and her smile resumed its sparkle.

They rounded the corner and both broke into a run, like

children, rushing up the steps to the green door with the brass knocker. Viv pushed inside and was met with a cheer of excitement from Mrs. Weatherford and Sarah, who made quite the welcoming committee with streamers of painted newspaper and a cake Mrs. Weatherford had been setting aside sugar and flour to make.

In the weeks that followed, Grace and Viv picked up where their friendship had left off, filling their newfound free time without the ATS and ARP with cinemas and cafés and nights out at the theater and, of course, jazz clubs and dancing.

Through it all, there was the bookshop for Grace. As children returned from the country and soldiers from war, the familiar faces who had become friends now began to show up with their loved ones. She met husbands and wives and children.

Jimmy enjoyed reading aloud as well and took it upon himself to do a children's book hour every Saturday afternoon. On one particular afternoon, Mrs. Kittering arrived with her daughter, a pretty brown-haired girl with proper manners and wide doe eyes like her mother. Never had Grace seen Mrs. Kittering smile as much as she did with her daughter, doting on her every move and word with the eternal love of a mother. And eagerly awaiting her husband, who would undoubtedly be released from his service soon.

It was on one such afternoon on a sunny Saturday in August that Grace found herself with a moment's respite. With the customers all occupied, she made her way to the sunlit window with a copy of *Forever Amber*, leaned against the wall and opened the book.

The familiar scent of paper and ink drew her in as she

fell head over heels into a new story. She was so lost in the literary world being spun within her mind, she missed the bell chime at the front door.

"I never thought reading could be more beautiful," a familiar, rich voice said. "Until this moment."

Grace's head snapped up and the book fell from her hands. "George."

He stood several paces away from her, handsome as ever in his neatly pressed RAF uniform, holding a head of purple cabbage. "It appears cabbages are still all the rage in place of flowers."

"Only because you're not the Ritz." She ran to him and threw herself into his arms as the cabbage head tumbled to the floor with a soft thump.

They'd grown far closer in the years of war, with letters unveiling deep parts of their souls and all the time they could squeeze in together on the rare moments of leave he was afforded.

"Are you home for good now?" she asked, gazing into his eyes, never able to get enough of him. She enfolded a hand into the warmth of his in an attempt to convince herself he was real. Truly standing before her.

"I am." He stroked a finger down her cheek. "For good."

She closed her eyes and leaned her head against his chest, breathing in his clean, wonderful smell and savoring the rasp of his wool uniform against her cheek that had grown so familiar.

"Do you really not plan to ask if I brought you anything at all?" His voice rumbled under her cheek.

She looked up in surprise. "I couldn't possibly think of anything more that I'd want."

"Couldn't you?" He grinned and reached into the pocket

of his jacket. "Not even a book?" His hand hovered, his brows lifted with expectation.

She straightened and clapped in delight. It had become tradition, after all, for them to exchange books with one another. His often were battered, well-read copies that had been shared between countless soldiers, but the stories within were always captivating.

"I couldn't possibly return to you empty handed." He withdrew a rectangular green book.

It was an oddly shaped thing, scarcely bigger than her hand.

"They're made in America, specifically for soldiers to carry about in their uniform pockets," he said, answering her question before she could even ask it. "It's quite brilliant, actually."

"It is." She turned it over in her hand to study it before reading the bold yellow title aloud. *"The Great Gatsby?"* In the far left corner was a black circle declaring the book to be an Armed Services Edition.

"All the Americans are raving about it."

"You haven't read it?" she asked in surprise.

"I'm rather keen on the idea of having it read to me from the infamous shop owner of Evans and Bennett." He put his large, warm hand over hers, so they held the book together.

"I'm sure I can arrange that." Grace's smile grew even wider. "I don't know if I ever thanked you."

He lifted a brow, making him look as dashing as Cary Grant. "What would you have to thank me for?"

"For teaching me how to love books." She regarded the bookshop with fondness.

He furrowed his brows with a genuine expression. "You

did that, Grace. Not me. That passion was something you found inside of you."

Her chest swelled with his words. Deep down, she knew part of her newfound passion had started with him, with that old battered copy of *The Count of Monte Cristo* he'd given her. Part of it had been Mr. Evans and everything the bookshop stood for. Still another part was the people she read to, the dark times those stories had guided them through with distraction and love and laughter. It was even the war itself, the desperation to have a means to escape, a longing to feel something other than loss and fear.

It was everything and everyone coming together as a community, drawn by the power of literature, that truly made her love of books complete and what put the heart into Evans and Bennett—or as some of her long-time patrons still referred to it, The Last Bookshop in London.

★ ★ ★ ★ ★

ACKNOWLEDGMENTS

WRITING A WWII HISTORICAL FICTION NOVEL HAS always been a dream of mine. Thank you to my editor, Peter Joseph, his editorial assistant, Grace Towery, and my agent, Laura Bradford, for helping make that come true.

Thank you to Eliza Knight for her constant support. This has been such an amazing experience for us to go through in our careers together. Thank you to Tracy Emro and her mother for always helping keep me in line. Thank you to Mariellena Brown and my wonderful mother, Janet Kazmirski, for taking the time to beta read for me.

And an enormous thank you to my family: John Somar for being by my side through all of this, always willing to step up and help with the kids so I can make deadlines. To my sweet daughters, who are my biggest fans and are so excited to finally get to read one of my books. To my parents for always being so proud of me. I have so much love in my life and am so grateful to each one of you.

And a heartfelt thank you to all the readers out there who make dreams come true with each book they hold in their hands.